19/11/19

FRAZER LEE

HEARTHSTONE COTTAGE

To all the staff,
volunteers and readers at
Great missenden / Bucks
libraries, with best
wishes,
[signature]

This is a **FLAME TREE PRESS** book

Text copyright © 2019 Frazer Lee

FLAME TREE PRESS
6 Melbray Mews, London, SW6 3NS, UK
flametreepress.com

Distribution and warehouse:
Baker & Taylor Publisher Services (BTPS)
30 Amberwood Parkway, Ashland, OH 44805
btpubservices.com

Publisher's Note: This is a work of fiction. Names, characters, places, and
incidents are a product of the author's imagination. Locales and public names
are sometimes used for atmospheric purposes. Any resemblance to actual
people, living or dead, or to businesses, companies, events, institutions, or
locales is completely coincidental.

Thanks to the Flame Tree Press team, including:
Taylor Bentley, Frances Bodiam, Federica Ciaravella, Don D'Auria,
Chris Herbert, Josie Karani, Molly Rosevear, Will Rough, Mike Spender,
Cat Taylor, Maria Tissot, Nick Wells, Gillian Whitaker.

The cover is created by Flame Tree Studio with
thanks to Nik Keevil and Shutterstock.com.
The font families used are Avenir and Bembo.

Flame Tree Press is an imprint of Flame Tree Publishing Ltd
flametreepublishing.com

A copy of the CIP data for this book is available from the British Library
and the Library of Congress.

HB ISBN: 978-1-78758-327-6
PB ISBN: 978-1-78758-325-2
ebook ISBN: 978-1-78758-328-3
Also available in FLAME TREE AUDIO

Printed in bound in Great Britain by Clays Ltd, Elcograf S.p.A.

FRAZER LEE

HEARTHSTONE COTTAGE

FLAME TREE PRESS
London & New York

This one's for Alan Stewart,
who always has an eye for a story.

PART ONE

Under dark, dark skies
There are dark, dark mountains
And beneath the dark, dark mountains
Is a dark, dark road.

CHAPTER ONE

Mike opened his eyes and saw the looming shapes of the Kintail Mountains through the sunroof.

He yawned, stretched and sat up in the back seat. His mouth was dry, and he reached for the bottle of spring water that lay in the space between him and Helen. As he picked it up, his fingers brushed her hand. She smiled at him, and he reciprocated through his yawns.

"Welcome back to the land of the living," Helen said.

He took an enormous thirst-slaking gulp from the water bottle. Feeling more awake now, he became aware of the talk show chatter on the car radio.

"Of course nonhuman animals feel pain and emotions just as keenly as we do," a woman was saying. She sounded annoyed. The male presenter cut her off and began inviting listeners to call in. Mike drained the rest of the water from his bottle. He belched, then dodged Helen's backhander as she made a swipe at him.

"Pig," she said.

"Sorry," he yawned. "Whereabouts are we?"

"Nearly there. Another twenty minutes or so, Alex reckons."

A huge Ordnance Survey map lay partly open in Helen's lap, just as it had before he'd fallen asleep. A Google Maps smartphone app didn't fare so well in the Highlands, where the signal was as unpredictable as the weather. Mike had watched Helen diligently follow their progress across the map, unfolding and refolding it as she went, before he had fallen asleep. Now he saw her trace a line with her finger to a dark outline indicating the foot of the mountain range. The map elevation was emblazoned with the legend 'KINTAIL MOUNTAINS'.

"Blimey. How long was I asleep for?"

Alex's gruff voice boomed from the driver's seat. "Too fucking long, man. I could do with a kip myself."

Mike laughed. "You're forgetting – he who drives the first leg gets to snooze for the second. You missed your chance to sleep earlier."

"Oh, you mean when you were playing Guns n' Roses at full pelt? Fat chance I had to sleep then, man."

"You and me both," Kay said. She winked at Mike and Helen from the front passenger seat. "I have to admit a fondness for a bit of hair metal, though." She made devil horns with her right hand, teasing Alex with them.

"Pipe down, woman, I'm bloody well trying to drive here." Alex hit the off button on the steering wheel column and silenced the advertisements blaring out of the radio.

"Both you *men* were bloody well asleep when Kay and me took turns to drive," Helen countered.

"Yeah, curled up together on the back seat like lovebirds," Kay said, before adding, "The bromance continues."

They all laughed at that, except for Alex, who scowled ahead at the winding country road. Mike knew the constant grump act was a bit of a put-on, but he also knew Alex could get spectacularly grouchy if the girls teased him too much. He suspected that was why they did it so often – just to get a rise out of Alex.

Mike reached into the seat pocket in front of him and pulled out his tobacco tin. The friendly marijuana leaf design on the lid greeted him as it always did, along with the legend 'Born to... Born to... No, it's gone'. He took out a couple of rolling papers and started building a joint, using the lid of the tin to offset the movement of the car as it weaved along the country road. Mike heard Helen exhale just a little too loudly between her teeth. She had made it clear several times that she did not approve of his smoking. But it was happy holiday time and Mike needed it to relax. And relax he could – he had graduated with upper second class honors, and now all he had to do was build a nice, fat doobie, kick back and wait for the job offers to come rolling in. Mike sparked up and breathed out a little cloud of smoke. It drifted across the back seat, toward Helen. Her heavy-breathing act turned to loud tuts of disapproval as she made a show of waving the smoke away from her face.

"Open the window, you bloody menace," Helen said.

Mike activated the little window switch set into his armrest and watched the smoke escape. It curled up and out, creating the illusion of yet more mist above the mountains as it went.

"Want some?"

Helen rolled her eyes and turned her attention back to the map.

"Don't know what you're missing," Mike said.

"I know what you're missing, smoking that all the time – a fair few brain cells."

Now it was Mike's turn to roll his eyes. Much as he was into Helen, he wished she would lighten up sometimes. She, like his friend Alex, had studied law. Mike had started out on a law degree too before switching to business partway into his first year – a decision that had incurred the wrath of his parents, who were paying his fees. He had enjoyed the business course much more than he had law, though he was thankful he had started out on that track since he'd met Helen in classes. Watching her through the haze as she pored over the map, he noted how tired and strung out she looked. She'd been that way all through her finals, but they were long over and Mike was still waiting for her to snap out of it. He took another toke, hoping she might ease up later, after a couple of drinks and a sizeable dose of fresh Highland air.

"Mike!"

"Shit, Helen."

Lost in thought, he'd allowed the joint to go to ash and had inadvertently hot-rocked the seat upholstery between his legs. Mike patted at the angry orange nugget of burning ash, but that only made it worse. His heart sank as he saw the cinder smoldering into the plush seat cover. He looked up, and his eyes met Alex's in the rearview mirror.

"Idiot," Alex said. His quiet tone carried more dread than any exclamation ever could. "The rental company told us it was no smoking when we signed the form – when I signed the form – and you said—"

"I said I'd be careful. I know, I know, I'm sorry. Pass me that bottle of water, will you, Kay?"

Alex's girlfriend hailed from Palo Alto on the west coast of the USA. She had studied classics, also in Edinburgh, and had met Alex through a mutual friend. Mike liked her, though she could be a bit aloof sometimes. Her bookish ways softened the often by-the-book approach adopted by Alex, who was a natural-born lawyer if ever there was one. Mike's and Alex's fathers both worked at the same company, The Consortium

Incorporated, which had a regional office in Glasgow. Mike's dad was in business development, or 'Biz Dev' as he called it, and Alex's dad was high up in the legal department. While their respective fathers had fallen prey to office politics – they no longer went for after-work drinks together – Mike and Alex had remained friends all through university. And Mike and Alex often joked about how, in spite of themselves, they had followed their fathers into the same line of work.

Mike knew how bitterly disappointed his father had been when his son, his only child, had opted to switch courses. He suspected his dad had really wanted to be a lawyer like Alex's father. Every Christmastime for the past three years, Mike had to endure lengthy lectures from his father about how the legal profession had better prospects and job security. Still, he had graduated now, and he hoped his father might chill out a bit in the knowledge that Mike had achieved a B+. He doubted it, however, and felt sure he'd get 'the lecture' again come next Christmas about how a first class degree in law would serve Alex much better than Mike's mere upper second in business.

Mike unclipped his seat belt and reached forward to take the water bottle from Kay. He shuffled aside, eliciting more protests from Helen, and surveyed the damage. It was a small burn mark, but it had gone deep. He splashed a little water onto the burn and rubbed at it with his thumb.

"Shit!"

His attempts had only made matters worse. He had made the black stain bigger, making the burn look worse than it was.

"Who makes seat covers *this* beige anyhow?"

"Oh, so it's the car's fault now, is it?" Alex's voice bubbled with anger.

Mike tried to cover the damage with his hand as Alex craned his neck around to see. But Kay pointed out something through the passenger window.

"Is that it?!"

Mike felt relieved to hear the excitement in Kay's voice, hoping it would be enough to keep Alex's mind off the singed seat cover.

"Aye, that's the place all right," Alex murmured as he returned his attention to the road. They each craned their necks to get a better look out of the passenger side.

The landscape on the left-hand side of the road had opened up, giving a full view of an enormous, stunning loch. The still surface of the water was like a mirror, reflecting every detail of the sky above it. Tall, ancient trees lined its banks, and, between them, the stark white of a small building stood out from their dense green foliage. Mike tilted his head with the car's movement around the loch and peered out at the building he knew so well.

"Hearthstone Cottage," he said, "venue of legends!"

"It looks…smaller than I'd imagined," Helen said.

Kay hissed through her teeth. "It's beautiful!" she exclaimed. "It looks freaking beautiful!"

Alex cracked a smile at her enthusiasm, playfully tousling her hair.

"Thank you for bringing us here," Kay said softly and kissed Alex on the nose.

Alex's eyes were taken off the road for just three seconds.

But three seconds was all it took.

"Alex!"

Helen's horrified scream jolted Mike from the stunning view. He almost screamed too from the sudden pain of her fingernails as they dug into the flesh of his forearm. The gasp died in his throat when he glanced through the windscreen. A massive, dark shape loomed dead ahead on the dirt road in front of them. It was a stag. Mike saw, almost in slow motion, steam rising from the creature's back in subtle wisps like the smoke from his joint.

"Christ!" Alex yelled, gripping and yanking the steering wheel to the left.

The car drifted as it went into a skid. Mike felt the entire rear end of the vehicle lift from the ground. He saw the stag's eyes, twinkling dark in the daylight. Then the car hit the dirt, righted itself on its new trajectory and clipped the stag as it hurtled onward. The car shook from the impact. Mike pressed his hands over his ears at the grinding of metal and the sickening crunch of bones. Helen dry screamed, a hollow croaking sound that did not stop until the car had trundled to a halt.

The engine died, its death rattle giving way to the sudden hiss of steam escaping from the ruptured cooling system. Steam billowed from beneath the crumpled bonnet, cloaking the cracked windscreen in vapor.

"Shit!" Mike saw the joint at his feet, now smoldering on the mat in the footwell. He stomped it out and, on instinct, opened his door and climbed out of the ruined car.

"Are you okay, babe?" he said through the open door. But Helen's gaze was fixed dead ahead, as though she was replaying the point of impact over and over in her mind.

Mike heard a click and saw Kay frantically trying to climb out after him. Her seat belt was still on. Pinioned like a butterfly beneath a pin, she struggled against it for a few seconds. Then, with a trembling hand, she reached for the seat belt clasp and thumbed the catch. Kay tumbled out of the car and staggered past Mike toward the roadside. Mike watched her stop dead in her tracks when she saw the massive deer lying in the road.

"I'm sorry," she sobbed. "I'm so sorry. If I hadn't been so.... It's all my fault."

Alex caught up to her and put his arm around Kay, holding her upright as she convulsed with each sob.

"Are you...okay?" Mike heard himself say once more.

His words trailed off as he realized he had wandered over to where the stag lay. Plumes of steam still rose from the animal's powerful back and haunches. A dark slick of blood had streaked from its nose across the rough surface of the road, like a chef's statement flourish over slate dinnerware. Mike moved closer through the silence and saw that the animal still had a pulse. One of its legs was twisted beneath its huge body, the yellow of bone poking out of a tear in its hide. An angry gash, between the struts of the stag's ribcage, spurted blood in time with each beat of its ailing heart.

"My god, it's still breathing."

Helen's voice at his ear shocked Mike from the quiet. He hadn't even noticed her leave the car and join him. No sooner had she spoken than the deer trembled.

It's cold, thought Mike. *I'll get a blanket from the car.*

He wondered if it felt afraid. Wondered if it knew it was dying. He recalled the voices on the car radio, discussing sentience—

Of course they feel pain, of course they experience emotions like we do!

Mike swallowed dryly and wished he could somehow ask the stag. To know for sure if it felt and, if so, *what* it felt. But then he heard a death rattle emanating from between the creature's bloodied teeth. The animal's eye widened and fixed Mike with its gaze.

You did this, it seemed to say. *You and your friends.*

"What are we going to do?" Kay's distraught wail pierced the silence.

Alex sighed, his expression grim. "We'll have to walk if I can't get the car running again," he said.

Kay slumped to the ground, defeated. Alex wiped the tears from her eyes with his thumbs, then let her be.

Mike tore his gaze from the creature's accusing eye and glanced across the loch.

"It's a long walk," Mike said.

"Yes, it fucking well is," Alex replied. He was already on his way back to the 4x4.

Mike heard a torrent of further expletives as Alex wrenched open the bonnet, engulfed in steam from the engine cooling system. He approached the car to offer Alex a hand, eager to be away from the dead stag and its dark, accusing gaze. He felt something knock against his shoe and paused. Looking down, he thought it was a rock. But then he noticed the blood and stooped to pick it up. Roughly six inches in length, it was the curved, pointed tip of one of the stag's antlers, bone yellow beneath the blood spatter. The shard felt warm and heavy in his hand. On instinct, he pulled a tissue from his pocket and wiped away the blood spots. Mike tucked the antler into his pocket and ambled over to the car.

CHAPTER TWO

Daylight was fading by the time they reached the cottage. Alex had, with Mike's help, patched up the coolant leak, but the 4x4 was on its last legs. The engine groaned its last as Alex steered the car into the narrow dirt track that led to the drystone perimeter wall.

"That's us, thanks tae fuck," Alex announced. He sat back in the driver's seat for a moment and breathed a sigh of relief.

"Come on," Helen said, reaching out and squeezing Kay's shoulder over the seat. "I'll help you with your things."

Mike climbed out and stretched, clicking out the vertebrae in his neck. He looked over the rough, low wall at the cottage. It was exactly as he remembered it, though it had been several months since his and Alex's last fishing vacation. The cottage was set back from the loch and built into the curve of the land. Constructed in the classic crofter's style, the low building always looked to Mike like it was hunkering down, huddled away from the icy water just a few hundred meters away. The narrow windows of the ground floor reflected the darkness of the landscape, while the upper windows were mirrors to the dusky sky.

Mike craned his neck to try to see inside, but he knew the cottage would betray none of its mysteries until it was opened up. He took a deep breath of moist lochside air and caught the rich, bracken scent of an open fire. Glancing up at the roof, he noticed wisps of gray smoke billowing from the chimney stacks at either end of the cottage.

"Someone knew we were coming," Mike said, nodding to the chimneys.

"It cannae be," Alex replied. Then he, too, spied the smoke. He pushed open the gate and started up the winding, paved path to the front door of the cottage.

Mike watched as Alex tried the front door latch. It was locked. Alex then opened the combination lockbox that housed the front door key.

"Fucking key's gone!" Alex cursed. "Hello?" Alex called through the letterbox. No answer came, save for the echo of his own voice.

Alex looked back at Mike, who saw his friend's confusion. No one else was meant to be at the cottage. Though Alex's parents rented it out sometimes, they had arranged that it would be theirs – and theirs only – for the week.

"Oh, no. It's not double booked?" Helen asked.

This seemed to further trouble Alex, who darted around back, calling out again to whoever had lit the fire. Mike caught up to him and found him hammering on the back door with his fist. Mike peered in through one of the rear windows. The interior of the cottage was in darkness, save for a flicker of orange firelight from the hearth within.

"D'you think it's squatters?" Mike asked.

"I hope not, for their sakes," Alex seethed.

They both turned away from the rear of the cottage and made their way across the muddy yard, past a rusty, old brown Fiat Panda that sat half-covered by a tattered tarpaulin, and toward the outbuilding.

"Maybe we can get Meggie's old banger running, at least," Alex said.

His sister, Meggie, was a fine art undergraduate at Glasgow School of Art. Mike had happy memories of drinking and chatting with Alex and Meggie beneath the sloping roof of the wood store, watching the cloud formations over the landscape, during his previous visit. They passed the wood store, beyond which was a wicker enclosure for the bins and recycling boxes. Mike followed Alex's path as he strode past these and arrived at the door to the outbuilding. Alex's family used the structure as a studio space and for storage. Alex's mother, Shona, was a keen painter, no doubt the source of Meggie's artistic DNA, and Mike could just make out a half-finished canvas standing on an easel through the grimy windows.

Alex moved to the window at the other end of the outbuilding, and Mike followed him. Looking inside, he saw Alex's trusty old trail bike leaning up against his father's older, rustier model. Mike recalled the last time they had rode the bikes out to the lake, and how much they had enjoyed the rough terrain that snaked through the woods.

"Hey, do you think your parents might be here?"

"Surprise visit, you mean?" Alex said. "No, they would have said something. They're in Switzerland for the skiing – Mum would'nae miss that for the world. And Meggie's still living it up in Thailand, far as I know."

Mike could almost hear Alex's growing frustration amid the quiet of the yard.

"Whoever lit the fire will have to come back at some point," Mike said.

"Aye, they will," Alex growled, and Mike noticed his friend had balled his right hand into a fist.

Hitting the stag had been stressful enough, but now that they were locked out, Mike felt the last wisps of his warm, smoky glow leaving him cold. They had just started retracing their steps around to the front of the house, when they heard Helen's familiar voice calling out to them.

"Boys! Boys?"

Alex and Mike rounded the corner leading back to the front of the cottage to find the girls waiting for them on the front doorstep. Another figure was visible, walking down the winding track that led from the hill path to the cottage. She was wearing an ankle-length skirt and carrying a huge bundle of dry twigs in her arms. A Border collie dog bounded along faithfully at her side. Seeing the young woman's shock of long, tousled red hair, Mike recognized her at once.

"Meggie?" Alex called out. "What are you doing here?"

"I've missed you too, big brother," she laughed as she made her way through the gate and up the path. She put down her bundle of twigs on the front porch and gave Alex a hug. The collie barked his welcome and jumped excitedly at Alex, who looked a little taken aback at the sudden display of affection from both dog and owner.

"When did you get back?" Alex asked, helping her with the twigs.

"Oh, a few days ago," Meggie muttered vaguely. She really was the stark opposite to her big brother. Then, looking around at the others' faces, she said, "Aren't you going to introduce me to your friends?"

"Kay, this is my sister, Meggie," Alex said, giving his girlfriend a proprietary squeeze.

"Pleased to meet you at last," Meggie said, smiling and shaking hands with Kay, who lurched forward to give Meggie air kisses, then awkwardly withdrew, settling for the handshake.

"Mike you already met last time," Alex went on, "and this is his girlfriend, Helen."

"Lovely to meet you," Helen said to Meggie, keeping her hands to herself.

Meggie nodded in reply. "And this unruly child is Oscar," she laughed as the dog barked and ran rings around the legs of all the visitors. "Oscar! Behave!"

"You could have left us the bloody key," Alex said.

"I just popped out for more kindling. Thought I'd get the place warmed up for you. Me and Oscar have been hanging out in the studio mostly, next to the electric heater." Laughing at Alex's stern look, she added, "You're very welcome."

"We're grateful, even if he isn't," Helen said. "A warm fire is what we could all do with right now, after the journey we've had."

"Traffic bad, was it?" Meggie asked.

"Look at the bloody car, Meg," Alex said.

Meggie peered over the perimeter wall, and her eyes widened at the sight of the crumpled car. "Oh my goodness! What a mess! Is everyone okay?"

"Kay's still a bit freaked—" Alex began.

"I'm all right." Kay scowled at him.

"What happened?" Meggie asked.

"We hit a stag and—" Mike explained.

"Technically the stag hit *us*," Alex cut in. "And it did'nae get up again afterwards."

"Poor wee beastie," Meggie said.

"Poor wee beastie? Have you seen what it did to the fucking car? I doubt the insurance even covers it. Christ!"

The dog barked as if in solidarity with Alex's anger.

"Okay, okay. Calm down. And you, Oscar! Hey, the damage is done, right?"

Alex shrugged, frustrated. Meggie forced a smile at the others.

"Let's get you all into the warm, eh? We can have a nice cup of tea."

"That sounds great," Helen said. "Bring the rest of the bags, will you?" she said to Mike.

He nodded and headed back to the car to retrieve the rest of their luggage. Pausing to watch Alex and the others as they entered the cottage, he realized that Meggie hadn't even said hello to him.

★　　★　　★

A warming fire crackled in the grate with the fresh wood that Meggie had added to it. Smoke swirled into the wide, dark flue above, casting flickering shadows on the old hearthstone, which lay like a toppled monolith in front of the fire. The impressive stone mantelpiece and supports were fashioned from the same weathered stone.

Mike breathed in the smell of the burning wood. It was sweet and earthy, an olfactory description of the cottage he stood in. He remembered being intoxicated by the smell of the hearth on his very first visit to the cottage. It smelled like home, somehow. The months since he'd last stayed there had done nothing to diminish the effect. In fact, if anything, he felt more drawn to the old place than ever. He settled into the old armchair and took a warming sip of tea.

Alex, ever the hunter-gatherer, was unpacking their food and stowing it away in the open-plan kitchen cupboards. Kay was already rifling through the bookcases, which were filled to bursting with an eclectic mix of local guidebooks, paperback fiction, and elderly hardback editions of shooting, fishing, and sporting almanacs. Helen had generously made a pot of tea for everyone, while Meggie tended to the fire, leaving Mike in the position that came most naturally to him – sitting comfortably on his arse, watching everyone else do the work. He savored another sip of tea from his mug and sighed contentedly. Despite their earlier tangle with the stag, he now felt sure this was going to be a good break for all of them.

"Looks like the Cheshire cat, that one," Meggie said as she fed the last of her wood to the fire.

Mike looked over to her but found she had her back to him. The firelight made her red hair dazzle. She was evidently talking *about* him, not *to* him.

"Aye, never happier than whenever other folk are doing all the hard labor," Alex said.

Mike lifted his mug of tea in a mock toast. "Cheers," he said.

"On your feet, soldier," Helen said before draining the last of her tea. She popped her mug on the kitchen counter and walked over to their luggage. "Help me carry these upstairs. I'd like to get unpacked before we all get too settled."

"Why don't we settle first? We are on hols," Mike protested.

"I hate living out of a suitcase," Helen replied, "and you'll never get unpacked if you don't do it right now. If you think I'm going to—"

"All right, all right," Mike sighed. "No need to mother me."

"I think your mother would disagree with that," Helen countered, eliciting sniggers from Alex and the others. "Come on, get up off your arse and help me with these."

"Shall we?" Kay said to Alex, tearing her attention away from the cottage's makeshift library.

Alex nodded and grabbed their bags from the pile.

Meggie stood up from the hearth and smoothed down her skirt. Tucking a long strand of red hair behind one ear, she said to Helen and Kay, "I'll give you the tour. I have a feeling you're going to love your rooms. Did my brother show you any snapshots?"

"Of course he didn't," Helen replied.

"Bloody men," Meggie muttered as she led the way aloft.

Alex went up first with his and Kay's bags, followed by Mike. The staircase was narrow and turned a sharp left toward the top, making it difficult to carry the bags without knocking against the walls.

"Try not to demolish the place on the way up," teased Alex. Reaching the landing, he added, "Bagsie the master bedroom," before quickly ducking inside with his luggage.

"I guess that leaves spare bedroom number two," Mike said. "If you don't mind?" he added, nodding to Meggie.

"Oh, no, not at all. I already took the single. Oscar's happy to share." Meggie winked.

"What are those?" Helen asked, pointing at a series of wooden carvings hanging above each bedroom door.

Mike looked up to see they had been carved into a series of runic symbols – four for each room. He didn't recall seeing them on his last visit. Probably Meggie's artwork, or her mum's.

"They're Haelu charms, aren't they?" Kay interjected.

Meggie looked impressed. "You know your folklore, I see. Yes, they are. It's an old tradition in this neck of the woods to hang these up around the house, especially over the thresholds."

Mike looked at the charms, mesmerized. He reached out slowly and took one in his hand before recoiling as if a sudden shock of pain had jolted through his arm.

"Ouch! It bloody burned me!"

He looked at Kay's shocked expression and couldn't help himself. He cracked up laughing. Alex punched him playfully on the arm.

"Dick," Helen said. "Almost had us going there." She nudged Mike aside and took a closer look at the charms.

Mike grinned, noticing that she didn't touch any of them.

"What's their significance?" Helen asked Meggie as her eyes scrutinized the charms. "Do they mean something specific?"

Meggie pointed out each symbol in turn. "The Anglo-Saxon meaning is 'health', 'wealth', 'luck'—and that one on the end there means 'blessings'."

"I like them," Helen mused. "Do they sell them in local gift shops, or museums round here?"

"You made them, I reckon, eh, Meggie?" Mike said.

Meggie chuckled. "Oh, no, I couldn't make those. They're very old. Maybe someone is making copies. The old crafts are certainly coming back. You'd have to try eBay."

"Not that you'll have any luck getting online here," Alex said.

Helen had already unlocked her phone screen. "No wi-fi?"

Mike shook his head, smirking at Helen's growing look of horror.

"Nobody told me there was no bloody wi-fi."

"Welcome to the wilderness," Meggie giggled. "There isn't even a landline."

The sound of her mirth was infectious, and they all shared a laugh.

★　　★　　★

Unpacked and settled in, Mike and the others sat around the fire, which roared in its grate beneath the fireplace. The golden light flickered across the impressive mantelpiece. Mike followed the line of the flickering light and noticed that the mantel's supports and the slablike hearthstone appeared to be fashioned from the same weathered rock.

"That fire's lush," breathed Kay, the light dancing in her eyes. "The hearthstone looks really old. Like someone lugged a chunk of Stonehenge all the way up here."

HEARTHSTONE COTTAGE • 17

"From Salisbury? No need," Meggie said with a smile. "Plenty of local rock in these mountains. All the houses in the village are made from the same stuff."

"Grub's up!" called Alex from the kitchen.

Mike followed his nose to the conservatory. The most delicious wafts of hearty beef stew guided him in to land at the big, old dining table. The others soon joined, and Alex made a show of popping the cork on a bottle of cava.

They each helped themselves to a steaming bowl of stew and passed around a wooden chopping board laden with crusty bread. Mike delved in before the others had even finished dishing up, and caught Helen's look of admonishment as he did so.

"What?" he asked through a delicious mouthful of food. "It's not like anyone's gonna say grace."

He wiped his mouth on the back of his sleeve and took the glass that Alex offered to him.

"A toast," said Alex, and they all raised their glasses. "To still being alive after hitting that bloody stag."

"And to still being alive after our fricken finals," Kay added.

They all clinked glasses, and the first drinks went down quickly enough for Alex to have to pour refills before his stew had even had time to cool down. Finally he sat down and tucked in while Mike helped himself to seconds.

"The view is just stunning," said Kay. "I could never get tired of it."

Mike looked out over the loch. The conservatory windows gave a widescreen view of the landscape. Dark clouds drifted overhead, the gaps in between them directing dappled light onto the surface of the water. The sun was setting behind the mountains, turning the sky a ruddy shade of orange.

"It can get lonely out here, but there's no shortage of inspiration for painting and sculpting," Meggie said.

"So, you're an art student?" Helen asked.

"Was. I went to Glasgow School of Art."

"When did you graduate?"

"I didn't. I...took some time out to travel."

"She bloody well dropped out is what she means to say," Alex said.

"Bit harsh, brother mine," Meggie said softly. Then she blushed a little. "I might go back and finish my studies...."

"If Pa and Ma cough up for another year's fees, eh?" Alex laughed sarcastically.

"Where did you travel?" Kay cut in, elbowing Alex in the arm and throwing him a cautionary look.

"Thailand mostly," Meggie replied. "I was at a yoga retreat for a while, and I took some art classes to keep my brush-hand in."

Meggie glanced at Alex, her eyes twinkling, and rose from the table. She began gathering up everyone's dishes.

"Oh, no, I'll do that," Helen offered.

"No, you guys relax. I'll do the washing up. We can take turns each day after that. So don't worry, you'll all get your chance," she laughed, carrying the dishes to the sink.

"Even you," Helen said to Mike.

"Hey, I'm a dab hand at...air-drying," Mike replied, provoking laughter from the others.

As the laughter subsided, Mike saw Kay glance over her shoulder. She leaned in close to Alex and lowered her voice, almost to a whisper.

"Hey, you shouldn't be so hard on your kid sister like that."

"She's no kid; she's twenty now. My folks were absolutely bloody furious when she dropped out of college. Even more furious when she went cap in hand to them for more money to go gallivanting off halfway around the world."

Kay elbowed him again, making him lower his voice.

"Come on, I'm just joshing with her. She knows that."

Mike watched Meggie in the kitchen. She didn't look like she knew Alex was joking. Far from it. As she worked on the dishes, scrubbing them hard beneath the trickle of hot water from the tap, he saw her blink something away from the corner of her eye. He felt sure she must be crying in silence over there all alone. She must have sensed him staring at her because she turned and looked straight at him. He felt his arms turn to gooseflesh at her blank look, like she was staring right through him.

"Jesus!"

Mike jolted at the sensation of something cold and wet brushing against his right hand. He looked down and saw Oscar sitting right next to his chair, tongue lolling out of the corner of his mouth.

"Blimey, you're jumpy," Helen said, smiling at Mike and then getting up from her chair to fuss over the dog.

Kay looked troubled. She folded her arms and shivered. "It's hard to forget the look in that poor stag's eyes."

"Aye, and it's hard to forget we totaled the bloody car," Alex said.

Mike could tell that Alex was trying to make light, but the annoyance in his friend's tone was evident.

"Another drink, anyone?" Alex asked, holding aloft the empty cava bottle. "We made light work of this one. Something a wee bit stronger next...."

Alex sloped off to investigate the bottles of spirits on the sideboard.

"I'll chuck another log on the fire," Mike said. "It's getting chilly in here."

CHAPTER THREE

Mike savored the peaty scent of the single malt whisky that Alex had poured for him. It tasted earthy and good. The afterglow of the drink warmed his throat and stomach. He felt almost content and was confident he would achieve full contentment after another stiff measure.

The fire crackled on in the hearth, making flickering shadows dance across the rug and the pale walls. Mike wondered how many nights had been spent like this in the crofter's cottage, sipping whisky next to a roaring fire after a hard day's toil. Helen and the others were milling around in the kitchen, checking out the tourist leaflets that Alex's parents kept stacked up next to the vegetable rack. He ambled over to the table to join them, placing his hand on Helen's shoulder. She took it in hers – her hands were always cool to the touch, the opposite of his – and squeezed it before continuing her chat with Kay and the others.

Just then, the clouds parted, allowing a brilliant shaft of moonlight to appear. It shimmered, silver-white on the black surface of the loch. The moon was full and so bright that it caught the attention of everyone in the room. The conversation subsided as they each gazed out at the beautiful sight of it. Mike supposed they had all become too used to the light pollution in the city. It certainly felt like he was seeing something they all took for granted for the first time, standing there in the conservatory.

Oscar growled and gave a tense little bark. He darted between the table legs and emerged on the other side. He began scratching at the back door with frantic front paws, knocking over some Wellington boots as he did so.

"Call of nature, is it, wee Oscar?" Meggie said.

Oscar pricked up his ears and ran around in a little circle next to the door.

"*Wee-wee*, Oscar," Kay quipped tipsily.

Alex smirked, then kissed Kay on the cheek. "Oh, well done, Yankee Doodle Dandy," he said.

"Effortless," Mike added, smiling as Helen laughed, long and loud.

Good, thought Mike, *she's loosening up*.

"Come on, Oscar," Meggie said, opening the back door. She dodged to one side as Oscar made a swift and clumsy exit into the night air. "Anyone coming?" she asked the room. "It's a lovely night."

Mike turned to Helen. "Fancy some fresh air, babe?"

"Sure." She smiled back.

"What about you two?" Meggie asked her brother and Kay.

"Oh, I'm a bit busy with the contents of this glass right now," Alex chuckled.

"Suit yourselves," Meggie said, "but remember – it's bad luck to look at the full moon through glass."

Meggie stepped out, leaving Kay looking puzzled.

"What did she mean, bad luck?"

"Superstitious bloody claptrap," slurred Alex.

Helen looked at Mike, clearly amused. He decided to play up to it.

"Come on, Alex, Kay – you don't want to be cursed by the full moon!"

He made the last word into a howl for good measure. From outside, Oscar barked in reply. Even Alex laughed, hearing it, and they all headed out into the night air.

★   ★   ★

Helen had started snoring within minutes of her head hitting the pillow. Mike envied her ability to sleep on demand. He, more often than not, needed a smoke before he could sleep, and even then he'd have to listen to his heartbeat throbbing in his inner ear for at least an hour before he dropped off. The booze was still in his bloodstream, too stimulating – and entirely the wrong kind of buzz if he wanted some shut-eye. He turned over under the covers and let out a sigh of frustration. He heard a giggle, then low laughter through the wall. The sounds soon gave way to moans of pleasure.

Great, he thought, *now I have to listen to Alex and Kay shagging*.

He prayed that the amount of booze they'd put away would mean it would be over quickly, at least. As the muffled moans reached their climax, Mike rolled out of bed and crossed to the window. The full moon was high in the sky, painting the surface of the loch in silver light and making it look frozen. He knelt on the window seat and pressed his forehead against the glass, eager to feel its coolness on his hot skin. The drinks had given him the night sweats, and he relished the respite the windowpane was giving him. His breathing slowed as he watched clouds drift darkly across the moon, a halo of light dancing on the windowpane. The tips of fir trees moved against the invisible breath of a breeze, their shadows cast on the loch like the bows of ancient boats long since sailed for other shores. The tree nearest the window joined the dance, the tips of its branches skittering across the glass and making a faint scratching sound.

As his breath fogged up the window, diffusing the moonlight, Mike wondered how many other sleepless souls had gazed out of this very same window in the middle of the night. The thought troubled him, somehow making him feel insignificant in the grand scheme of things.

He heard another sound then, fainter and more distant than that of the branches. As it repeated, muffled yet shrill, it made the hairs on the nape of his neck stand up. He tore his gaze from the window and glimpsed a shadow breaking the dim light between the door and the floorboards. He grabbed his check shirt from the end of the bed and tugged it on over his t-shirt, then crossed to the door and opened it carefully so as not to wake Helen. Another shadow flickered across the wall down the hall from the doorway, and he heard the sound again – much clearer this time.

It was the sound of a child's laughter.

He stood at the threshold between the bedroom and the hallway, uncertain whether he wanted to investigate. Another shimmer of youthful laughter came, from downstairs now, and he wondered if Alex and Kay were playing tricks on him, restless after their bout of obnoxiously loud lovemaking. He glanced back at Helen, watching the covers rise and fall gently with her breathing. She could sleep through a thunderstorm, that one. He felt too wakeful to climb back in beside her under the covers. He pulled the door shut behind him quietly, stole out of the room and padded down the hall to the narrow stairwell. His skin turned to gooseflesh as he heard a high-pitched giggle.

Kay, it has to be. The giggling continued, becoming maniacal as he made his way down the creaking stairs. *Yeah, keep telling yourself that, buddy*, he thought and swallowed against the dryness coating his throat.

"Alex? Kay? This your idea of a windup? Well, it isn't funny, you bastards," he whispered. "You'll wake Helen."

He reached the foot of the stairs and paused for a moment, clenching his teeth at the piercing sound of child's laughter. As soon as his bare foot touched the stone floor, the sound stopped dead.

"Alex? You there? Kay?" he called out, all the more conscious of the apprehension in his voice now that he was standing in the silence of the living room.

No answer came, save the faintest crackle from the fireplace. Amber light pulsated on the stone floor, cast by the last embers of the fire. He entered the room and walked toward the light. The smell hit him before he saw it fully. A stench like salt meat burning on a spit.

The enormous shape of the stag lying across the hearth made him gasp. Its ribcage rose and fell as it took a labored breath. The animal's eye was open and its unflinching gaze upon him. Unable to speak due to the shock of finding it there, Mike watched the animal die all over again, just as he had at the roadside. As the weary animal breathed its last, Mike noticed a piece of antler in the grate. He walked over to the fireplace and crouched low to try to rescue it from the heat of the embers. It was the same broken piece he had brought back to the cottage. He reached out, tentatively because of the heat, and touched it with his fingertips. It felt cold to the touch, but how could that be? His fingers closed around the shard, and he retrieved it from the hearth, marveling at the cool sensation of it in his hand. But as he did so, the fire erupted in a sudden, angry ball of flame. The hot gust knocked him back from where he crouched. Sprawling to the floor, he sliced his hand open on the jagged end of the antler. Cursing, he tossed the antler aside and saw that the fire was out. Gray ashes littered the grate, cold and lifeless.

Impossible, he thought, *it was a raging bloody inferno a moment ago.*

He opened his hand and saw blood pumping from a deep wound at the center of his palm. The sight of so much blood made him gag. He swallowed his revulsion and smelled that salt meat stench again, felt hot breath ruffle his hair. The shadow of the beast loomed large over him. He knew it lived. Knew it wanted to exact its revenge upon him. The scrape of a hoof on the hard stone floor made his heart skip a beat.

Mike woke up thrashing, a choked scream dying in his throat. He sat up, vaguely aware of Helen lying asleep in the bed beside him. His hand was gushing with blood, and his head swam at the sight of it. He was bleeding out all over the white sheet, which had become an enormous bandage to swab the relentless flow of his lifeblood. He tried to scream, but no sound would come. He tried to move his other hand, intent on rousing Helen. Try as he might to waken her to his agonies, he felt paralyzed. Helen slept on with her back to him, in the oblivion of dreams. He struggled to find his voice, to cry out for help, but still no sound would come.

Breathe, he told himself, *just breathe.*

It was difficult. There was so much blood. But he managed to focus and slow his breathing just enough to make a difference. He felt a sensation like pins and needles passing through each of his limbs and then out through the extremities of his fingers and toes. Then the paralysis was gone. Able to move freely again, he looked in panic at his hand. There was no blood, no wound to be seen, nothing. He examined the bedsheets and found them drenched only with sweat, not a single drop of his blood.

He lay back as the first light of morning flickered through the trees, casting its glow on the bedroom wall. Shadows of branches moved above him, phantoms haunting the ceiling. Helen stirred beneath the warm cocoon of the covers and murmured something softly under her breath. Mike tried hard to hear what it was she was saying. Unable to hold onto the conscious, waking world, he fell fitfully asleep.

★ ★ ★

Breakfast was a welcome tonic to Mike's night of disturbing dreams and nightmare injuries. He had awoken to find Helen already gone and the delicious smell of frying bacon and fresh toast wafting up the stairs. After a quick shower to wash away the sweat of the night before, he joined the others in the conservatory and was welcomed with fresh coffee and a kiss from Helen.

"Sleep well?" she asked, taking a bite of buttered toast. "You were still out for the count when I got up, so I decided to leave you to it.

Knew the smell of brekkie would wake you up, if nothing else. You're like Oscar." She laughed, and he shrugged, smiling before taking a few welcome gulps of strong black coffee.

"Save some bread for us, lassies," Alex said. "Mike's going to need to make some sandwiches. Long day's fishing ahead of us. Hungry work, and thirsty too." As if to illustrate his point, Alex tapped the lid of a beer cooler he had placed on top of the counter.

"Make your own bloody sandwiches," Mike replied.

"I'll make the sandwiches the day that you can row us out onto the loch. Remember last time? You had us going round in circles for so long it was like being trapped in a bloody whirlpool."

Alex and the girls laughed, entirely at Mike's expense, but he had to relent. Alex was right; he really was lousy at rowing.

"All right, all right, I'll make the frigging sandwiches," Mike said. "Then I can eat them all while I watch you doing all the rowing."

Alex threw a tea towel at him, and Mike caught it.

"I'm having some bacon and eggs first, though; they smell amazing." Mike loaded up his plate and took a place at the table opposite Kay. He shoveled food into his hungry mouth and watched Meggie wander in, toweling her hair.

"Breakfast?" Helen asked, offering her the last of the bacon.

"Oh, no, no thanks," Meggie said, looking more than a little horrified. "I'm vegan."

Alex rolled his eyes. "Not that shite again. Have some bacon, you need the bloody protein."

"I get all the protein I need, thank you very much," Meggie replied. She crossed to the refrigerator and poured herself a glass of orange juice. On her way to the table, she paused and patted her brother's stomach, using her free hand. "You could do with a bit less saturated fat yourself, Captain Cholesterol."

Alex scoffed, red-faced, making Kay and the others laugh. Meggie sat down nearest the window, the morning light adding an orange glow to the red curls of her hair.

"Good first night?" she asked the table.

"Oh, yes," Helen was the first to reply. "Slept like a baby."

Mike felt himself wince at the memory of the child's laughter from the night before. Dipping his toast into his fried egg, he put his nightmares to one side, focusing instead on the view over the loch. It looked to be a fine day for fishing.

Meggie gulped down the rest of her orange juice and placed the glass on the table, idly turning it around and peering at the fragments of fruit coating the inside of the glass.

"We wondered if we could ask a favor, Kay and I," Helen said.

"Ask away," Meggie replied.

"Well, we don't want to spend the day watching this pair of lummoxes fishing." Helen ignored Mike's and Alex's noises of protest, adding, "Can't think of anything more boring, to be honest."

"I'm with you there, ladies," Meggie replied, with a twinkle in her eye.

"We wondered if we could borrow your car, go and explore the village?" Kay said rather bluntly.

"We'd walk, but it's a bit much after a big night," Helen explained apologetically, "and we'd like to get a few more provisions. Maybe there's something you need?"

"I'll drive you," Meggie offered.

"Oh, you don't have to do that," Helen said.

"Oh, no, no. It's no bother at all," Meggie replied.

Mike saw a flicker of discomfort on Helen's face. She looked more than a little uncomfortable at the prospect of spending time with Meggie. Or perhaps it was merely reluctance to ask a favor from a relative stranger. Mike couldn't be sure – Helen could be pretty tightly wound and was nothing short of impenetrable at the best of times. Her 'lawyer's poker face', as he liked to call it.

"Really, it's no bother," Meggie said. "My car is a bit… temperamental anyhow."

Alex chuckled dryly. "One way of putting it," he joked.

Meggie ignored him. "So it's probably best if I drive. And I know the way. I can be your tour guide for the day. Not that there's so much to see in Drinton, of course."

"To be frank, there's more to see on the loch," Alex said, and Kay elbowed him softly. "Still, it'll be an adventure, taking your chances in Meggie's old rust bucket."

"It's in better shape than your four-by-four," Meggie said pointedly.

Alex grimaced and turned his attention to the coffee pot for a refill.

"I still can't shake the image of that poor stag," Kay said with a frown, the shadow of a memory darkening her eyes. "I had a dream about it last night. I could hear it breathing. Poor thing was in agony, and I–I just couldn't do anything to help it." She looked sorrowfully around at the others. "Did any of you dream about it too?"

Mike felt cold all of a sudden. The breakfast sat heavy in his stomach, and a bead of sweat trickled onto his brow. He gazed out of the window, once again willing away half-remembered fragments of his nightmare. The stag looming large, the sickening scrape of hoof on hard stone floor. He felt his heart beat faster, just as it had during his bad dream. No one said anything, the conservatory now quiet and the atmosphere no longer convivial but strangely somber. Then a sudden and enormous bang shattered the silence as a black crow smashed into the conservatory window.

Kay shrieked with fright at the sound, causing Alex to startle and spill hot coffee down his shirt. Alex's unfettered cursing prompted Oscar to bark loudly. The panicked dog began clawing at the door, desperate to get out. Mike reached out and grabbed Oscar's collar, pulling him back from the door and trying to calm him down. As he did this, Meggie opened the door and dashed outside. Oscar turned on Mike, barking at him and snapping his jaws. Mike let go of the collar, narrowly avoiding being bitten.

"Oscar!" Alex exclaimed and gave chase, forgetting about his coffee burns for a moment.

Mike followed and stumbled outside. He saw Oscar run straight for Meggie, who was crouched beneath the section of glass where the bird had hit. She stood up, and Mike noted that she had the feathered bundle cupped safely in her hands. Seeing Oscar, she sidestepped the crazed animal and shouted at him until he backed off, turned tail and ran full pelt away from the garden and under the fence until he was out of sight.

"Is it still alive?" Helen had emerged from the conservatory, followed by a queasy-looking Kay. Alex put his arm around Kay to comfort her.

Mike and Helen followed Meggie as she carried the bird to the outbuilding studio. Mike held the door open so Meggie could enter, still cupping the bird's body in her hands. Helen followed her inside, and then Mike. The air in the room was calmingly cool and the cluttered space filled with old crofter's tools, furniture, and a collection of boxes over-spilling with assorted ornaments. An unfinished watercolor painting, depicting an ancient stone circle set in a twilight landscape, sat atop an easel. The artwork was accomplished, even though it was incomplete.

"Empty out one of those, could you?" Meggie asked Helen, nodding toward a couple of small cardboard boxes filled with tubes of paint.

As Helen set about her task, Meggie nodded at another cardboard box, this one resting on a pile of old magazines and newspapers. "You'll find plenty of ribbon in there," Meggie instructed him.

Mike grabbed a roll of pastel green ribbon at random. Meggie carefully lowered the bird onto her workbench and, gripping it with one hand, used the other to take the ribbon from Mike.

"Thanks. Now, tear some of that newspaper into strips, will you?" she asked.

Meggie carefully bound the bird's wing with the soft, green ribbon as Mike walked back to the stack of old newspapers. A cloud of dust billowed when he took the topmost one from the pile. The dust made him cough and sneeze, and he dropped the newspaper to the floor. He glimpsed part of the headline – 'DISASTER' – then succumbed to a coughing fit again.

"Clumsy," clucked Helen, pushing past him and grabbing a newspaper from the pile. She began tearing strips of the paper, which she then placed in a lattice work of layers inside the empty paint box.

"Thanks," Meggie said, lowering the bird into the makeshift nest of torn paper.

Mike absentmindedly stroked his hand where Oscar had almost bitten him as he watched them fussing over the crow.

Meggie noticed him doing this. "Oscar didn't hurt you, did he?" she asked.

"Oh, no," Mike said, "his bark was worse than his bite."

"He has his moments," Meggie said, sighing. "Always off chasing rabbits if I don't keep him to heel."

"He's not vegan then, I take it?" Helen asked, smiling.

"No, he's not. Seems I'm the only one here who is." Meggie's voice sounded a little clipped. Her eyes narrowed, and Mike saw a flash of deeper meaning there for a moment before she carried the box over to some shelves and placed it there. Presumably so that it was out of reach of wild predators such as Oscar.

"We went veggie for a bit, didn't we, Mike?" Helen said.

Mike nodded. Awful memories of couscous and other nonedibles came rushing back. The worst three and a half days of his entire life. He remembered going for drive-through the day that Helen had announced their culinary experiment was over. She was as much a meat eater as he was. The cheeseburger had never tasted so good as it had on that day. "I don't think I could physically live without bacon," Mike thought out loud.

"Sure you could," Meggie said, "and the poor wee pigs certainly would, if you abstained." She whispered something musical and unintelligible to the bird in the box.

Mike thought it might be Gaelic. He hadn't known she could speak other languages.

"Couldn't hack it for long," Helen said. "A week, wasn't it, Mike?"

"Three and a half days," Mike corrected, seeing Meggie roll her eyes.

Helen hadn't noticed. "I think it was the soya milk that did it," she continued. "Disgusting." She shuddered and pulled a face.

"I always find it strange," Meggie said, "that meat eaters can claim to be such animal lovers."

Mike glanced at the little box containing the bird.

"I don't claim to…I *do* love animals," Helen said.

"Only *certain* animals," Meggie replied. "You two rushed in here to help me with the bird. But at breakfast you were eating dead pig. See, to me, this bird and the bacon on your plates are one and the same thing."

"The bird isn't part of our food chain though," Mike said. All this talk of bacon was making him hungry for seconds – a development he decided to keep to himself. For now, at least.

"Neither is Oscar," Meggie retorted, "but they do eat dogs in China."

"Oh, Jesus. That's gross. It would never be socially acceptable over here," Helen said.

"And yet, eating pigs is. Cows and lambs, chickens. All 'socially acceptable' murder meat. And what did you both have in your coffee this morning? Cows' milk."

"I read somewhere that if you don't milk a cow, it dies," Mike offered.

Meggie laughed at that and then threw him what could perhaps best be described as a pitying look, although withering have might been a better fit. "Well, wherever you read that they forgot to mention that they also fit dairy cows with these horrible contraptions they call milking preventers so the calves can't feed from their udders."

"Pull the udder one," Mike quipped.

Helen scowled at him and mouthed silently for him to shut up.

Meggie went on, oblivious, her voice building in intensity until she was almost sermonizing. "Humans are literally stealing milk from baby cows. How has that become socially acceptable? If people didn't breed cows for dairy production, then they'd just feed their young as nature intended. The male calves are sent for slaughter, of course, because they're of little or no value. They end up in cheap supermarket burgers, no doubt. I never want to be in a food chain that does all that...."

Mike swallowed, and his stomach gurgled at all this talk of dairy products and hamburgers. He really hoped that Meggie had not heard it.

"Fair enough," Helen said, breaking the uncomfortable silence that had crept into the studio like a fog.

Outside and far away, Oscar barked. The sound echoed off the trees that surrounded the loch.

"Better try and get that one under control," Meggie said, and Mike noticed she had tears in her eyes. "I'll check how the bird's doing later, when we get back from the village, Helen."

"Sure," Helen replied as Meggie left the outbuilding.

"Well, that went well," Mike muttered, making sure that Meggie was out of hearing range.

"Bit on the intense side, isn't she?" Helen ambled over to the unfinished painting, tracing the sweeping lines made by the brushstrokes with her fingers. "She's a good artist though," Helen mused. "Completely mental, but good."

Mike joined her, placing his arm around her shoulders. Helen leaned into him, and he welcomed her warmth in the slight damp of the studio.

Mike studied the painting for a moment. "Artists always have to be a *bit* batshit though, don't they?"

"True enough." Helen shrugged before kissing him on the cheek. Something about the way she was looking at him gave Mike pause.

"What's wrong?"

"Nothing," Helen said, smiling at him. She glanced at the little box on the shelf. "Think that poor bird will live?"

"If it doesn't, we can always eat it," Mike chuckled.

"Don't!" Helen said, laughing.

"What? Few breadcrumbs, nice dollop of murder gravy...."

Helen broke their embrace and led him by the hand toward the open door. "Just don't let the vegan avenger see you," she said, and they both laughed.

Mike strolled outside after her and listened to Meggie calling Oscar's name in the distance as they walked. The dog's barking had ceased. Coast clear, he and Helen headed back toward the kitchen.

CHAPTER FOUR

"Relax the line, din'nae lose it! Din'nae bloody lose it!"

Mike gripped the side of the rowing boat with both hands, watching the powerful silhouette of the fish break the water as it struggled against Alex's hook. It looked to be a fine trout.

"I know what I'm doing, don't distract me, man." Alex was half-standing, half-kneeling at the dead center of the boat, struggling to keep control of his catch. "Move around to the other side, will you? Or you'll capsize the bloody boat. Slowly now!"

Mike shuffled backward, then ducked under Alex's arms to avoid getting caught up in the fishing line. The reel made a high-pitched whirring sound as Alex let more line out before he started reeling it back in again.

"Come on, you bugger," Alex muttered under his breath. He was in silent concentration now. It was just him and the fish, bonded by the line that joined them. But the fish did not want to join its captor on land, that much was certain. Mike watched Alex as he skillfully began to play the trout closer to the boat, allowing it enough of a run to keep it on the hook but not so much that it could free itself from his grasp.

Mike watched the darting fish as it powered through the water, just feet away from the boat now. It swam deep, and Alex made a frustrated smacking sound with his teeth. Gripping the rod tight in both hands, he shifted his weight to compensate for the movement of the fish.

"Cannae let the bastard swim under the boat or I'll bloody well lose it," he said, breathless. "Get the net ready, mate."

Mike grabbed the net and held it aloft, ready to plunge it into the water the moment Alex instructed. Leaning over the side of the boat, Mike saw the fish retracing its sideward path through the water. Alex used the line to close the gap slightly. Now it would have to swim ever closer to the boat. As the fish tried to swim deeper, Mike's gaze followed its dark shape down beneath the glassy surface of the loch. The clouds broke, and the afternoon sun reflected on the still surface, making Alex's job even harder. With the glare in his eyes, he could no longer see where the fishing line met the water.

"Never let me say you don't need sunglasses in Scotland," Alex sighed. Then he sighed again, but this time in relief as the clouds obscured the sun once more.

Mike searched the depths, looking for the fish beneath the water. He saw a shape – much bigger than a fish – and recoiled, dropping the net inside the boat.

A human body lay floating just below the surface of the black depths, facedown. She was dressed in a white nightgown that billowed out around her, shroud-like. Her skin was pale as death and mottled gray from who knew how long in the water. Mike gagged at the sight of the tangled hair, floating like seaweed with its strands now and then licking at the surface of the water. Bubbles rose up from the deep, breaking on the surface of the water, and Mike smelled the foulness of corruption and decay as each bubble popped. He clamped a hand over his mouth as the body started to roll over in the water. The surface of the loch smoothed over the pale skin like the sickly film on a cataract eye. As it righted itself, the dead body floated closer to the side of the boat. It was directly beneath him now, dead face revealed to the sky above.

The face was Meggie's. The hair that undulated like fronds in the water was of a ruddy hue. It was definitely her, but how? He had seen her driving her car, with Helen and Kay in the passenger seats, just a couple of hours ago. She should be in the village, shopping, not dead in the water. His jaw dropped open, and a sound that he didn't recognize came out of his throat. And then the sound became a strangled scream like all the animals in a slaughterhouse dying all at once – for he saw Meggie's dead eyes open. They were milk-white and lifeless but still seeing somehow, and they looked right through him. Or, rather, deep into him. Mike felt the cold grip of fear at his heart, and he fell back into the boat, rocking it violently as he went.

"What the fuck are you doing, man?" Alex was shouting. "I told you to grab the bloody net!"

Mike floundered, then willed himself into action. Her eyes had opened. She was still alive. He had no idea how, but that must be it. Either she was still alive or he was totally losing his mind. Mike grabbed hold of the net and crawled back to the side of the boat.

"Quickly, man!"

Alex must have seen her too. Mike felt a rush of relief that he hadn't taken leave of his senses after all. He readied himself to thrust the pole of the net across the water so Meggie could reach it. They would have to hope she still had enough strength to grab hold of the net so they could then pull her closer to the boat and haul her inside. Leaning over the side of the boat once again, Mike peered back into the water. She was gone. There was no dead body. What he had mistaken for tangled red hair was a cluster of algae that drifted by just beneath the surface of the loch.

"Nearly bloody lost it, no thanks to you," Alex spat as he maneuvered the exhausted fish to the side of the boat. "Do not fuck this up, mate."

Mike scooped into the water with the net. Even now, he was fearful he might feel the dull snag of lifeless fingers on the net. Dread dulled the beating of his heart as he swept the net through the spot where he had seen her, bloated and pale and – nightmarishly – neither dead nor alive.

"It's a beauty! It's a fucking beauty!" Alex exclaimed, dropping his rod and taking the net pole from Mike's trembling hands.

Mike tried to smile, to act normal.

What the actual fuck did I just see? he thought.

Whatever it was, it had gone now, and he laughed, more in hysterics than anything else. Alex misread his laughter as celebration for the fish and slapped him on the back, hard.

"We'll eat well tonight, hey, mate?" Alex chuckled. The tension had gone between them; now there was only Alex's elation at a successful fishing expedition.

And now that his apparently dead sister wasn't floating in the water in her nightgown.

Mike shivered uncontrollably. He watched Alex as he set about removing the hook from the enormous trout's dying mouth. Beating a retreat, Mike sank back against the unyielding wooden surface of the boat and wanted, more than he had ever wanted anything, to be back on dry land and away from the still, black waters of the loch.

★   ★   ★

The girls were waiting for them on the jetty when Alex triumphantly rowed them back in.

Mike winced when he saw Meggie, his nightmarish hallucination of her dead body in the water still so vivid to him. He didn't know whether he needed to have a smoke or to pack it in. Meggie was very much alive, sitting, laughing and joking beside the water with Helen and Kay. They had shopping bags with them, from which they were passing around snacks. Alex seemed particularly pleased to see bottles of booze poking over the top of the bags. His blood was up after catching the fish, and Mike felt sure his friend would be indulging in some single malts as soon as he was on dry land again.

"Hey, hunter-gatherers! Catch anything for us poor, hungry womenfolk to eat?" Kay laughed.

"Aye, you look like you're wasting away there!" Alex called out in reply. "Save some bloody crisps for us at least, you gannets!"

The girls laughed and teased Alex and Mike with the snacks, pretending to devour all of them. They looked like they'd had an enjoyable day. Mike felt relieved to be back in the fold after all the weirdness on the water. He secretly enjoyed being surrounded by the girls, especially when Alex was at peak machismo – as he was right now. Alex guided the boat to the jetty, and it rocked slightly as it bumped against the mooring post. He threw the rope over the side, and Meggie stood up and helped him tie it off.

"Thanks, sis," Alex said, ignoring her disapproving look at the dead fish.

"Don't suppose you heard anything of Oscar while you were out there?"

"Not a peep. Still not back then?"

Meggie shook her head, and Mike could tell she was trying not to appear too worried. It wasn't working. She was clearly concerned about her best four-legged friend.

"Bloody liability, that pup. He'll come back soon as we start cooking this beastie," Alex said and proudly lifted up the net containing the enormous fish.

The girls laughed and cheered.

"Look, girls, they sneaked off to the fishmonger's while we were gone," Kay joked.

"Bloody cheek of it," Alex said, turning to Mike, who shrugged.

"We'll have to eat it all, I reckon, mate," Mike said. He too was trying not to look worried, and he hoped it was working. He didn't want to have to explain that he had hallucinated seeing Alex's sister dead in the water while they were on their fishing trip.

Helen's eyes met his. She looked quizzical for a moment and then guarded. If anyone could read that there was something on his mind, it was her. She looked as though she was about to say something to him, but then Meggie spoke and the moment was gone.

"That's quite a catch," Meggie said.

"Yes, I am," Kay said, laughing at her own joke.

"In your dreams," Alex said before trying, and failing, to dodge her punch to this arm.

"Shame you boys couldn't set it free," Meggie muttered.

"Shame you're being so vegan and virtuous," Alex said to his sister. "Don't know what you're missing – this beauty is going to be bloody delicious."

Meggie just shrugged and helped Alex with the net as he clambered out of the boat. He turned back for the gear, which Mike passed to him before hopping onto the jetty beside him. Helen grabbed Mike's hand and hugged him tight. She stared into his eyes, and he noticed that hers looked wet and filled with emotion.

"You all right?" she asked him.

"Yeah," Mike mumbled, "I was just going to ask you the same thing."

"Never better," she replied.

Wiping a tear from the corner of her eye, she led him by the hand toward the cottage. Her hand was small and warm in his, and he could feel her pulse through her wrist against his. This unspoken connection made him feel closer to Helen, but also alienated from her. Helen was given to mood swings – he'd been with her long enough to know that – but he'd never seen her get weepy over anything other than her favorite Netflix show. Mike didn't know how to read her right now. He pulled her hand, slowing her down for a second.

"You sure you're okay?" he said.

She nodded, breaking into a wide smile, her eyes still glassy. "It's just this…this place," she said, as though that would explain everything.

"This place," Mike repeated. He glanced back at the dark, still waters of the loch.

"I don't know," Helen went on. "We've been in the city for so long, studying and cramming for exams."

"Speak for yourself," Mike said. "I've been partying, mostly."

She nudged him to shut up. "I don't want to sound like I'm away with the fairies. Like Kay, or Meggie for that matter, but...."

"Helen, I shall have to tell them both that you said that about them."

"You bloody dare, mister."

"Sorry, only kidding around. Go on, what was it you wanted to say?"

Helen sighed. "It's...it's just...coming here, it's just kind of magical. I feel, well, *connected* is perhaps the best way I can put it."

"Makes sense, I suppose," Mike ventured.

"You've been here before, I know. Was it like this the first time for you?"

"Yeah, a bit. It's a total change from the city, you know, from Edinburgh. But I think the wide-open spaces can get to you after a while. And no bloody wi-fi."

"Oh, the wi-fi, thanks for reminding me," Helen said. "Still, we girls got our Instagram fix in the village today."

"You had a signal?"

"Yes, we did," Helen said boastfully.

"No fair," Mike replied.

"I just feel like we're on the cusp of something new, here at this place," Helen said. "Like everything will change now that we've graduated. Nothing will ever be the same again, somehow. Don't you feel that too?"

Strange fish, Mike thought as Helen squeezed his hand and led him back toward Hearthstone Cottage.

★ ★ ★

Mike and Alex helped the others unpack the food and drink provisions they had brought back with them from Drinton village.

Alex made appreciative noises about the bottle of single malt Kay had picked out for them, and Mike counted eight bottles of wine in total. They were in for a good night – or two at a push. As they placed dried goods in a cupboard together, Helen told him about her trip to the village and how the place seemed to be a snapshot of time stood still. That was exactly how Mike remembered the old place, with its tiny post office and grocery store. The local pub held particular appeal for Mike, and he felt a pang of alarm when Helen reported it had been shut when she and the others had passed by. Mike hoped it hadn't closed down entirely, although he would understand if it had. Drinton got approximately two weeks of sun per year if it was lucky, according to Alex.

Helen talked on, describing how Meggie had shown them an artists' studio at the far end of the lane that led out of the village. The owners of a smallholding were renting the space, previously a barn for livestock, to artists interested in staying and working in the area. Helen said most of the work on display was overpriced and unimaginative, but one piece had caught her eye. She took a low, wide box from the grocery bag and placed it on the counter. After removing the lid, she tore aside layer upon layer of thin white tissue paper until she had revealed the object inside. It looked to Mike like a black dinner plate, smoothly curved upward, creating a shallow bowl shape. Helen lifted it out, and Mike marveled at the sheer, black reflective surface.

"Meggie told me it's a scrying mirror," Helen announced. "Handcrafted."

"It looks...cool," Mike said, trying to sound convincing.

"It's traditional to the Celtic healing arts," Helen went on, oblivious. "Apparently if you gaze into it for long enough, you can enter a deep meditative state."

"All that from a bit of black glass?" Mike said, his interest piqued. He was beginning to wonder what the effect might be if he smoked a blunt and stared into this mirror thing. It could be trippy.

Helen tilted the mirror to place it on the little wooden display plinth that lay folded up in the box, and her reflection stretched and elongated, growing thin. The image made Mike think of Meggie's dead face under the loch. He shuddered. Maybe he'd be better off not looking into the damn thing after all.

"I think we should display it," Helen said. "It's far too pretty to keep in its box until we go home."

"How about here?" Kay asked, standing at the bookcase where she was rifling through the dustier old tomes.

"I'd worry about it being knocked over and broken," Helen said before crossing to the fireplace. "Here," she said, placing it carefully on the mantelpiece. "It belongs here."

★   ★   ★

"Listen to this, you guys!"

Kay was sitting cross-legged near the fire, poring over a tatty, old book on local folklore that she had selected from the shelves.

Mike was in the kitchen, washing the trout that Alex had landed while his friend peeled some potatoes. It was the boys' turn to prepare a meal for the holidaymakers while Kay held court beside the fire. Meggie sat at the piano, idly fingering the keys.

"It says here that the last witch to be executed in Scotland was put to death near here."

"That's a cheery thought," Helen said, peering over the top of a tourist map.

"Spooky to think, though, isn't it? She was put on trial after several villagers died of a strange illness.... Oh, some of them were just poor wee kids...."

"Learning to speak Scots already, I hear," Meggie said. She didn't sound too pleased at Kay's appropriation of her accent.

Kay carried on, seemingly oblivious. "They blamed the woman for poisoning their water and making their crops fail. She confessed to being in league with Satan and begged for a merciful death."

"Well, she would say that, wouldn't she?" Helen suggested. "Poor woman was probably being tortured. That's what they did back then, isn't it? You'd say you rode a flying unicorn home every night if that would make them take the thumbscrews off. I know I would."

"A woman with principles similar to my own," Meggie chuckled. She began improvising a gentle tune on the piano that sounded halfway between a Celtic reel and a nursery song.

"The witch did not go quietly, according to eyewitnesses," Kay read on. "She spoke in tongues...."

"What did she say? Put the bloody fire out?" Helen giggled.

"Listen," Kay pleaded, "it says here the minister who said the last rites implored the dying woman not to curse them with her witchcraft, and she exclaimed, 'You have all cursed yourselves!' Kind of creepy, hey?"

"I find it kind of...typical that a man who was burning a woman alive at the stake only had a care for his own safety," Helen replied.

"How times have changed," added Meggie, with more than a hint of sarcasm. She beat out a few bars of punk rock to make her point.

"Us lads had better know our place – in the kitchen," Alex chuckled. "They're making ready to smash the patriarchy in there. How's the main attraction coming?"

"Time to gut the beast," Mike answered, "before we sacrifice it."

Mike carried the heavy fish over to a chopping board. He took a sharp knife from a drawer and inserted it beside the rear lower fin. He pushed the blade forward.

The smell hit his nostrils so hard he thought he might throw up all over their dinner. He gagged at the sight and smell of a flood of thick black fluid that gushed from the incision in the fish's flesh. Writhing maggots spilled with the noxious fluid, coating the chopping board in a living mass of corruption. The flesh inside the fish was charcoal black, and the stench that rose up from it made Mike retch. He stumbled back from the chopping board and lost his grip on the knife. Slicing his thumb open on the sharp cook's blade, he cried out in pained surprise.

"Jesus, Mikey." Alex was at his side, looking in shock at Mike's hand.

Not just my hand, Mike's mind raced, *look at the bloody fish. It's black inside. Foul, foul thing.*

"Rinse it under the cold water, bud," Alex was saying, though to Mike he sounded a million light years away. He felt cold, like the water of the loch, where he had seen Meggie's dead eyes open—

"I said you're not going to faint, are you?"

Mike's nausea dissipated, and he found himself standing over the sink. Cold water ran from the tap onto his wound. A fuzzy spiral of blood coiled into the plughole, carried by the water flow. Alex passed him a clean tea towel, and Mike wrapped it around his thumb. Alex lifted Mike's arm and told him to keep it above his head since that would stop the bleeding. As Mike walked numbly through the kitchen, he glanced at the fish and stopped in his tracks.

Impossible.

Where there had been a mess of black fluid and maggots just moments ago, now there was only a patch of blood – whether it was the fish's blood or his, he couldn't be certain – and the discarded knife that lay on its side against the chopping board.

"I...."

"Hold on, Mikey, we'll get you a bandage or something."

"Don't call me Mikey."

"You'll live. Mikey."

Alex led Mike into the living space. The fire made it feel too hot in there. Helen had gone; only Kay and Meggie were in there. Kay was still engrossed in her book, and Meggie was tinkling away at the piano. It really was too hot in there, and too close, like being in a sauna. Mike wished he could go outside.

"Meg," Alex asked, "have we still got the old medical kit?"

"Don't call me Meg, you know I hate that," his sister said. Then, seeing Mike's bloodstained tea towel, her eyes registered her surprise. "Oh! Come with me, Mikey, it's in the studio, I think."

"Fuck's sake. Don't you call me Mikey, either. Where's Helen?"

"Bathroom, I think," Kay murmured, then noticed Mike's hand for the first time. "What did you do?"

Meggie rolled her eyes at Kay and led Mike out of the room. "Come on," she said.

CHAPTER FIVE

Mike stood outside the studio, smoking a welcome blunt. Meggie had patched his wound up with all the skill and care of a field medic. He glanced at the bandage she'd fixed around his thumb, after first cleaning the cut with saline solution from the little first aid box and then applying a small square of sterile gauze to the wound. It was a deep cut, and she'd told him that there'd be a permanent scar. If being an artist didn't work out for her, Mike reckoned she had a bright future in medicine, and had told her as much. The early-evening air was fresh and invigorating and he felt a million times better already. He looked over at the cottage, warm lights glowing in each of the downstairs windows. Only one upstairs light could be seen, and that was the one in the bathroom. Mike heard water flowing down the outlet pipe that led to a drain just a few feet away from where he stood. He wondered if Helen was in the bathroom. Mike was glad she had missed out on all the carnage in the kitchen. He felt a little embarrassed now about how he'd nearly fainted when he'd cut himself. Alex would no doubt crack a few jokes later at his expense, particularly after he'd had a couple of drinks. At least his friend had been left to take care of prepping and cooking the fish. Alex did seem besotted by the slimy thing after all.

A flicker at the periphery of his vision jolted Mike from his thoughts, and he saw a shadow pass by the open doorway of the outbuilding. He took a few steps closer, and his blood ran cold when he heard the same childlike laughter he had heard in his dream, shrill as a bell, coming from inside. He stubbed out the joint and then peered through the nearby window to see if anyone was in there. He had not heard Meggie leave and assumed she was still inside. Maybe she was listening to the digital radio or something.

"Meggie? You there?"

The door swung back slightly on its hinges as he approached

the threshold. He heard another giggle, more distant this time, accompanied by little footsteps.

"Who's there?" he called out as he rushed inside.

Meggie squealed in alarm. She was standing over by the corner shelves with her back to him. He had clearly startled her.

"Made me jump out of my skin, so you did!" she exclaimed. Then, calming herself, she said, "You look white as a sheet, what's wrong?"

"I heard—I mean, I thought I heard…"

"What?"

"…someone come in here. It sounded like a kid. You sure you didn't see anyone?"

"No children around here," Meggie said, "except for my man-child of a brother."

"Well, I definitely heard laughter."

"Maybe you heard Kay, or Helen, from inside the cottage?"

"Yeah, it could have been them, I suppose. But it really sounded like it came from in here."

"The wind could be playing tricks on you, making noises from the cottage sound like they're coming from somewhere else. I imagine all sorts of things while I'm working out here, especially at night. And Oscar barks at anything.…"

Mike saw a pang of regret at the mention of her pet's name. "Still no sign of him?" he said.

"No. I'm trying not to be worried about him, but he hasn't been gone this long ever before. Usually his stomach brings him back, so.…"

"I'm sure he'll turn up." Mike hoped he sounded convincing enough. He didn't like seeing Meggie so upset about the dog. But he couldn't help thinking the animal had got himself into some kind of trouble out there in the wilderness.

Meggie turned her attention back to a little box on the shelf. "Looks like this one will be okay, at least."

Mike sidled over to her and knew then what had kept Meggie in the studio. She was tending to the crow, and he watched as she fed it water carefully from a clean artists' pipette.

Meggie noticed him standing close by. "Here, want to try?"

"Oh, I don't know if I—"

"It's easy; you just have to hover the water over the wee beastie's beak, and he'll do the rest."

Before Mike could protest, she took his hand in hers and placed the pipette between his fingers. The bird moved suddenly, startling Mike, but Meggie gently stroked the bird's feathers, all the while shushing them both. She guided his hand until the tip of the pipette was above the bird's beak. "Now give it a little squeeze," she said softly to avoid spooking the bird.

Mike squeezed the plastic bulb of the pipette until a drop of water appeared. The bird took the cue and gobbled it up, snapping its beak thirstily. Mike squeezed again and repeated the process, with the bird eager to take more water from him.

"Thirsty little blighter, isn't he?" Mike said.

"He is that," Meggie said with a smile. "I find it quite relaxing, feeding animals. Makes you feel connected to them in the most primal way possible."

Mike did feel connected to the little bird. The simple stuff of life – water – was flowing between his hand operating the pipette and the bird's beak. He marveled at how fragile the bird looked in the box but also how startled he had been when it had moved. It was still vital and filled with life – and potential.

"How long do you think until it flies again?"

"Oh, a day or two at most," Meggie said, and the bird snapped its beak, as if on cue. "You're a natural."

Looking into her smiling eyes, Mike couldn't quite believe how long it had been since he'd first met Meggie, here at the cottage. She had changed a fair bit since then. Traveling must do that to a person, he supposed. She seemed more mature, more assured about what she was saying. She was no longer in her big brother's shadow, as she had appeared when they had first met.

"What is it?" she asked.

"I, uh...." Mike realized he had fallen silent and was staring at her like some kind of lunatic. He struggled to find the words and then faltered, realizing she was still gently holding on to his hand.

"Hello? Mike? You in there?"

"Shit," Mike said.

It was Helen. In a clumsy reflex action, Mike wrenched his hand away from Meggie's and, in doing so, dropped the pipette into the box, alarming both Meggie and the bird.

Mike turned to see Helen standing in the doorway. Her face looked flushed, and she was a little out of breath.

"How's the patient?" Helen asked.

"Oh, I was just helping Meggie to feed him. I mean *it*," Mike replied.

Helen looked from the bird box to Meggie and then threw Mike a quizzical look. "I meant you, you daft sod. Kay and Alex told me you mortally injured yourself in the name of fine dining."

"Oh," Mike said, "the fish." He raised his thumb, proudly displaying the bandage.

"Looked like he might faint from the sight of blood at one point," Meggie said, "but he'll live."

Helen laughed, and it sounded like a reflex action of her own. "That's what Alex said."

"Bet he did," Mike growled, "the unsympathetic bastard."

"Talking of which, I'd better check he isn't murdering the vegetables," Meggie announced, positioning the bird box safely on its shelf. "He always boils them into a soup-like nonexistence." Meggie popped the pipette on the drainer next to the little sink unit. "See you guys in a wee bit," she said on her way out.

"Nurse Meg saves the day," Helen teased, admiring Meggie's handiwork with the bandage. "Is she going to find a little cardboard box to keep you in too, Mike?"

"Bugger off," Mike said in mock protest. "Thought I'd sliced my bloody thumb off, didn't I?" He winced at the memory of the black fluid seeping from the fish's innards, and the pulsing mass of writhing maggots that had seemed so real to him—

And the stench, oh, Jesus, the filthy stench of the thing.

"Are you listening to a single word I just said?"

"About the box?" Mike knew from the look on Helen's face that he had zoned out again.

"Bloody stoner," she said.

"Hey, don't turn into Alex. One of him is already more than bloody enough," Mike said.

"I was saying, before you decided to go on a mental trip to la-la land, that we need to talk."

"How d'you mean? A *talk* talk?"

"Yes. A *talk* talk." Helen looked serious.

"Well, can it wait 'til later? How about after dinner? I'm ruddy starving. Cutting my thumb like that, I think I lost a fair bit of blood...."

Helen's laughter echoed off the walls of the studio. "Mummy's poor 'ickle soldier!"

"Well, let's go outside, yeah?" Mike took Helen gently by the wrist and led her away from the shelves. "Don't want to freak the bird out."

Helen resisted, giggling all the while.

Mike tensed up. "Please, Helen, you'll startle the bloody bird."

At this, Helen shot Mike a look of exaggerated surprise. "Who are you, and what have you done with my boyfriend?"

Mike relaxed his grip and sighed. He needed to be out in the open. The studio seemed suddenly very small to him, still fuzzy with the atmosphere of the intimate moment that had passed between him and Meggie while they had tended to the bird.

"Let's just get out of here, okay?"

"Good idea," Helen said, her mood cooling along with her subsiding laughter. "We can have our chat down by the jetty."

*　　*　　*

Mike sat next to Helen, their legs dangling over the black waters of the loch. The final, straggling rays of sunlight painted distant clouds in hues of burnt orange. A light breeze blew across the open water, bringing with it the wet scent of a season on the cusp of giving way to the next.

"I'm so glad we came here, to this special place." Helen's voice broke the silence softly but with purpose.

"And I'm glad you like it here," Mike said.

It was evidently the right thing to say. Helen reached out and took his hand in hers. *Just like Meggie had done,* Mike thought for one guilty moment.

"You remember what I said before, about how everything will change?"

"Yeah, of course I do," Mike said.

He felt a little uncomfortable at Helen's intensity. Since cutting his thumb, he had just wanted to eat. To be back in the cottage with his noisy friends and to gorge himself on whatever was available, and then to get as drunk as a lord, fuck his girlfriend and pass out until the hunger to do it all over again woke him up. That was what the word 'holiday' meant to Mike. And he was just working out how to best articulate all of that to Helen when she pressed something into the palm of his hand. It felt like a pen, and for a crazy moment he wondered if she was gifting him with one—

Congrats on your graduation!

—but when he opened his hand and looked down at the object, he saw a flat length of white plastic, about four inches long.

"What...? What's this?" he asked, dumbfounded.

"Turn it over and take a look," Helen said.

Mike took the plastic object by one end, wincing as he gripped it with his bandaged thumb, and flipped it over. A little indicator halfway along the object's shaft had a symbol on it. He peered closer and saw in the encroaching twilight that it was a thin blue line.

"I'm pregnant," Helen said.

Mike's head swam. The whole jetty seemed to lurch and tilt beneath him. He was about to stand up but realized if he did so he'd fall feetfirst into the cold waters of the loch. Instead he reached out behind him with his good hand for support. In his bandaged hand, the pregnancy test felt awfully heavy for a little piece of plastic. He didn't know what to say. The shock was too great. But he had to say something.

Helen was crying now and smiling at him and speaking words he couldn't quite hear. A maelstrom of emotions whirled inside his head, dizzying him. He leaned forward, over the water, and saw his face reflected on the dark filmy surface of the loch – an indistinct blur. A bubble broke the surface of the water, the ripples distorting his reflection until the dark slit of his mouth looked like it was screaming.

"But you have a say in this too," Helen was saying. "Mike? Say something. Please?"

He exhaled, trying to get a grip on solid land, but the planks of the jetty creaked unreliably beneath him.

"It's...it's a lot to take in."

Helen looked slightly confused. "That's all you have to say? After what I just told you? You can open up to me, Mike. Here and now. It's okay. It's going to be okay...."

Mike did not feel that confessing to having zoned out again would help in any way right now. So he forced a smile and said, "I'm sorry. Just getting used to the idea, that's all. I thought we were, you know, being careful."

"So did I."

"How, then?"

"I don't know. I already told you...."

Mike bit his lower lip, still unwilling to confess he hadn't heard what she'd been saying before. "I know, babe. I know, I'm sorry."

"You don't have to keep saying you're sorry." She paused for breath, and Mike saw her shiver as she exhaled. "I am a bit terrified, to be honest," Helen said. "I was all set to do my master's, but now...."

"Pregnant women go to uni all the time," Mike said, trying to sound upbeat. "You remember that mature student the year above us?"

"The Swedish woman?"

"Yeah. Her."

"She dropped out, Mike."

"Really?"

"Really. Never completed her course of studies. Awarded one of those token diplomas instead."

"Never get a decent job with one of those."

"Happens a lot with female students apparently. Easier for you bloody blokes." Helen sighed. "As per usual."

Mike reached into his jeans pocket and pulled out his stash tin and the cardboard packet of rolling papers. He started building himself a smoke.

"You'll have to pack those in, you know. If you're going to be a baby daddy."

Mike tried to stop himself wincing and failed. He could feel his brow furrowing and conspiring against him, betraying his worry. He licked at the strip of adhesive on the rolling paper, but his tongue was too dry. Feeling his hands trembling, he took a breath.

"You don't have to...have it, you know. There are alternatives." The words escaped his lips before he could think twice about saying them.

Helen blanched and averted her eyes from his, looking out across the water. The evening breeze tugged at her hair, tousling it across her face and obscuring her emotions from Mike. When she brushed her hair away, he saw that she had tears in her eyes again.

"Is that what you'd prefer – for me to have an abortion? To kill our child?"

"No, I mean...." Mike paused and tried to seal the rolling paper again.

Miraculously, he managed to muster enough saliva to close the weed inside the roll-up. He fumbled in his pocket for his lighter, the bandage on his thumb making it into more of a struggle. He stopped and fumbled for the right words to say instead.

"I mean, it's your body, so it's got to be your decision ultimately. And I want you to know that I'd respect whatever you decided."

"So, you don't have strong feelings either way?" Helen sounded hurt now.

Great, he had only succeeded in making things worse.

"I'm trying to—"

"To what? Pass the buck?"

"No, not that. Honestly not that. I'm trying to tell you that I love you, no matter what happens, no matter what you...I mean what we decide."

"What we decide. Yes, that's it," Helen murmured, and he could hear the strain in her voice. She leaned into him for a hug. "We'll be okay, won't we?"

"'Course we will," Mike said. "I'm not sure what your parents will think, though."

"Me neither. Yours will hit the roof, obviously."

"My dad will. Mum will be picking out a dress for you. Total control freak."

"Well, that makes two of us – control freaks, I mean – not the wedding dress thing, *obvs*, that's—"

"A whole other issue, I know."

Mike felt like he was having an out-of-body experience. This particular '*talk* talk' had escalated quickly, far too quickly.

"Let's go back inside," Helen said, and she sounded calmer and more in control when she added, "We don't have to tell the others yet if you don't want to."

Mike was horrified at the merest suggestion. "I think it's best if we wait."

"I was just teasing, Mike. Why don't you smoke your last ever joint and come join me in a bit?"

Last ever joint. Now Mike really was getting the Fear.

"Sounds…good."

Helen laughed and kissed him on the nose. "Don't stay out here too long." She stood up and started walking back to the cottage.

Mike waited until he could no longer hear her footsteps on the wooden boards of the jetty before he finally sparked up.

When he was done smoking it, he would smoke another.

Then another.

CHAPTER SIX

Alex passed the whisky bottle to Mike so he could refill his glass. Mike poured an ample measure – his second since returning – subdued from smoking on the jetty.

"You're quiet, old chum, everything all right?" Alex asked.

Mike just nodded.

"Probably the blood loss," Alex chuckled. "Another wee dram will sort you right out. Cheers."

They clinked glasses, and Mike drank deep, enjoying the nullifying effects of the single malt on both his tongue and his state of mind. Every now and then, he caught Helen smiling conspiratorially at him from the other side of the room, where she was propped up on a little pile of cushions. The firelight glinted in her eyes, making Mike feel conflicted. He had come to the cottage hoping to have some fun, and to get away from responsibilities for a while, when each of them knew there would be bigger responsibilities to come now that they had graduated. With Helen's shocking news, Mike wondered if he'd be able to relax at all in the coming days. He wondered if they might be better off leaving the cottage early. Perhaps he could invent some kind of family emergency. He smiled grimly to himself, recognizing that it was kind of a 'family emergency' that was giving him the impetus to up and leave.

"No luck?" Helen asked Meggie, who walked in and removed her sweater and tossed it onto the nearest chair.

"Nope. Stupid dog," Meggie sulked.

Mike offered her the whisky bottle, which she took gratefully, swigging it straight from the bottle. She looked stressed as hell about Oscar.

"Oh, I give up. Can't find it at all." Kay dropped the large Ordnance Survey map she had been poring over into her lap and sighed in defeat.

Meggie looked perturbed, maybe even a little offended, at Kay's outburst. Mike thought it was a bit of an insensitive thing to say, given Meggie's worry about not being able to find Oscar.

"Find what?" Alex asked in a clear attempt at diplomacy.

Kay reached beside her for the old book on local folklore. She had tucked a drinks coaster inside as an improvised bookmark.

"I was reading about the witch, you know, the one who they executed in the village? Apparently, she performed rituals at some stone circle near here. The Spindle Stones, the locals took to calling them. They said she sacrificed animals there—"

Mike glanced at Meggie, looking for a reaction to this, but saw none. In fact, she looked distant. Probably still worrying her head off about Oscar's disappearance.

"Gross," Helen said, and shuddered.

"Chickens, goats, you name it," Kay went on. She flipped open the book at the page she had bookmarked, her keen eyes scanning the pages as she spoke. "But when the livestock ran out, she started kidnapping children. A child going missing was a tragedy that hit the community hard. They even asked the witch for help in finding the kid, but then they discovered little bones in a smoldering fire at the stone circle and accused the witch of abducting children to use in her rituals and potions." Kay ran her finger down the page, scanning each line intently. "Yes, here it is, it says that the local pastor said she had used the fat of a virgin child to make flying ointment for her broomstick...."

"That's horrible," Helen said, looking queasy at Kay's description from the book.

"I thought it would be neat to go find the stone circle. Maybe take a picnic...."

"Oh, yes, lovely," Helen deadpanned, "tuck into our ham and mustard sandwiches, followed by some invigorating *ritual sacrifice*. How bucolic."

"But I just can't find it on the map – I mean anywhere," Kay went on, regardless. She held the map out to Alex, then Meggie. "Do you guys know where it is?"

Mike saw Alex and Meggie smile at each other in that particular, conspiratorial and unspoken way that siblings do when they know something that you don't.

"It's all around us," Alex said.

"What's that supposed to mean?" Kay said.

"He means we're surrounded by the stone circle," Meggie said, her eyes twinkling in the firelight.

"What? The cottage was built in the middle of it? I don't think it would be so large."

"No, it's not bloody Avebury, you numpty," Alex scoffed. "That's in...." He trailed off, clearly struggling to remember.

"Don't be rude," Kay retorted and hit him on the forehead with the crumpled map, which fell into his lap. "But top marks for remembering Avebury. It's in Somerset, for your information. One of my all-time favorite ancient sites. Remember the long barrow? And the maypole dance the locals put on for us at the summer fair? Oh, it was bliss," she sighed.

"I remember the beer festival," Alex joked. When Kay tapped him on the shoulder, he added, "I do listen sometimes, my darling." Alex shrugged. "That's how I got a first in law."

"All right, show-off," Kay said. "So what did you guys mean, anyway, about the Spindle Stones?"

Meggie glanced around the cozy room they were all sitting in. "Most of the houses around these parts are so old that the people who first built them incorporated what stone they could find into their foundations and into their walls."

"You mean they used stone from the stone circle? To build houses?"

"Aye," said Alex, "it was quite a common practice in those days, wasn't it, sis?"

Meggie nodded, adding, "Ancient sites weren't as revered as they are nowadays. To the local people, they were simply raw materials to be recycled and put to better use than just standing there, being ignored. There's a fair few churches with stones from pagan circles holding their altars up. Not content with plundering the old ways for their religious holidays, they went and stole the sacred sites too."

"How do you mean, plundered?" Helen asked.

"Come on," Meggie scoffed, and Mike saw that Helen really didn't like that. "Easter is about as Christian as I am a carnivore."

"I don't follow," Helen said, her tone decidedly clipped.

"The Celtic tradition predates Christianity by a long mark. Pagan worshippers venerated Eostre, a goddess at the time they called Imbolc.

A festival of renewal and rebirth. The Christians came along and turned it into Easter. That's where all the bloody chocolate eggs sprang from." Meggie's eyes glinted in the firelight.

"I bloody love chocolate eggs," Mike said.

"Well, you learn something new every day," Helen said.

"You do. And don't let's get started on Halloween," Kay added.

"Why? What about Halloween?" Mike asked.

Meggie and Kay shared a laugh. "All Hallows' Eve used to be Samhain," Meggie explained, "which was basically the Celtic New Year."

"How do you guys know all this stuff?" Mike asked.

"Read a book – broaden your mind, Mike," Kay said, making Helen chuckle.

Kay reached out and scooted her hand over the rough stonework of the hearth. "So this cottage is really made from ancient standing stones? That's crazy. Kinda cool too, but crazy."

"Not the whole cottage, just bits of it," Meggie pointed out.

"Which parts?" Kay asked.

"No one knows for sure," Meggie said.

A thought seemed to strike Kay. "You're messing with me, aren't you?"

"Not at all," Meggie said. "When we pop into the village again, ask any of the old folk about it. They'll be able to tell you more, though you may regret asking. Some of them can talk the hind legs off a donkey, given half the chance."

Meggie offered Kay the whisky bottle. Kay refused. "I'll stick with vodka, thanks." Kay looked over at Helen. "Hey, my main girl, you haven't got a drink."

"Oh, I'm fine without, thanks," Helen said.

"No, no, I insist," Kay protested. "Let me get you a glass."

"No, really, I'd better not. Not in my condition—"

Helen clamped her hand over her mouth, but it was too late; they had all heard her.

Mike almost crushed his glass tumbler in his fist, he was gripping it so tight. He felt his cheeks begin to burn with embarrassment.

Kay's jaw dropped.

Alex nearly choked on a mouthful of whisky.

Meggie simply raised an eyebrow.

Each of them looked at Mike and Helen, and – seeing both of them blushing profusely – a series of amazed gasps, then delighted laughter, filled the living room.

"Who'd have bloody thought it, you dog," Alex said, sloshing an ample measure of whisky into Mike's glass. "You look like you're in shock, old chum. Better get malted!"

Mike took a slug from his glass, wishing for the night to be over. He felt numb, from whisky and from the unexpected outing of his impending fatherhood. Unless Helen changed her mind, and judging from the way she was laughing and smiling with Kay and Meggie – and now even gently smoothing a hand over her belly – that seemed increasingly unlikely. Meggie looked especially happy at the unexpected announcement, and Mike watched as she toyed with a loose strand of Helen's hair. This intimate act struck him as strange. Until now, Meggie had kept her distance from Helen and vice versa. But with the news that Helen was pregnant, Meggie seemed to have softened and, very suddenly, closed the distance between the two of them. Kay, on the other hand, seemed a little subdued. In between sips of his drink, Mike caught fragments of the girls' conversation. He heard Kay asking Helen what she was planning to do about her studies and about her travel plans, and he wondered if he detected a slight look of distaste in Kay's expression. There was something aggressive in the way she was abruptly interrogating Helen. Mike couldn't really tell if Kay was jealous of Helen somehow or disapproving of her – maybe a bit of both.

Alex refilled Mike's glass, even though Mike tried to protest. He felt a bit drunk already and more than a bit nauseated. He hadn't eaten much, finding his hunger had turned to nausea when he'd sat down to a plate of pan-fried trout earlier – he had been unable to shake the nightmarish image of plump, slimy maggots wriggling from the fish's stomach cavity.

Mike glanced up at the piece of broken antler on the mantelpiece above the fire. It sat next to the black scrying mirror Helen had bought from the village arts and crafts shop, reminding him of the stag's dark, accusatory eye gazing at him as it died on the road. Mike felt cold sweat trickle down the back of his neck. He wiped it away with his bandaged hand and shivered, remembering the imagined hot breath of the beast on the back of his neck from his bad dream the night before.

"A toast, to the happy couple! I mean, happy trio!" Alex exclaimed, his naturally booming voice louder than ever now that he had more booze inside him. He lurched to his feet suddenly, raising his glass. As he did so, the huge map fell from his lap.

Mike felt strangely transfixed by it. Time seemed to slow down as he watched the map in freefall, floating down and onto the hearthstone. Then, the noise of the room snapped Mike from the moment. Alex was in full sway and clinked glasses first with Mike, then Helen, who was drinking water. He was about to do the same with Meggie when Kay cried out in alarm.

"Shit, the map!"

It had caught fire in the hearth. Mike saw the flames spread from the corner of the map until the whole thing was ablaze. It was too late to rescue it from its fiery fate.

"Bloody hell!" Alex said.

Alex reached down and grabbed the poker from beside the fire and used it to shove the burning map into the grate.

Mike placed his whisky glass on the floor. Feeling queasy, he decided he didn't want any more to drink. The heat from the fire was making him sweat, and he felt the need to lie down on his cool bed upstairs. As Alex made a show of warming his hands on the fire, cheered on and jeered at in equal measure by the girls, Mike saw the flames devouring the elevation lines representing the Kintail Mountains. Torched paper floated up into the chimney, incinerated little moths of flame and smoke.

He watched the remains of the map turn black as it burned away to ashes.

*   *   *

Mike slept fitfully. The unpleasant onset of acid reflux woke him as it took hold in his chest.

The burning aftertaste of whisky lapped at his throat, and he puffed up his pillows and tried to prop himself up in order to quell the fire, but to no avail. He was awake now and feeling much the worse for wear after drinking so much on an empty stomach. Mike decided it might help him sleep if he sneaked downstairs for a snack – that might give the acid something to feed on other than his insides. He swung his feet over the side of the bed and caught the flicker of a shadow passing under the door. Mike froze, dreading what he knew in his heart would happen next. Seconds later, he heard it. The piercing sound of a child's laughter, echoing down the stairs. Mike looked to Helen to see if the sound had woken her, but she was still fast asleep.

He shot out of bed, the drink almost making him lose his footing as he lurched toward the door. Opening it quickly, he rushed out onto the landing. He heard the child laughing again and footsteps on the stairs. He followed the sounds downstairs and found himself standing alone in the living room.

"Who are you? Hello?"

Mike felt ridiculous even asking out loud. Chasing phantoms. He glanced around the room and saw nothing except the detritus of the evening – a few empty glasses, and his own still half-empty by the fireside. The only sound to be heard now was the faint crackle of dying embers in the hearth. Mike felt a rush of acidity at the back of his throat and padded barefoot into the kitchen. He opened the fridge and searched for something to eat. The remains of the cooked trout lay on a plate under clear plastic film. It looked gray and unappetizing in the artificial light of the refrigerator. After closing the fridge door in frustration, Mike crossed to the sink and filled a clean glass with water. Even the water looked slightly off to him in the gloomy light, and cloudier than it should have been. He glimpsed his reflection in the window, beyond which was the total blackness of night, and found himself thinking of the loch again. It was out there somewhere, vast, deep and dark. He sipped his water and watched himself do so in the reflecting glass of the window.

Then he heard a cry.

At first, he thought it was the child's voice again, but when it came again he realized it was an adult's voice, a woman's. It had come from the living room, he was certain of that. He placed his glass on the drainer and made his way back through the conservatory and into the living room. There was no one there. But again he heard the woman's cry. It was a cry of unmistakable pain. He rubbed at his throbbing temples with his fingertips, wondering if he was simply drunk or going stark, staring mad. The cry was coming from the mantelpiece – and more specifically from the black scrying mirror, which stood there alongside the fragment of stag's antler.

"Hello?" he said again, now feeling more self-conscious than ever, speaking to a bloody mirror in an empty room.

Only the crackling embers answered him. But he was drawn toward the mirror, intrigued by what he had heard, and wondering if by approaching it he might hear the woman's cry more clearly should it come again. As he drew close, the smooth, inward curve of the black glass seemed to latch on to him, filling his field of vision with its void. Something flickered darkly there, and Mike blinked. No, he had definitely seen something. But what was it? He moved closer, until his toes were touching the rough stone of the hearth, and gazed deeply into the mirror.

Reflected there, he saw a half dozen men. They were workmen but not from Mike's era – they wore clothes from centuries ago. The room behind them appeared half-built, and even though it was the middle of the night for Mike, in the reflection he could see daylight through the gaps in the unfinished walls.

Four of the men each had a thick rope over his shoulder, which they were pulling on in order to move something across the floor of the room. Something that was clearly incredibly heavy. The other two men were leaning and pushing against the object, which Mike suddenly realized was the very same hearthstone that was at his feet. The surface of the enormous slab of stone was rough-hewn, and it did not surprise Mike that six men were required to shift it. Mike ran the big toe of his left foot over the hearthstone. It was as though tactile contact with its surface would rid him of the strange reflections in the mirror. He looked into the shallow black bowl of glass again and saw the men reflected there, as though they could be working in the room where he stood. Spooked, he glanced over his shoulder into the physical room behind him.

No one there.

He heard the woman's cry again and looked once more into the mirror. What he saw there made him take a step back from the hearth in surprise. The workmen and their slab of stone had disappeared, replaced by the reflection of a young woman. She was lying on her back with her legs parted. Either side of her, half-obscured by the dark shadows at the edges of the mirror, stood silent figures. Each wore dark robes, their features hidden by cowls that hung black over their faces. The woman cried out again, her voice echoing like breaking glass through the glossy surface of the mirror. She appeared to be in a lot of pain, writhing on the floor with her hips thrusting out in sudden spasms. The robed figures appeared to be coaxing and placating her, two of them gripping her wrists – to assist the woman or to restrain her, Mike could not tell. Seeing her huge, distended belly as she gave an almighty thrust accompanied by an agonized scream, Mike understood that he was witnessing the birth of a child – or at least the memory of it.

He glanced behind him again into the room and saw the slightly crumpled rug on the stone floor where, in the mirror, the woman lay in the throes of childbirth. Her cries stopped short, suddenly replaced by the hysterical laughter of a child.

Mike felt afraid to look once more at the mirror, but he felt compelled to know what was reflected there. He tried to resist, but it was as though his head was being forced back to look, urged on by some unseen and powerful force. The scrying mirror was black and empty once more, the woman and the dark figures nowhere to be seen. An echo of the child's laughter rang out, the sound seeming to travel around the dark perimeter of the looking glass.

Then an idea struck Mike.

Here he was, standing close by the mirror, looking straight at it. The phantoms – for he was sure that was what they must have been – were gone. Why then could he not see his own reflection? He leaned in closer to the mirror's surface to test his idea, then swayed on his feet from side to side. Nothing. He cast no reflection in the mirror. It was as though the mirror and the hearth were there but he somehow didn't exist at all. The sensation of not existing made him feel nauseated, and he tried to tear his gaze away from the mirror, intent on turning his back on it and getting the hell away from this creepy nighttime room.

But he could not budge. The mirror had a hold on him so intense that he could not even blink. He felt a rush of air, how he imagined it might feel to be in an airplane cabin when it depressurized, and his face was pulled closer to the mirror. The air was freezing cold, making his eyes water. He opened his mouth to scream as he was sucked into the black circle of the mirror. He reached out and gripped the mantelpiece with both hands, fighting against the vortex pulling him in. His head was at the center of a cold, whirling storm of blackness.

Mike looked down and saw, impossibly, the waters of the loch. The storm was sucking him down, closer and closer to the water. He saw his face reflected there, a pale oval with a black hole for a screaming mouth. As he plummeted closer to the water, feeling sure he would be drowned in it, he saw that the reflection was not his face at all. It was someone else, peering up at him from beneath the surface of the dark, briny water.

Meggie's face, pale and drowned and screaming in silent anguish.

*   *   *

Mike's eyes blasted open, and he awoke from his nightmare, struggling for breath.

His heartbeat slowed as he realized that what he had seen in the mirror, all of it, was a disturbing nightmare. He glanced at Helen beside him, curled in a fetal position, fast asleep. Mike wiped sweat from his brow and sat up. His t-shirt was drenched with perspiration, and he peeled it off, ready to toss it onto the floor. As he lifted the shirt up and over his face, he was astonished to see someone standing at the foot of the bed.

Meggie was naked, her red hair hanging loose over her alabaster skin. She was looking right at him, her eyes becoming as black as the glass of the scrying mirror. Though her intense gaze troubled him greatly, he felt powerless to look away. Her lips curled into a thin smile, and he saw that she held an infant child at her breast, wrapped in a white swaddling blanket. She moved around to Helen's side of the bed—

No, no, don't come any closer, please don't come any closer.

—her darkening eyes impenetrable, unreadable to Mike. Something about the way she moved seemed spiderlike and utterly threatening to Mike, and he wanted more than anything to raise the alarm, to wake Helen and to warn Meggie to keep away. But any such sound stayed locked inside his throat, and all he could do was watch as Meggie scuttled, naked and savage, to Helen's side.

Meggie took the baby from her breast and held it out in her arms, lowering it onto the bedsheets next to Helen. All the while, she stared at Mike, her eyes fully black now with no whites to be seen in them at all. And she laughed – a vile chuckle that froze Mike's heart and would have sent him scurrying beneath the covers if he could only move.

In her sleep, Helen moved her arm, embracing the child.

Meggie's horrid chuckle increased in volume until it was a constant loop, sounding all at once like the crackling of the fire in the hearth, the breaking and re-breaking of millions of jagged fragments of sharp black glass, and the anguished, pitiful cries of an infant. Mike clamped his hands over his ears to try to blot out the sound, but it only increased in intensity until he felt that his skull was caving in. He roared along with it, his own scream an attempt to dispel the sound but instead becoming part of the concert with it. Mike felt the weight of the baby on the sheets next to Helen and in that moment knew how fragile it was. He felt afraid that the explosive noise filling the room, and his skull, would somehow break the child's little body apart.

★　　★　　★

He jolted awake and found himself tangled in sweat-drenched sheets once again. Mike looked at the space in the bed next to him, where he had dreamed Helen and the child. He sat up, still in a panic, and looked toward the foot of the bed, half-expecting to see black eyes staring back at him. He was alone. Morning light bled through the gaps in the curtains. He swallowed dryly, the acid aftertaste of whisky lingering in his throat, and looked fearfully around the empty bedroom.

PART TWO

Under dark, dark skies
There are dark, dark mountains
And beneath the dark, dark mountains
Is a dark, dark road.

On the dark, dark road
There is a dark, dark turn
And beyond the dark, dark turn
Is a dark, dark cottage.

CHAPTER SEVEN

"Oscar! Oscar!?"

Meggie's voice echoed off the wall of trees skirting the edge of the loch.

Mike and Alex walked on ahead, carrying backpacks full of snacks and equipped with two-liter bottles of water tucked in the plastic holders.

"Oscar!" Mike called out, while Alex whistled.

"Good thing my sister loves that wee mongrel so much," Alex said. "I'd be inclined to bloody well kill him for making us walk this far."

"You always liked a walk," Mike said.

"True enough," Alex replied, "but I prefer sitting on my arse and fishing even better."

Mike laughed but inwardly felt glad to be out and stretching his legs. His nightmares of the past couple of nights were still casting their gloomy spell over him, and he had begun to dislike being cooped up in the cottage with the others. He breathed in the fresh mountain air, finding it refreshingly energizing with its scents of bracken and pine.

As they pushed on up the twisting path that led away from the lochside cottage and into the hills, he began to feel the color returning to his cheeks and with it his appreciation for being outside in the amazing landscape. The farther they trudged, the thicker and higher the banks of heather rose on either side of the path. A slight breeze made the stems sway, creating a vivid display of purples and greens as far as his eye could see. As the tree cover became denser, the path split into two. One track led deeper into the trees, and Mike recalled that Alex had told him this was the bridle path, carved out over decades by countless horses' hooves traveling to and from the village. The other track led up the hillside to higher ground, twisting and turning like a giant stairway. Mike and Alex stopped for a while and waited for the girls to catch up. Mike was glad of the rest, conscious that he and Alex had both put a bit of spurt on in order to get ahead of the girls.

He chuckled, slightly out of breath, and Alex looked at him with a quizzical expression.

"Thought they were just behind us," Mike said.

"Probably chatting," Alex growled. "Slows them down."

Mike chuckled again.

"What's so funny?"

"We are, mate," Mike said.

"Oh? How so?" Alex asked.

"I don't know. It's just the differences, you know? We'd much rather push on ahead in relative silence, while that lot.... Oh, here they are."

Mike saw Meggie's red hair first, as vivid as a hi-vis vest against the green backdrop of the wild landscape. To Mike, she looked just as wild as her surroundings – her long, flowing skirt and baggy cardigan adding to the effect. Helen and Kay walked close by Meggie but looked like urbanites in comparison to Alex's younger sister. Mike wondered how he might look if he left the city for good, to go live in a rural area. He had toyed with the idea of growing a beard while in his final year of university, but Helen had made it clear that she did not even approve of the slightest shadow of stubble. If he dared grow a beard, she'd hold kisses for ransom, she'd told him. Mike had stocked up on disposable razors that same day, and they had not mentioned the topic since. Yet, as he watched the carefree, fluid way in which Meggie navigated the path, he envied her. She seemed entirely at home here, at the foot of the mountains. He didn't really know where he belonged. University had given him anonymity for the past three years. Now his girlfriend was pregnant and he didn't have a job, or anywhere to live other than his parental home. He knew from crashing there for a few weeks during his first summer break that his parents were not keen on him overstaying his welcome.

They had managed a fortnight before raising the unwanted specter of rent and bills, and had badgered Mike into taking a crappy job in an even crappier bar just so he could 'pay his way' a little while he lived under their – more than ample, it had to be said – roof. He could imagine how they might react if he returned home and told them that Helen and little Mikey Junior would be along for the ride. His father, in particular, would no doubt go mental about it. His mother would get upset and retreat into herself, allowing her husband to call the shots about Mike's future. He didn't blame her for adopting this coping strategy – his dad was a forceful personality, and he too would avoid confrontation with the man whenever he could. A bead of sweat trickled from Mike's temple, and he wiped it away with the back of his hand. His bandaged thumb throbbed along with his and Alex's footsteps up the twisting path.

"What kept you?" Alex said, in between gulps of water from his plastic bottle.

"Pacing ourselves, unlike you two,' Kay said. "You both look a bit sweaty. Not overdoing it, are you, boys?"

"Not at all," Alex replied. "We didn't know whether to crack open the sandwiches or send out a search party."

"Yeah, yeah," Helen said, "it'll be us waiting for you on the way back. You'll have run out of energy."

"Typical men," Kay said, "always a sprint and never a marathon." She winked at Helen and Meggie, who both burst out laughing.

The girls passed around their water bottles, and Mike saw that Helen was taken by a shrub with clusters of strangely shaped pink berries. He strolled over to take a look at what it was that had grabbed her attention.

"Aren't the berries just absolutely gorgeous?" Helen said as she gently tilted a drooping stem toward the light.

"Aye, they are that. But don't ever eat them; they're fearsome poisonous," Meggie warned. "They look like wee Halloween pumpkins, don't they?"

Mike couldn't see it. To him, the pinkish-colored berries looked like fragile little hearts. He pinched one between his thumb and forefinger, and it disintegrated in a little flood of juices that coated his skin.

"Careful, Mike," Helen said.

"That's a spindle bush," Meggie said. "The berries split apart when the weather gets properly cold and reveal their orange insides."

She sounded as though she was relishing every word. Mike wiped the slimy juice of the poisonous little berry away from his skin on some nearby leaves. He was glad he hadn't crushed it with his wounded thumb, for fear that he might get poison inside the cut.

"Guess we know where the Spindle Stones got their name from anyways," Kay mused before she took a welcome sip of water from her reusable bottle.

Helen and the others continued rehydrating themselves and, in between sips, resumed calling out for Oscar. The only reply was the distant cry of a kestrel, circling high above the loch. Mike watched the bird, wishing for a moment that it was on the lookout for Oscar too. It would make finding the stupid dog a lot easier.

"We'll cover more terrain if we split into two teams," Alex said. "Which do you girls prefer? The high or the low ground?"

"I vote low," Helen said, and Kay and Meggie agreed.

"Good choice," Meggie said. "Plenty of tree cover on the lower path. My main concern is that Oscar chased something into the woods and injured himself. He could be hurt. I've got some basic first aid stuff with me in case we need to dress a wound or anything."

"Poor Oscar," Helen said, sounding horrified.

"He may be fine yet, just lost," Meggie reassured her, but the concern was still written in her tense expression.

Mike didn't like the look of the steep path, but, seeing the look on Meggie's face, he said, "Best we get going then."

"Aye," Alex said, hoisting his backpack straps over his shoulders.

Mike blew Helen a kiss, and he followed Alex onto the path that led up the hill. Glancing back over his shoulder, he saw Meggie leading Helen and Kay into the woods on the lower path.

When the girls were out of view, Mike and Alex settled into a slower pace. It was as though an unspoken agreement had passed between them. Out of sight of their partners, they had less to prove, Mike supposed. The thought kept him amused all the way to the higher ground while he listened to Alex's labored breathing. And his friend had the audacity to pick fault with him about his smoking all the time. Mike began to chuckle under his breath.

"What's so funny all of a sudden?" Alex asked.

But Mike ignored the question. As they climbed over the ridge onto a flat, green promontory, he spotted a dark shape lying in the grass.

"Hey, what's that?" he asked, drawing Alex's attention.

The two increased their pace to investigate. Flies buzzed in an ever-shifting black cloud as they made their approach. The smell hit Mike then, too, bringing back unpleasant memories of the dead fish with its belly full of maggots.

Oscar lay on his side, his body stiff and still beneath his muddy and matted fur. Something had torn open the dog's throat and abdomen. Congealing blood had spilled from the dog's wounds and onto the strands of grass poking out from beneath. The trauma to the dog's body stood out vivid crimson against the muted green of the long grass.

"Jesus bloody Christ," Alex said.

Mike thought of what Meggie had said about her first aid kit. Oscar was beyond any help that mere bandages might bring. "How long do you think he's been out here like this?"

"I don't know," Alex replied. "He was an old dog – about to get his bus pass, in dog years. A predator probably got the better of him. He was always off chasing after some prey or other. Maybe this time he decided to chase something else's supper and didn't live to tell the tale. Had to happen sooner or later, to be honest. Though I doubt that will make my poor wee sister feel any better about it."

"She loved that dog, didn't she?"

Alex nodded. He blinked into the wind, and Mike thought he may have glimpsed a tear in Alex's eye. Maybe Alex loved the dog, too. But his carefully maintained alpha male persona would not allow for any outward expressions of sentimentality about Oscar. It would be different with Meggie, of course. Mike knew that Oscar's death would shake her to the core. And her grief would put a damper on their vacation; that was for sure. He felt a little selfish even thinking it, but he couldn't help himself. He'd already had more than his fair share of grim morbidity, what with hitting the stag on the road and all the weird dreams he'd been having since they'd arrived at the cottage. An idea occurred to him, and the more he tried to push it away, the simpler and more attractive it seemed to him.

"We could decide to…*not* tell her."

There. It was out in the open, his idea becoming a potential action, a viable solution. Alex blinked back at Mike blankly.

"Look at it this way. If we tell her, she'll want to see him," Mike said. "You know she will."

Alex looked from the dead dog's corpse to Mike, and back again to the dog.

"Dead right. You cannae show *that* to a vegan, no matter what you think of all that tofu-munching bollocks," Alex said with his usual air of sensitivity.

Maybe that tear in his eye really had only been a result of the wind.

"We're agreed it's for the best then?" Mike asked.

"Aye," Alex said and nodded, "we'll bury him as best we can, but it'll be bastard difficult without any tools."

Mike and Alex set about locating a suitable spot but found only hard, rocky ground. Burying Oscar was clearly not an option. They decided instead to gather up the biggest, heftiest rocks and stones that they could find to conceal Oscar's body. Then they began piling on loose turf and foliage as camouflage. The work took just over an hour, but when they were done, the spot where Oscar lay concealed was pretty much indistinguishable from the surrounding landscape.

Mike took a few steps back from their handiwork, searching out any gaps he and Alex might have left. If there were any gaps, then other animals – attracted by the smell – might be able to burrow inside easily. If they did so, they could uncover Oscar's body. Satisfied that they had done a thorough enough cover-up job, Mike nodded to Alex, who was taking a breather on a rocky outcrop toward the edge of the ridge. Alex took a hip flask from his backpack, unscrewed the cap and took a swig before offering it to Mike. Alex's concept of a picnic lunch always included a nip of something strong to take the edge off, and Mike was gladder than ever to see that today was no exception. Just as Mike began to approach Alex to take the flask from his outstretched hand, he noticed something about the rocks upon which Alex was perched.

They had purloined a fair few of the rocks from the perimeter of the ridge around the spot where they had discovered Oscar. Something about the curve of the land from the rocky ridge to the burial spot struck Mike, and he stopped in his tracks to glance around the area where he stood. Among the rocks were bigger, darker plinths of stone. That was it, the reason why his eye had been drawn to them – they were the exact same hue as the stone fireplace at the cottage. He followed them, picking up speed as his eyes searched them out between the smaller rocks, stones, and long grass.

"What's gotten into you? D'you want a drink or not?" Alex shouted.

"These stones!" Mike replied. "The dark ones. Don't they look familiar to you?"

Alex placed his hip flask on the rocks beside him and stood up. Mike continued around the perimeter, each step confirming his suspicions.

The dark stones marked out a circle, about fifty feet in diameter, with their little grave mound at the dead center of it.

Making his way around to Alex, who stood frowning next to his flask, Mike said breathlessly, "It's a circle, Alex, I knew it! It's a stone circle, or at least what used to be one."

Mike leaped up onto one of the rocks next to where Alex had been sitting. Then he climbed up onto another, the highest of the stones. From this elevated position, he could see it even more clearly.

"We're at what I would guess is the southernmost side. If you start with those darker rocks over there, and follow them around, ignoring the grass and the scrub, you'll see it."

He pointed out the perimeter, tracing its circumference with his finger in the air.

"Bloody hell," Alex muttered. "I never even noticed that, until now."

Mike's mind raced with possibilities. Perhaps this stone circle site was the same one that Kay's book at the cottage had mentioned. The Spindle Stones. He looked around again at the layout, trying to imagine how it might have looked before the circle had been plundered for building materials. It would have been an imposing sight, he imagined, to anyone who climbed the steep, winding path he and Alex had taken. Maybe ancient feet had created that path as they made their pilgrimage to the stones. All of which begged another question.

"Don't you think it's weird, though?" Mike asked.

"What?"

"Oscar just upped and died. Right in the middle of it. In the dead center of an ancient stone bloody circle."

Kay had only been talking about it the night before, after all. About the witch and her curse and the children going missing. Mike recalled the childlike laughter from his nightmare and shuddered.

Human sacrifices, the book had read.

Suddenly cold, Mike felt that he might take a drink from Alex's hip flask right about now. He clambered down to retrieve it. Mike unscrewed the cap and tipped it back. Feeling a warm wave pass down his throat, he realized Alex had filled it with good honey malt whisky. The perfect tonic for the shivers he was experiencing at his discovery of the stone circle.

"Ah, I would'nae read too much into that if I were you, pal," Alex said, now sounding as gruff as ever.

"You don't think it's even a little bit weird, though? After what Kay told us yesterday?"

Alex shrugged, then reclaimed the hip flask for another drink. "It's a coincidence, that's all. I mean, there are a lot of places an animal as daft as Oscar could've met his maker."

"Well, I think it's a bit spooky. Of all the places out here in the vastness of the Scottish countryside, he chooses this one to give up the ghost – pun intended."

Alex groaned. "Maybe I should'nae let you take any more of this whisky. You're half-cut, man. Bloody mumbo jumbo and superstitious nonsense. You sound almost as batty as my poor wee sister."

Mike sighed. Whatever his friend said to try to normalize it, he felt an unshakeable feeling that this place had somehow drawn Oscar to it. Either that or whichever predator had killed the poor pooch had dragged him up here. Which pointed to the same conclusion, at least in Mike's mind – the stone circle that had stood here for centuries still held some power over the surrounding landscape that it had dominated in its heyday. Those same stones were now tucked away in the walls, floors, and chimney stacks of the houses in the village. And in Hearthstone Cottage.

Mike found little solace in that revelation as he and Alex made their descent back down the hillside path in search of the girls.

CHAPTER EIGHT

The trees became taller and their trunks thicker the deeper Mike and Alex walked into the forest. Mike felt relieved to put some distance between them and Oscar's grave up at the stone circle site. The atmosphere up there had seemed pregnant with unease, and Mike had been eager to leave it behind. Even though they had done a bloody good job of burying him, the fact that Oscar's corpse lay just inches under a layer of rock, dirt, and foliage stayed with Mike all the way down the hill. Every time he blinked, he saw the dog's ruined body and its tongue lolling lifeless from between its teeth, a grotesque and cartoonish image of decay. The buzz of a fly passing close by his ear reminded him of the torn fur and ruptured flesh. Death's red gash was staring him in the face, undeniable in its finality the more he tried to blink it from his memory. It was as though they had buried a problem but had inadvertently carried the guilt of that apparent quick fix with them.

The woods, though, felt different, and for that Mike was thankful. Here, the foliage was dense and dark green. Shade-loving ferns lined the forest floor, which was carpeted with fallen pine needles from the high branches. Mike luxuriated in the cool calm of the fresh air, each breath becoming a balm as they walked on. The occasional cry of a predatory bird was muted by the canopy of strong branches that formed a complex interlocking ceiling high above their heads.

Mike heard another sound as he and Alex navigated a steep, downward slope in the forest floor. It was a female voice, though it was too far away for him to make out if it belonged to Helen, Kay, or Meggie. As the natural dip began to slope upward again, presumably the result of heavy rainfall and subsidence in the soil, Mike saw more daylight between the branches of the trees. At the top of the slope, he and Alex passed through a line of younger, more spindly trees until they reached the edge of a clearing. Mike spied the girls at the other side of this clearing. They looked as though they were taking a breather.

Mike heard laughter among the girls as they spotted him and Alex. "Found them," Mike said.

Mike and Alex continued across the clearing, the ground softening beneath their feet as the leaf-littered forest floor gave way to an open expanse of rough scrubland.

"Hey!" Alex shouted as the girls turned and ran into the trees on the other side of the clearing, laughing as they went.

Mike glanced at Alex, and the two exchanged grins. The girls had challenged them to a game of chase. Caught in the reverie of the moment, Mike took off after them. Competitive as ever, Alex pushed past Mike, knocking him aside slightly as he hurtled across the clearing and beyond the line of trees.

"Cheating bastard!" he called after Alex. His friend hurtled on, oblivious.

Mike stumbled, losing his already tenuous footing on the uneven ground, and fell to his knees painfully. He reached out with his hands on instinct to break his fall. He scraped the soft skin of his palms on the rough ground and the pine cones that were scattered there. He felt his injured thumb twinge with a violent stab of pain. Cursing under his breath, he rolled over and stood up again. Pressing his smarting hands together, he was now facing the trees through which he and Alex had just emerged. His flesh turned cold at the sight of a low, dark shape as it darted between the trees. It looked like a dog.

"Oscar?" Mike called, incredulous at the sound of his own voice.

Of course it couldn't be Oscar. They had left the pooch buried under a pile of earth, stones, and bracken about half a mile up the hillside. The dark shape flitted between the trees again, and this time Mike saw something else.

The flash of sickly yellow eyes.

He gasped at the sight of them, searing into his vision from across the clearing. His feet moved as if of their own volition. He felt a broken branch – or at least, what he hoped was broken branch – against his heel as he backed up and away from the disturbing shape in the trees. Mike listened to the sound of his breath, coming in rapid, staccato bursts. Whatever he had glimpsed in the trees had put a primal fear into his very bones. He wanted to turn on his heel and run away, catch up with Alex and the others and pretend he hadn't seen anything out there at all.

Hadn't seen something with yellowy eyes glaring at him hungrily from the shadows of tall trees.

Then he heard a low growl. It was a guttural sound, the sound of something that had not eaten for a while and was, even now, savoring the taste of Mike's fear on its pink tongue and in its red throat. The growl came again, louder this time, and Mike heard the snapping of teeth. That was enough to get his legs moving again. They felt numb beneath him as he ran full pelt for the opening in the trees through which the girls and Alex had disappeared. It was as though he were running outside of his body for a few disturbing moments, with the growling and snapping of teeth growing ever louder and all too close until he fancied he could feel something dark and immensely powerful bearing down upon him. He willed himself not to look, to just keep on running until he caught up to the others. He broke the tree line and hurtled between a confusion of saplings, which swayed from their contact with his panicked body. Only then did Mike risk turning around fearfully. The swaying young trees were like flags, alerting whatever dark beast was pursuing him to his presence on the other side of the clearing.

Blackness erupted across his vision, and his hands shot up over his face protectively. He stood there, locked in a cage of his fear, until he realized what the black shape was. It flitted out of his eyeline and into the sky – a crow on the wing, startled by his crashing footsteps. He scanned between the trees, looking for any glimpse of those horrible, sickly looking eyes but saw only shafts of diffused daylight as they fell between the tree branches.

Mike turned and ran on in the direction he had seen Alex go. Within seconds, he heard another sound, this time a panicked yelp from one of the girls. He increased his speed, pushing on until he felt his lungs might burst—

You have to quit smoking, baby daddy.

—and found Alex and the others standing beside a rough track in the woods. Kay had fallen over, and Helen and Meggie were rushing to her aid.

"You all right?" he heard Helen ask.

"Yes, but my damn foot is stuck," Kay replied, sounding embarrassed.

Mike jogged closer to see what was up and saw that Kay was struggling to retrieve her foot from a tangle of tree roots.

"Let me help," Helen said. She crouched down and took Kay's foot gently in both hands, trying to free it from the roots.

Alex rushed over and, leaning over Helen and Kay, lifted the largest of the roots, creating enough of a gap through which – with Helen's help – Kay managed to wriggle her foot.

"Wow, these trees look ancient," Helen said as she and Alex helped Kay to her feet.

"They are," Meggie said.

Mike looked around at the surrounding trees. They were so established that he could scarcely make out where one branch began and another ended. It was as though the forest had fused into one continuous, arboreal organism.

"Careful," Meggie said, seeing Helen pick up a length of broken branch from where Kay had fallen. "Like the spindle berries, the needles of a yew tree can be harmful."

"Really? I never knew they were poisonous." A worried look passed over Helen's face. "Are they diseased or something?" She threw the broken branch to the ground.

"Not diseased, no," Meggie said. "The yew is a powerful symbol in the folklore of the Highlands. To our ancestors, the trees represented the cycle of death and resurrection. The branches drop off and die so that new life can spring up in their place."

Meggie pointed out a young yew sapling and smiled at Helen.

Mike saw Helen absentmindedly run her hand over her belly. He knew his girlfriend was making a connection between Meggie's folktale and the new life growing inside of her. He also saw a clear flash of jealousy in Kay's eyes as Helen did so. Mike wondered if Kay and Alex had talked about marriage, about settling down and starting a family. He doubted that his stoic friend would tell Mike even if they had. The truth was that Alex was much more the settling down type. He didn't smoke dope, and on those occasions when he did have a skinful, he was still the early-morning type – first off the mark to be cooking and/or devouring a cooked breakfast after a big night. Alex was more like his father than Mike reckoned he was aware. He was driven, and that drive made him more serious than Mike, somehow. A contender for inheriting his father's mantle of successful lawyer and breadwinner. Mike tried to ignore the dawning realization that he and Alex really were becoming like their fathers.

Mike's dad had married young, and he had overheard him – on more than one occasion – complaining that he was trapped in a never-ending cycle of mortgage payments and university fees. His dad always cut loose over Skype with his work buddies when he'd had a couple of beers—

"When I'm reincarnated I want to come back as a bloody housewife; I swear to god, all I'll have to do is spread my legs every now and then, squeeze out another fucking mouth to feed and boom! Hubby darling can do yet more fuck-bollocking overtime."

—and he always seemed to go on a lengthy business trip soon after. Mike had stumbled across the webpage for a lap-dance club in Central London in his father's browser history one day when he had borrowed his iPad. He remembered how tempted he had been to casually ask his dad about it over breakfast – in front of his mother. That would have rocked the boat for sure. But after giving it some careful consideration, Mike had remembered the not insignificant matter of his allowance, not to mention his tuition fees and rent, and had decided to give the old bastard a break. Mike had cleared the browser history and kept quiet about it. Though, he did wonder if his dad detected anything in Mike's knowing smile when his father had returned from that business trip looking particularly relaxed and with his suitcase filled with gifts for Mike's mother.

Mike's memories stayed with him as they followed the winding path through the forest and down to the lochside. Each of them hardly spoke a word on the return walk to the cottage. Mike felt nervous all the time they were among the trees, finding himself glancing between them and searching out that black shape and those yellow eyes. But he saw nothing out of the ordinary, and it wasn't until they had reached the shore of the lake that anyone thought to mention Oscar. Mike let Alex do the talking and pretended to be half-listening as his friend described in detail the route they had taken in search of the dog, and that they had found nothing. In reality, he was taking mental notes of everything Alex said, in case the subject came up again later – they would have to get their story straight to avoid arousing any suspicion from Meggie.

Meggie fell completely silent on the final approach to the cottage. Even she had given up on calling out Oscar's name. Mike felt a knot of guilt coiling in his stomach as he saw the dirt beneath his fingernails from when he and Alex had buried the dead dog. He held the gate open for Meggie as they reached the cottage and noticed she was carrying a broken length of yew branch in her right hand.

It looked like the one Helen had thrown away.

CHAPTER NINE

Mike awoke to a welcome cup of tea from Helen. She placed the steaming mug on the bedside table, then threw open the curtains to let the morning light in. Mike rubbed his eyes and sat up in bed, propping himself up against his pillows. The night before had been more subdued than their first boozy gathering at the cottage. Mike supposed they were all feeling pretty tired after their lengthy walk in search of Oscar—

And the hour you spent burying him.

—and Helen's self-enforced sobriety seemed to be putting a bit of a dampener on things, too. Mike sipped hot tea from his mug and watched Helen as she folded clothes, tutting loudly at the discarded underwear he had seen fit to leave abandoned on the bedroom floor.

"How are you...? How are you, you know, feeling?" Mike asked.

"Disturbingly like I'm seeing into our future, Mike. That's how I'm feeling."

What the bloody hell did that mean? "I don't follow," he said cautiously.

"No, I don't suppose you do," Helen sighed.

"My mind reading isn't so good, you know that, babe. You'll need a clairvoyant for that."

Helen glared at him.

"If you think I'm picking up after you all week? Think again," she said and threw his underwear at him. "Does that make it any clearer for you?"

Mike recoiled and spilled some of the tea on his bare chest.

"Ouch!" he exclaimed. "Watch it, woman!"

"Don't *woman* me," Helen replied, "or else I'll tip the whole bloody mug over you, just see if I don't."

"Bit early for your hormones to be kicking in quite so badly," he muttered.

"What?"

Mike laughed but noticed that Helen wasn't laughing.

"What did you just say?"

Mike sipped his tea, feeling suddenly vulnerable in bed.

Helen glared at him. "Sounded like everyday sexism to me."

It *was* a bit early for her hormones to be kicking in, he thought, feeling suddenly uncomfortable at the prospect of the great unknown of her pregnancy. Mike had no idea how to broach the subject with her without it coming off as yet more everyday sexism, so he decided to keep his mouth shut.

"Sorry, babe," he said, "I didn't mean it that way. It's just...." He faltered, hyperaware that anything he said might be taken down and used against him as evidence in a court of law with his legal graduate girlfriend.

"Just what?" she snapped.

"You've always known me to be a bit messy. I thought you found it endearing?"

She rolled her eyes. "For your information, I only told you once that I envied how you can amble through life with that devil-may-care attitude of yours."

"And now you're using it as an excuse to hurl dirty boxers at me. No fair."

Mike's blood ran cold. What might she be like when she was six months pregnant? Or after she'd had the baby? She'd be hassling him to do laundry, go to the shops, maybe even change nappies. He shuddered at the merest thought. Mike decided to try a different strategy. Hangovers always made him feel horny, and the best cure was becoming pretty obvious to him as he watched Helen selecting a cardigan from the drawer.

"Why don't you climb under the covers with me? We can kiss and make up."

"Not bloody likely, with your booze breath." She pulled a face. "Thanks, but no thanks."

He watched her pulling on the cardigan and wondered how she might look when she was further along. Mike loved Helen's tight body and felt a pang of regret that it might change for the worse if she decided to keep the baby. He would definitely keep that thought to himself. His honest fears would only be taken by Helen as criticism – more everyday sexism. Mike felt ashamed that he was even having such thoughts. He tried to push them aside, forget about them. Much better to focus on the now rather than what might happen in the future. Besides, he'd much rather drink his tea than bathe in it.

But his thoughts kept circling back to that pivotal point. *If* she decided to keep the baby. Who was he trying to kid? Ever since she'd told him, she'd been acting like a Mother Teresa of the Highlands, refusing a single sip of wine and even rejecting a bacon sarnie for breakfast in favor of some probiotic muesli concoction that Kay had mixed for her. He sipped more tea and sighed, thinking how much better it would taste with a roll-up. He began planning when he could have a crafty smoke. That was it, he had the perfect cover.

"Thought I might head out again to look for Oscar," Mike said, his voice trailing off into an almighty yawn.

"No need," Helen said, sounding clipped. "Alex's sister has a plan for us all today."

Mike tried to hide his disappointment that his illicit smoking plan had failed at the first hurdle. He pictured himself smoking a fat one behind a tree next to the lake. He imagined the smoke billowing up into the branches. Trees could keep secrets. Then he recalled the yellow eyes he'd seen watching him the day before, and the black shape darting between the tree trunks. Maybe he'd just risk smoking out of the bathroom window like he used to at home when he was a kid.

"Bit annoying really," Helen continued. "I mean, it's our holiday. I understand she's worried about Oscar, but does she have to monopolize our entire stay looking for him?"

Mike gulped down a mouthful of tea. It had cooled down, and, in lieu of a smoke, he felt ready for his second mug. Helen struggled with the sticky drawer in the chest housing their clean clothes. It took her a couple of attempts to slide it shut. Mike knew that if she said something was a bit annoying, it really meant she was absolutely steaming about it. He would have to proceed with caution.

"What's going on then?" Mike said.

"Come downstairs and see for yourself," Helen said. "And tidy up your bloody underpants before you do."

"I was going to. Honest, I was," he said without really even convincing himself.

"Let's just not succumb to the tiresome, bloody gender stereotypes before I've even had a scan," Helen replied. "Tomorrow, you can bring me tea in bed while I have a lie in, work off that burgeoning dad-bod."

"Sure thing," Mike chuckled, blowing her a kiss. "Watch that everyday sexism, though, babe."

She rolled her eyes and left the room.

Some holiday this is turning out to be, thought Mike.

He glanced at the mess of clothes on the floor. He really had better tidy them up. But first he'd sit back and enjoy the rest of his tea.

★   ★   ★

"How many of those have you made?" Mike asked.

"A few," Meggie replied.

It was an understatement. The kitchen was a mess of painted sheets of paper of all sizes. Meggie had apparently been up since the break of dawn, working on them. The table was completely obscured by a haphazard gallery of makeshift posters. Mike picked one up at random. It was emblazoned with the words 'MISSING DOG' above a – admittedly rather cute – sketch of Oscar and the address for Hearthstone Cottage.

"What are you going to do with them?"

"We," Meggie corrected, "are going to distribute them around the village."

Mike glanced at Helen, who made a 'told you so' face. He looked away quickly so he wouldn't laugh inappropriately.

"But we won't all fit in the car," Mike said.

"You can go in the boot," Alex chuckled dryly.

"Not bloody likely," Mike said.

"Meggie and Alex will go into the village with Kay first, then Alex will come back for me and you," Helen said helpfully.

Alex pulled a face. "Thanks, Helen, but I was going to string soft lad here along a wee bit more." Alex raised his eyebrows at Mike's disheveled appearance. "Good of you to join us, by the way. Enjoy your cryogenic sleep, slacker?"

"Bugger off and make me a coffee, mate," Mike said. "It's your fault I'm tired anyway, dragging me halfway across the mountains yesterday in search of some d—"

He had almost said 'dead dog'.

Alex shot Mike a stern look. Luckily, Meggie didn't seem to have heard him. She had started rolling up the posters that had dried, and was placing them carefully inside a plastic poster tube.

Mike put his hand over his mouth and widened his eyes.

Alex rolled his. "Get your own bloody coffee. If there's any left."

Thankfully, there was. Mike poured the dregs from the filter carafe into a clean mug, which was decorated in garish tartan with the legend 'I LOVE BONNIE SCOTLAND' in metallic gold script. A real tourist-trap item. Mike guessed it must have come from one of the tacky gift shops in the village. He had only visited Drinton once, during his first stay months ago, and then he and Alex had only made it as far as the local pub. He sipped his lukewarm coffee and started to feel a yearning for something stronger to drink. He hoped the pub was still open. A lot of local watering holes were closing down all across the country. There had been a campaign at his university in Edinburgh, encouraging students to drink in the union bar. So many undergrads did their pre-drinking from cheaper supermarket bottles of cider and spirits – and their actual drinking from cans on the quad – that the bar had been threatened with closure. Happy hour at the bar had been extended to a full three hours, which helped, but even then it was still cheaper to load up your shopping trolley with booze than it was to get a round in at the local boozer. Mike hoped he could entice Alex away from teetotal Helen and the girls for a game of pool and a couple of pints while they were in the village.

The opportunity presented itself in the form of Meggie's posters. By the time Mike and Helen had arrived, with Alex at the wheel of Meggie's cranky old car, Kay had already volunteered to take some to the post office and general stores so she could ask the proprietor to put some up in the window. Meggie handed a stack to Alex and instructed him to go off with Mike and knock on a few doors down toward the church. Mike did a mental fist pump hearing that – the church was not too far away from the pub, from what he remembered. Helen paired up with Meggie, who was intent on attaching some posters to telegraph posts at strategic locations around the village high street where there would be the most foot traffic. She had made it sound like she was launching some kind of major advertising campaign, but, glancing up toward the main thoroughfare of the village, Mike could not see a single soul out on foot. He kept this observation to himself, fully aware that the only real purpose of the exercise was to give Meggie some peace of mind that she was doing *something* about Oscar's disappearance.

"Try and get a couple on the church noticeboard," Meggie said to Alex and Mike.

"Will do," Alex said.

"Fancy a pub lunch when we're done?" Mike asked.

"Sounds good," Meggie said.

"Just so long as there are actual solids involved," Helen said. "Your reputation for having liquid lunches precedes you."

"Spoken like a true lawyer," Mike said before turning to Meggie. "Don't worry, with these up all over the village, someone will have seen him."

Meggie flushed a little, looking hopeful.

Alex passed half the posters to Mike, urging him along, as if sensing that he might say the wrong thing at any given moment. They were halfway to the church when Alex made it clear to Mike that he already had.

"Why are you getting her hopes up like that?"

"What do you expect me to say? 'We may as well bin these'"—he fanned the posters around in the air—"'because sorry to say but we buried your dog yesterday'?"

"Pipe down, man," Alex said, looking over his shoulder.

"No one can hear. Because there's no one in this bloody village. It's a ghost town. I just hope the bloody landlord is out of bed. I could murder a pint."

"Ah, I see why you were so keen now, mate," Alex scoffed.

"Well, we are supposed to be on holiday. Celebrating our graduation – remember that? Only there hasn't been much celebrating, has there?"

Alex chuckled. "If you will get your missus knocked up, old chum."

"You say that like it's my fault."

"It takes two to— You know what I mean. If I didn't know you better, I'd think you were freaking out at the prospect of being a young father and seeking to hide it from those around you by rushing to the pub before lunchtime."

Mike glanced down at Meggie's cartoon image of Oscar. She had painted a little pink tongue poking out of the dog's mouth. Mike shuddered at the thought of flies landing on the poor animal's open, dead eyes.

"Let's just get these posters done and the first round's on me."

"All right then," Alex said, laughing at his friend's expense.

"Do you think we should bother posting them, though? I mean, it's not as if...."

"Don't even go there. If my sister finds a stack of missing pup posters in the bin, don't you think she'll be able to figure out who binned them? We have to go through the motions, keep up appearances. Just like you did in your finals, remember?"

"Okay, okay. No need to be such a complete and utter bastard about it."

They turned a corner in the street, and Alex stopped walking for a moment. They had reached the first of a row of houses. Alex knocked and waited. No answer came.

Mike saw the net curtain of the ground-floor front window twitch, then fall still. Some old dear was probably hiding inside, scoping them out.

"Someone's inside," Mike said to Alex. "I saw the curtain move."

"Perhaps they're worried we're Jehovah's Witnesses."

"That would'nae put them off. The old folk round here love a bit of old-timey religious banter."

Alex knocked again and waited a little longer this time. Still no answer. Then the curtain moved once more, and a fat white cat revealed itself in the window. It stared at Mike for a moment, then appeared to ignore him, as cats so often do.

"Let's see what that fat cat makes of poor old Oscar," Alex said, rolling up the poster and shoving it through the letter slot.

The little metal flap of the letter slot swung on its hinges, squeaking hysterically. The cat looked around and jumped down from the windowsill, making Mike and Alex laugh. Meggie could count one reader for her leaflets, at least, albeit a feline one.

"One down, about twenty more to bloody well go," Alex said. "Why don't you head down to the church while I finish off the houses? It'll be quicker, and you've got me thinking about a pint, you sly bastard."

"Ah, so you are a mere mortal after all, Alexander Buchanan," Mike chuckled. "Meet you outside the church in a bit then?"

"Aye," Alex said. "Just make sure you get a couple of posters on the community noticeboard. Then you can buy me that drink, Michael Carter."

"Will do," Mike said with a chuckle and, tucking his roll of posters under his arm, he headed off toward the church.

Saint Andrew's was a small, low building, the brickwork weathered and worn from many a Scottish winter. A saltire flag fluttered in the breeze atop the tower. Mike recalled Alex telling him that the main part of the church dated from the twelfth century, with the red-brick extension a twentieth-century addition. Alex had said that congregations must have peaked back then. The population of Drinton was now mainly elderly retirees, and Mike supposed they still attended services. But the rest of the dwellings, particularly the detached cottages on now disused farmland on the outskirts of the village, had been bought up by city workers and property developers keen on supplementing their pensions with holiday rentals. Alex often lamented how the community had become divided into those who never left and those who profited by their absence.

Mike thought his friend's position on this was hypocritical to say the least, though he'd never risk saying it to Alex's face. Hearthstone Cottage was only in use by Alex's family for a few weeks, sometimes only a few weekends, out of the year. The rest of the time it could be booked via a 'holiday cottages in Scotland' website, operated by the company that Alex's parents paid a handsome commission to in return for their services. To add insult to injury, the letting company was not a local business either. As far as Mike could recall, it had its head office in Glasgow and employed cleaners and contractors from outside of the local area. In truth, Alex's family were really no different than all the other out-of-towners who were buying up and renting out for a tidy profit. Still, Mike knew that even if Alex's family was to try to source locals to do it, there weren't any young local people left to physically do the work. All the people Alex and Mike's age had moved to the city years ago, no doubt to set up profitable businesses of their own. Mike understood why they would want to make the transition from Nowheresville to the city. And he fully intended to be among their number.

The plan was simple – earn enough money to be financially

independent, then develop a couple of properties to sustain his lifestyle into old age. He wondered if he could ever retire in a place like this, with its half-empty church, single pub, and random shops. Mike couldn't see it, somehow. He fancied somewhere more exotic, where he could idle his winter years away in a hot tub overlooking some tropical paradise. If he got bored not working, maybe he could open his own expat pub at a beach resort somewhere.

Daydreams of beach pubs spurred him on to complete his task at Saint Andrew's, and he pushed on down the lane to the church gate. The vicar was clearly trying to keep up with the times – a garish poster beside the gate displayed a picture of a smartphone with the caption 'YOU DON'T NEED ONE OF THESE TO HEAR JESUS CALLING YOU'. Mike unrolled one of Meggie's posters and tucked it into the frame, overlapping the main poster. As he did so, he began to chuckle at the humorous possibilities that careful poster alignment might offer. Sliding the missing dog poster farther across underneath the loose Perspex covering, he managed to obscure one word on the church poster. It now read, 'YOU NEED ONE OF THESE TO HEAR JESUS CALLING YOU'.

Amen, Mike thought as he stepped past the gate and up the winding path to the main entrance of the church. The outer doors were open, giving access to a small foyer within. Mike tried the doors leading to the interior of the church and found them locked. He guessed that Jesus was not calling him today, after all. To the left of the locked doors, a community noticeboard was wall-mounted above a bench housing three vases of flowers, each in varying stages of decomposition. Mike perused the little flyers and handwritten notices on postcards that had been affixed to the board with rusty drawing pins and saw that they advertised everything from counselling to gardening services. One particular postcard gave Mike a pang of guilt. It advertised dog-walking services for those too elderly to cope with long walks anymore. He thought of poor Oscar, buried under his mound of rocks and dirt. Grimacing at the memory, he quickly set about his task.

Mike cleared a poster-sized space on the board by removing, then repositioning, a couple of the classifieds cards. He prized away a couple of unused drawing pins from the board and liberated two more from a poster advertising beginners' Pilates classes. Missing dog poster affixed to the board in pride of place, Mike stepped back to look at it. Something about the vivid fleshy color of the dog's tongue on Meggie's painting made his stomach churn. He backed away from the church entrance, feeling suddenly cold. Something whipped past his legs, and he heard a sharp ripple of childish laughter. Whirling around, Mike caught a glimpse of a little figure in white dashing around the corner of the church.

"Hey!" he called out, giving chase. A narrow, tarmacked path led around the side of the building, flanked by flower beds to one side and the steep, weathered outer wall of the church to the other. The building loomed, casting its shadow over him as he followed the half-glimpsed figure around the back of the church. Mike reached the edge of a graveyard, dotted with gnarled, old trees and bordered by unruly hedgerows to the back and sides. Dozens of gravestones poked out above the unkempt grass of the graveyard, each with a different hue of moss or whatever lichen had grown on it over decades. He slowed to a crawling pace, scanning between the low branches of the twisted trees and the maze of headstones, looking for the child.

Another mischievous giggle came from the rear of the cemetery, and Mike's eyes searched out a large tombstone atop a plinth of weathered stone. The perfect hiding place, especially for a child. He darted between the grave markers, intent on finding out who was teasing him. Hearing the giggle again, he thought the child could be no older than five or six. Mike wondered why one so young was running about in the churchyard alone. Perhaps the kid was from a tourist family and had gotten lost in the village. Mike tried to ignore the way in which his arms had become pinpricked with goose bumps, and walked around the side of the large tombstone.

"Hello? You all right, kid?" he said in a wavering voice.

The giggle came again but sounded different somehow. It had taken on a disturbing, rasping quality, as though the child had learned to mimic the laughter of an elderly man. Mike did not like it one bit. His fear becoming indignation at the horrible sound, he dashed around to the back of the large tomb, intent on startling whoever was hiding there into a respectful silence.

The horrible laughter stopped, and Mike found nobody there. Only an upturned glass jar of dead flowers indicated that anyone could have been. Mike wiped the perspiration from his forehead and sighed. His mind was playing tricks on him again. He felt cold sweat at his back, and his legs turned numb. Concerned he might actually faint, Mike sat down on the tomb. A breeze rustled the leaves on the branches above him, and the sky darkened, adding to the chill that crept across Mike's skin. He reached out a hand to steady himself against the solid structure of the tomb. Only then did he notice the engraving in the stone. It was perfectly carved, and fresh, as though it had been made yesterday. The lichens he had seen covering the tomb had retreated from the carving, revealing the words to the subdued, cloudy daylight.

HERE LIES MICHAEL CARTER.

He blinked at the words, aware that his vision was becoming blurred and watery. They were still there, plain as day. He extended his fingertips, running them along the contours of the engraving. Mike could feel the sharp edges of the stonemason's work. It was real to the touch. He stood up as if in a dream and wandered away from the tombstone. Drifting through the long grasses, that cold sweat still at his back, and his heart pounding, Mike became aware of the other headstones all around him. There were many more of them than he had seen when he'd first arrived at the churchyard, but how could that be? They stood at insane angles, some jutting out and scraping against others like rows of crooked teeth. As he drew nearer to one of the headstones, he saw it too was carved –

HERE LIES MICHAEL CARTER.

No, that couldn't be. He was losing his mind, and he wanted it to stop. He tried to work his way between the headstones, each and every one decorated with the self-same mocking words –

HERE LIES MICHAEL CARTER.

The more he stumbled, the farther away he seemed to be from the church building, which loomed dark and distant as a vague memory. He heard the horrid childish laughter again, echoing around the graveyard, until he could not be sure whether the sound was coming from without, or within, his head. The roll of posters slipped from his hand and fell to the ground. He clamped his hands to his ears and charged through the ranks of headstones, feeling them closing in on him, the hideous sound of stone tearing through grass and soil adding to the dreadful cacophony of the man-child's laughter. Tears streamed from his eyes, and mucus dripped from his nose as he fought to endure the invasion of noise and deathlike stone all around him.

And then, no sooner had he thought he might succumb to the tumult and fall into the wet grass to be swallowed by stones, each bearing his name, than Mike found himself at the front of the church building. He clasped his hands to his knees, drawing deep breaths into his lungs and focusing on the welcome normality of the street beyond the church gate. He did not look back until he had passed beyond the gate and onto the pavement – and only then to close the gate firmly shut behind him. As he did so, a little flutter of white caught his eye and made his heart skip a beat. It was one of the missing dog posters, being carried away by the wind. He watched it snag on a tree branch before disappearing from view, into the graveyard.

CHAPTER TEN

The pub was perfect. Even more perfect than Mike remembered. The lounge bar still had the same old fusty, burgundy carpet that smelled of the cigarette smoke and spilled drinks of decades past. The old wooden beams of the ceiling framed expanses of yellowing paint that had presumably been white at one stage of its lifespan, many years ago. A faulty CD jukebox stood, lights blinking spasmodically in the corner, near to a scuffed old pool table. The last time Mike and Alex had been in the pub, Mike recalled, the jukebox would only play one CD – *Slippery When Wet* by Bon Jovi. Now it wouldn't even perform that basic service to patrons' musical requirements. All it was fit for was to be used as a handy receptacle for Mike's pint of beer as he lined up his next pool shot. Alex was losing, for once, and Mike felt he owed it to himself to become the victor before he had too much to drink. He always hit his losing streak on the second or third pint. He'd try to pace himself as he enjoyed his first.

Mike took his shot. The ball he had been hoping to pot rebounded off the corner pocket. He had cut the cue ball a fraction too tight.

"Ah, bad luck, old chum." Alex smirked at him over his cue as he chalked the tip and surveyed the arena of the pool table, looking for openings.

"Going easy on you today, man," Mike replied, "as you've yet to pot a single bloody ball."

"Yeah, yeah," Alex groaned before taking his shot. The ball thundered into the center pocket, making a decisive clunk as it dropped into the glass-windowed ramp inside the table. "You were saying?"

It was Mike's turn to groan now. He crossed to the blinking lights of the broken jukebox and took a sip of his pint.

"Winner stays on?"

Mike hadn't even seen the old man enter the pub, let alone the games area. Before either he or Alex could answer, the old man slammed his hand on the side of the pool table. When he removed his hand, Mike saw that he had deposited a coin there – muscling in on their next game. Mike was used to placing money on the table back at the students' union in Edinburgh, but he hadn't felt the need in the pub. It had been deserted, until now.

"Aye, all right," Alex said. "I will'nae be long," he added, winking at Mike.

The old man's eyes twinkled as he looked from Alex to Mike, as though sizing up his potential opponents. He was around seventy years of age, with a portly belly that was stretching the buttons of his check work shirt to the limits. He had the aspect of a farm laborer about him. His well-worn beige corduroy trousers were held up by braces and were tucked roughly into his Wellington boots. Wisps of white hair were visible beneath the peak of a tweed flat cap. He held a pint of stout in his left hand and took a sip, the thick white foam of the head coating his upper lip. He licked it away, the flick of his tongue lizard-like and, Mike thought, entirely unappealing.

"You boys on your holidays then?"

Another man, this one in his late fifties to early sixties, appeared at the pool table, carrying a tumbler of whisky. He was similarly attired but with a heavy waxed jacket over the top of his clothes. Mike glanced down and saw he was also wearing grubby wellies.

"Aye," Alex said, chalking his cue again.

"We just graduated from university," Mike offered. "We're taking a break to celebrate."

"Hear that?" said the first old man. "University graduates."

"What did you boys study at?" asked the second.

"I read law," Alex said, leaning over the table to take a shot at an easy green ball. "Mike there studied business."

Mike saw a flash of something unpleasant in the first old man's eyes. Then the old fellow blinked, and it was gone. "Well, well, two proper intellectuals we have here."

A sarcastic edge to the man's tone made this sound like an insult. Mike shifted on his feet, feeling uncomfortable. Couldn't they just fuck off and leave him and Alex to their game?

"Don't put him off his shot," the second man said, just as Alex miscued, sending the cue ball into a corner pocket.

"Oh, bad luck," his friend said.

Alex frowned and took solace from his pint while Mike stepped up for his turn. He had the freedom of the baize now, adjusting the placement of the cue ball until he got a clear potting angle, with the potential for another on the rebound. He leaned low over the table and tried to ignore the whispers of the old men as they stood hunched in the shadows over the far end of the table where he was aiming his shot. He exhaled slowly, feeling the cue slide back beneath his chin as he prepared to strike. Taking a sharp breath, he made the shot and the ball he had been targeting dropped into the corner pocket.

"Not bad for a young 'un," the first old man allowed.

"Studied business, he said." His friend sipped his drink and glanced over the table through narrowed eyes. "Where you fellers staying?" he asked Alex.

"Over at Hearthstone Cottage. You know it?"

"Know it? I should think so, son," the old man said through his whiskers. "We're going over that way tomorrow. For the grouse shoot."

"I thought shooting season was over. Usually runs October to January, doesn't it?"

"We have a special permit," the old man said boastfully, "from the landowner."

"Do you now?" Alex said.

"Aye. You met him, I suppose, if you're renting his place?"

"That'd be my dad."

The old man smiled through his rheumy eyes. "Of course! You're the Buchanan lad. Fancy that, Edward, the lawyer's son is a lawyer himself."

"Only a law graduate," Alex said, "not practicing yet. Though I hope to be soon enough."

"Oh, aye, you will be, no doubt about that," the first old man interjected. "Your father's well known around here. You'll be following in his footsteps. Do you wish to join us, ladies? Oh, my old brains, I meant to say laddies!"

The old man guffawed and made a show of correcting himself, though Mike felt sure his 'slip of the tongue' had been intentional.

"On the shoot?" Alex asked.

"Aye. It would be an honor to have such fine young fellows as yourselves along with us."

Mike made his way around to the other side of the table. His next shot was trickier than he had hoped it would be. The cue ball had traveled farther along the cushion than planned. He would have to put a bit of spin on the ball, or else risk giving Alex the advantage.

"And ye can keep whatever game you might be lucky enough tae bag," the other man continued. "Make a fine supper at that there cottage of yours."

"Aye, a traditional crofter's supper, for sure," his friend added. "Real men bring home the meat!"

Just as Mike was taking his shot, the two men slapped each other on the back and clinked their glasses in loud agreement.

"Oh, but now he's gone and fouled on the black," the first old man said.

Mike's heart sank into his stomach as he watched the curveball rebound off the cushion, potting the eight ball – and losing him the game. Mike saw something unpleasant in the old fellow's gap-toothed grin before his face reverted to a ruddy-cheeked mask of soft inebriation again.

"Let's hope he's better with a shotgun!" he said, chuckling.

"Aye, for all our sakes," his friend said, "or we'll all be dead!"

To Mike's dismay, Alex joined in with their laughter.

"Loser gets the next round in, mate. Just a half, I've got to drive you back," Alex said. "Hey, can he get you anything, gents?"

"Well, if he insists," joked the first old man, "a stout for me, and a scotch and a splash of soda for my pal here."

"Aye. I had a bit of a turn the other week."

"Oh, sorry to hear that," Alex said, taking the bait.

"The doctor said I was dehydrated," the old man went on, "and ever since then, I've been taking a little drop of water in my whisky."

They fell about with laughter once again, and, to Mike's immediate annoyance, Alex looked to be in cahoots with them.

Mike nodded as politely as he could through his grimace and trudged over to the bar. He ordered a pint and a half for himself and Alex, and the stout and scotch for the old locals. When the scotch arrived, it smelled so good that he ordered a chaser for himself. His mood had soured after losing the pool game, but Mike knew that the graveyard had rattled him most of all. Must be losing his mind. He blinked away the unpleasant memory of seeing his name engraved on tombstone after tombstone. After downing the whisky in one desperate gulp, he delivered the drinks to the old men, who took them eagerly but without thanking him. Passing Alex his half pint, Mike watched the eldest of the two men breaking the colorful triangle of balls.

"Shouldn't the winner break?" Mike asked.

"Aye," Alex replied, "but try telling this pair of jokers that."

Mike took a sip of beer. It cooled the whisky-induced fire at the back of his tongue. He could do this all day. Just as he thought it, though, the door to the saloon bar opened and he heard the familiar voices of the girls.

"Surprise, surprise! Told you they'd be boozing in here," Helen said to Kay and Meggie. She walked past the pool table, under the watchful gaze of the two old men, and gave Mike a kiss. Mike kissed her back, relieved that her mood seemed better than it had been earlier.

"How many have you had?" she asked.

"This is only my second," Mike replied, and set his pint glass down. He swayed slightly on his feet, despite willing himself not to.

"Liar," Helen said. "You stink of whisky, you old drunk."

An eruption of laughter came from the two locals by the pool table. Mike couldn't tell if they were laughing at him or just in general. He craned his neck around Helen to see that the one playing pool had missed his shot, and also caught his friend eyeing up Helen's backside.

"What is it? You seem rattled."

"It's nothing," Mike said, pretending not to see the old man's beady eyes.

"He's just a sore loser," Alex cut in, making an 'L' shape on his forehead with his thumb and forefinger.

"Aw, did the nasty man beat you?" Helen asked, giggling.

Mike felt himself blush and reached for his pint. The act of taking a sip put a distance between him and Helen and the men at the pool table with their unwelcome glances.

Over at the bar, Kay was ordering vodkas. "Still off the sauce?" she asked Helen, who nodded and asked if she could have a lime and soda. "Sure," Kay replied, and Mike detected a sharp look in her eyes, the same jealous disdain he'd witnessed during their walk in the woods.

"I'm all right, hun," Alex said from across the pool table.

"You bet you are, mister," Kay said flatly. "You're driving us girls back just as soon as we're done with these."

"Don't mind, do you?" Meggie asked. "You know I don't like to drink and drive." She was already sipping her vodka.

"Like I have a bloody choice," Alex growled as he cued up his next shot.

★   ★   ★

Mike noticed the poster he had affixed to the church advertising board outside Saint Andrew's had disappeared. He thought the wind must have snatched it away, though the afternoon air was now still. As he followed the others back up the lane toward the general store, he saw that the fat cat was absent too. It was as though it had been window dressing, arranged to amuse tourists on their way to the pub. The street was deserted once more, as it had been earlier, and an empty feeling hung heavy over the slate roofs, which were as drab and gray as the clouds above them.

The warm, fuzzy feeling from the booze helped Mike up the steep part of the hill. After reaching the general store, the girls went inside to collect the groceries the shopkeeper had put aside for them. Mike helped carry a couple of bags laden with tins and packets to Meggie's car, which was parked around the corner in the only occupied parking bay. The venerable hatchback could just about carry three passengers, but with all the shopping in tow, four were too many. Helen offered to wait with him, but Mike said not to bother; he could wait until Alex returned to pick him up. He put on his best and brightest smile in order to conceal his true intent. No sooner had the car disappeared from view than Mike ducked inside the shop.

The interior gave the impression someone had stopped the clock circa 1973. Mike suspected some, if not all, of the stock had originated in that decade. Many of the shelves were half – or even completely – empty. The others displayed seemingly random pairings of goods. An empty carton that once housed hot chocolate sachets rubbed cardboard shoulders with a stack of lurid pink-and-green sponge scourers. An assortment of different fruit-flavored jelly cubes occupied dusty shelf space with a stack of glue-backed envelopes, the kind you had to lick in order to seal. Mike pondered that the jelly could come in handy if you had the misfortune to lick one of the envelopes, which appeared wrinkled from the advent of a few too many wet autumns.

Frowning at the musty smell emanating from the envelopes, Mike made his way toward the rear of the shop. He gave a carousel of dubious-looking dried meat products a wide berth. Each was shriveled beneath its shrink-wrap, giving the pinkest of the snacks the disturbing aspect of severed tongues. One, paler and more yellow in hue than the others, looked like a pig's ear. After glimpsing what looked like a tuft of fine hair beneath the clear plastic, Mike hurried past the display.

Tucked away behind the gruesome carousel, Mike located his prize. Wall-mounted shelves groaned beneath the weight of dusty bottles, which Mike investigated eagerly, wiping away the dust with his thumb to reveal the labels. Cheap red wines stood alongside bottles of port and sherry. To his delight, this dark little corner with its dusty bottles was also the most generously stocked part of the shop. He stood on tiptoes to survey the lineup on the top two shelves, where the bottles of spirits stood proudly above their cheaper associates. There were a few blended whiskies and fairly decent brands of gin and vodka on offer. But it was the good stuff that Mike craved. He was on holiday, after all.

"Help you at all?"

Mike almost cried out in surprise at the sudden intrusion. He turned to see a diminutive shopkeeper standing next to the dried meats. She too looked like she had been preserved here in the shop since the earlier Seventies. Her greasy and gray-brown hair was clamped away from her high forehead with a hairclip, revealing a line of acne scars above her eyebrows. The National Health frames of thick spectacles framed her doughy face. Her hands were tucked firmly in the front pockets of a burgundy tabard, which she wore over a beige sweater and dark green trousers. Mike noticed a pair of scissors poking out of another pocket at her breast.

"I'm...just looking for a good single malt," he said.

"Ah, after a wee dram, are we?" She smiled, revealing a row of crooked and discolored teeth. "I keep the best behind the counter."

She turned and headed back to the front of the shop, turning the carousel of dried meats with one fat little hand as she did so. The display squeaked against its rusted old baseplate, and Mike was reminded of a turnstile at a rainy fairground he had visited as a child, as he navigated his way past the disturbing shrink-wrapped packages.

"Now," the woman said in a high-pitched voice, "was it the twelve, the fifteen, or something even older you were after?"

"Depends on the price," Mike said brazenly, his eyes scanning some out-of-date mint chocolate bars stacked in little wooden compartments beneath the counter.

Perhaps sensing a premium retail opportunity, the shopkeeper turned her back on him and began rummaging on the lower shelves behind her. He noticed her spine was crooked beneath her sweater and tabard. Her deformed back had forced her shoulders to lean toward the left. The unfortunate outcome was that she had a slight hump beneath her left shoulder. Mike found it at once repulsive and comical.

She turned sharply, holding a bottle in her hands, so sharply that she made him jump. Recognition flickered in her drab eyes behind those thick spectacles, and Mike wondered if she knew he had been staring at her twisted back.

"My husband made this, at his own still not two miles from here, where the old village well still stands. It's twenty years old now, the perfect age at which to enjoy it."

Mike began to wonder why the village well would be two miles away from the actual village, when she held out the bottle for him to take. It was heavy in his hands and had no label. He lifted it up to the dirty light of the shop window and saw that it had a beautiful golden color. The cork had been fixed into place with dark green sealing wax.

"Not much older than you, I'd wager," she added, and Mike felt queasy to see a flicker of scalloped tongue poke out from between her thin lips.

"How much?" he asked, craving fresh air. He needed to be out of this shop, with its dust and dandruff.

"Twenty-five," she replied. "Just over a pound a year. Not a bad price for a tried-and-true local malt."

"I'll take it," Mike replied. He fished out two notes from his pocket and handed them over. He winced as the shopkeeper's greasy fingers brushed his when she took the money from him.

"I'll wrap it up for you, so you can deliver it home safely," she said, pocketing the money in her tabard where she kept her scissors. She first wrapped the bottle in a sheet of brown paper before putting the scissors to use by snipping a length of twine. She tied the package off with a limp bow and handed it over to Mike. "If you like it, perhaps you'll buy some more to take home with you? A souvenir of Hearthstone Cottage."

"How did you know—" Mike began to ask, then saw that crooked, toothed smile again.

"The girls who came in before you said that's where you're all staying," the shopkeeper replied. "Nice girls," she added, managing to make it sound slightly like an insult.

"I'm sure I'll be back for more," Mike said, trying to sound friendly. He felt relieved to be leaving the shop and hoped Alex would not be too long picking him up. Maybe he would crack open the seal on the whisky and give it a taste.

"I haven't much left anymore," the shopkeeper said, then sighed. "Twenty years. One for every year since my poor husband passed."

"Oh, I'm – I'm sorry," Mike said.

"His last batch." The woman's eyes darkened behind the lenses of her glasses. "Enjoy it," she said as Mike slipped out through the door and onto the dusky street.

He heard the bell chime as the door swung shut behind him. The sound of the creaking door made him think of the groans of a dying old man. Glancing up the lane, he saw the top of the church bell tower looming shadow-gray above the slate roofs of the houses, the saltire flag hanging limp and lifeless. He found a low wall to perch on a short distance from the shop and cracked open the whisky.

★   ★   ★

"Found this sorry excuse for a university graduate drinking whisky at the roadside."

Alex chuckled and slapped Mike on the back. Helen took one look at the unlabeled bottle in Mike's hand and rolled her eyes.

"What on earth have you got there?" she asked. "Hooch?"

Mike held the bottle aloft proudly. "Actually, it's a fine local malt. The shopkeeper's husband made it at his own whisky still, she said. It's bloody delicious and bloody strong stuff. Anyone up for a wee dram? Not you, of course, babe...."

Helen scowled at him.

Meggie laughed. "Can't believe she duped you into buying a whole bottle of MacGregor's Death Juice."

"MacGregor's what?" Mike felt the color drain from his face.

"Did she tell you her husband's dead?"

"She did. That's why she only has a few bottles of the good stuff...."

"A few bottles!" Meggie laughed again, and Alex laughed along. "She's got dozens of them stashed behind that counter of hers. She can't give them away."

"How much did you pay for this?" Helen asked.

"I'd rather not say," Mike muttered.

Helen groaned, and Alex laughed mockingly.

"Did she tell you *how* her husband died?" Alex asked matter-of-factly.

"No, she didn't. To be honest, she gave me the bloody creeps, that woman. Couldn't get out of the shop quick enough."

Alex took the bottle from Mike's grip and waved it at him. "He died from drinking this stuff," he said, chuckling.

"Give that back," Mike said. He was sure MacGregor had simply been getting too old to take a drink. He was younger, with an Olympian liver.

"Don't," Helen pleaded from across the room.

"Buzzkill," Mike said. "Quitting smoking is one thing, but you never said anything about going bloody teetotal too. What kind of holiday is this?"

"I don't know," Helen replied, "you tell me."

An awkward silence fell between them. Mike could feel three pairs of eyes on him. He wished he could just take his bottle of MacGregor's Death Juice and finish it off down on the jetty. By himself.

"I'll tell you what kind of holiday it is," Alex said, raising his voice as if to purposely break the awkward silence. "It's the kind where we have grouse for supper tomorrow – if Mike can shoot straight after drinking so much firewater."

"Oh, no," Meggie groaned. "Tell me you guys aren't going out on a shoot."

"Oh indeed we are. Sorry, sis, but we just din'nae do tofu for supper."

Mike saw Meggie glance around the room, possibly looking for moral support. Finding none, she turned her attention back to her brother. "Fuck's sake, Alex. What have those birds ever done to you that you want to go around shooting them dead?"

"It's nothing personal, just good sport."

"It's a bloody...blood sport is what it is," Meggie spat, almost tripping over her words.

"They've had a really good life, those lucky old birds. Fresh Highland air, the best grain to feast on—"

"To fatten them up, you mean, so they can't fly too far from stupid men with their stupid guns."

"Hey, I resemble that comment," Alex said in jest, but Meggie wasn't laughing.

"All meat is murder," she replied, drawing a line under her point.

"Tasty, tasty murder," Alex taunted.

"You're going too?" Meggie's words to Mike were less of a question and more of an accusation.

Mike didn't know why, but her words made him feel uncomfortable. "Maybe you can...use the feathers in one of your artworks?" he ventured.

The look on Meggie's face showed him he had spoken out of turn. She skulked out of the conservatory and into the garden. Seconds later, Mike heard her calling Oscar's name and whistling to him. "Come on, boy!" Her voice sounded cracked and desperate. He tried not to think of the dead dog, its torn belly undulating with maggots beneath the burial mound he and Alex had built.

"Give me some more of that whisky," Mike said to Alex.

"The Death Juice? You sure?"

"Just get me a glass, will you, mate?" Mike replied.

"Think I'll bloody well join you," Alex said.

At that, Helen and Kay marched toward the conservatory door.

"Hey, where you going?" Mike asked. "You're not offended by grouse shooting, are you? It'll be amazing if we bag a couple for our meal."

Helen paused at the door and fixed him with a stare. "Fresh air," she said, her voice icy. "You should try it sometime."

"Worry not, laddie, we'll get plenty of fresh air tomorrow," Alex said, pouring two generous measures of whisky into their tumblers. "To the shoot." He raised his glass in a toast.

"To the shoot," Mike said.

They clinked glasses, and Mike enjoyed the sweet burn at the back of his throat. He saw the distant shapes of the girls as they walked toward the loch. Above the water, dark clouds were gathering as though eager to bring the day to an early close.

CHAPTER ELEVEN

The day of the shoot began in a bit of a haze for Mike. Firstly due to the weather, which had turned overnight into a gloomy, autumnal chill. And secondly because of the additional dram – or three – of MacGregor's Death Juice that he had put away after the girls had gone to bed. Alex had joined him for a while but had called it a day after his second glass and had advised Mike to do the same.

Mike just hadn't been in the mood to cut short his partying, so Alex's good advice had fallen on deaf ears. And aside from that, Mike had been reluctant to go to bed in case Helen was still awake. She would only have made a scene about him staying up drinking if he blundered into bed while she lay there reading. He had poured himself another ample measure of whisky and had savored each sip while staring into the fire in the hearth. Putting aside all of the nightmares and hallucinations – for that was what they must have been – he had decided there and then to enjoy the rest of his stay at the cottage as much as he could.

He had made a good start by staying up late and only crawling upstairs to bed after he had nodded off for a while in the chair by the fire. He had found it difficult to navigate the steep, narrow stairs with so much whisky inside him, but at least he hadn't woken Helen when he slid drunkenly under the covers beside her. She had still been sleeping when Alex woke him at seven that morning. Mike and Alex had both made coffee, wolfed down a couple of slices of hot, buttered toast, and managed to sneak out without waking Helen, Kay, or Meggie.

The two old men from Drinton village were waiting for them in a beaten-up old Land Rover at the lane that met the path to the cottage. The eldest man clambered out to greet them and finally introduced himself as Jamie. His friend, Edward, opened the passenger door and joined them.

Jamie took one look at Mike and cracked a sardonic smile, joking with Edward and Alex that he looked like he was sweating pure distillery water. Mike let it go. Truth was, a headache was forming between his temples that rivaled even the dark clouds brewing overhead in intensity. His stomach was gurgling, and his throat felt sore from the acid bile lapping there – an unwelcome tide on a sorry shore. He regretted drinking so much of the shopkeeper's Death Juice, though it had tasted glorious at the time. He supposed he could always duck behind a tree or some scrubby grass to puke if he needed to, though he hoped he wouldn't. He'd hate to give the wisecracking duo the chance to ridicule him some more. Mike swallowed down the acid sting at his throat and tried to soldier on as best he could.

Following the old men around to the back of their vehicle, he watched as they pulled back a heavy tarpaulin encrusted with dried mud to reveal a padlocked strongbox. They made a song and dance about which of them had the key before discovering neither did – it had been safely tucked away in the ashtray of the old Land Rover.

After unlocking the padlock and opening the lid of the strong box, Jamie revealed its contents with a grin. Four hunting shotguns were inside, along with a couple of air rifles that looked puny by comparison. Edward retrieved another padlocked box from the shadows deep inside the Land Rover and cracked that one open too. This box contained the ammunition. Mike tried to listen to the old men's instructions as they talked him through the process of loading and carrying the shotguns. But their thick accents, and the howling headache making his brow furrow, made it difficult for him to concentrate. When it came to his turn to handle one of the shotguns, he almost dropped it. His hands were slick with cold sweat, and – try as he might to style it out – he really did have a bad case of the DTs. Jamie snorted with laughter at him as Mike swallowed dryly and tried to get a grip on both himself and the shotgun.

"Would you prefer one of the wee air rifles?" Alex asked mockingly.

"Piss off, Alex," Mike said.

"He has...fired one of these before, hasn't he?" Jamie asked.

Alex chuckled. "Only on the range with my dad. Hardly a crack shot, but he knows the basics, don't you, Mikey?"

Mike didn't like the way his friend was talking about him as if he wasn't even there. He was about to say something he might regret – something involving the barrel of the shotgun and Alex's arse – when

Edward placed a paternal hand on his shoulder and began to talk him through the correct handling procedure for the shotgun.

"Ye'll get the hang of it eventually, laddie," Jamie said encouragingly when Edward was done with his lesson. "Though I would've thought you'd at least have bagged a bird or two for your table by now. Strapping, hungry young lad like yourself."

"First time for everything," Edward mused. "I remember my first kill like it was yesterday. Bloody well near blew my own foot off at one point, so I did."

"First shoot? That must have been wi' muskets or something," Jamie joked.

"Fuck off, you old bastard, you're one foot in the grave already," Edward laughed.

"This is going to be a fun day," Alex murmured.

"Don't we...need a license or something?" Mike asked as he did his best to shoulder the shotgun and line up the sights just as Edward had shown him.

"Oh, no, you din'nae need to worry about anything like that," Jamie said. "The beauty of it is, you see, the land out here is private. All we need is permission from the landowner to shoot here, and we're good to go."

"That'll be his da'," Edward added, nodding at Alex.

Mike still felt a little uncertain, and the old men's disingenuous smiles were doing absolutely nothing to put that feeling to rest.

Jamie took Mike's hand and helped adjust his grip, and then he tapped Mike on the shoulder, prompting him to improve his posture with the shotgun.

"That's better," Jamie said. "We may make a country squire of you yet."

Mike wasn't so sure about that. Looking up at the gathering clouds, he felt the first cold kiss of drizzle on his face. Great, it was going to piss it down while they staggered around in the wet countryside, trying not to shoot their own feet off. Mike wanted nothing more right now than a good fry up and another few hours – if not an entire day – in bed.

"Righto, that's us ready then," Jamie said chirpily. "Shall we be for the off then, lads?"

Mike declined to answer, sliding the shotgun's carry strap over his shoulder as instructed by Edward.

"What are we going to be shooting at, exactly?" Mike asked.

He realized as soon as he said it how green he must sound, but right now he didn't give a shit. It was more important that he keep talking, to keep his mind distracted from giving in to the nausea making his brain swim, and to keep his body distracted from puking.

"Red grouse would be our primary target," Jamie said, sounding sage-like and clearly relishing his role as shooting soothsayer. "They're difficult buggers to bag, though. They can fly up to seventy miles per hour. Quick on the wing, from land to air and out of range within a matter of seconds."

"Have you ever shot any?"

"Oh, aye. It just takes a bit of practice, like most things. The younger birds are the ones to bag, to be honest. They're the ones you want on your table."

Edward smacked his lips. "They're bloody delicious."

"There's black grouse out here too, though they're the rarer bird," Jamie went on. "Numbers are down in Scotland because of interference with their habitat."

"Interference how?" Mike asked.

"Oh, you know, deforestation and all that. Wetland drainage. Population explosion, all kinds of things."

"But not around here."

"No, not around here, laddie. Thanks to gentlemen like Alex's father."

"Because he's the landowner, you mean?"

"Not only that. The company he works for built a series of dams in the Highlands. One not far from here. Did'nae he tell you anything about it? Well, some parts that were dry now have a good supply of water running through them...."

"And some parts that were wet have more fields for growing crops, and trees for paper mills," Edward added.

Mike frowned. "That sounds like interference with habitat to me," he said.

"Aye, it does," Jamie said, "but it does'nae always mean it's a bad thing."

Mike thought about this for a few moments. He had always thought of his and Alex's fathers' jobs as being confined to the cities. Luxury hotels and shiny new office blocks seemed to be their thing. It was a surprise to Mike to hear they had real-world impact on the countryside and wildlife with their projects too. But he also knew it was a matter of some resentment that Alex's father had been rewarded with the cottage and land as a sizeable bonus package for sealing the Kintail dam deal. Mike's father had often complained about it at the time, believing that without his work in Biz Dev, Alex's father wouldn't have any contracts to draw up in the first place. Mike had broached the subject once with Alex, who said that his own father had told him Mike's dad had fucked up the terms of the deal with the local authorities, almost jeopardizing the project – until Alex's father had stepped in to play legal eagle and save the day. It was still the source of much friction between their fathers, to that day, and Mike's father had given him disapproving looks when he had mentioned he was planning a fishing holiday with Alex at the cottage.

"Should be ours, that place, Mikey. Ours by rights. But who am I to argue with the bloody Buchanans of this world? Even after all the hours of overtime I put in. He swans in, like a typical bloody lawyer. Robbed, we were. Still, we've got our timeshare on the Costa del Crime, I suppose...."

"All right, laddies," Jamie said, "time to get along with business. We'll walk up the high path, circle round behind the line of trees over there. That's where they're most likely to be roosting. When we get near to the loch, we'll have to cut the chatter. The wee beasties will take to the wing fast, just as soon as they've heard us. We'll only have a few seconds to bag a couple of birds."

Mike shouldered his shotgun and followed the others up the path toward the lower slopes of the hillside to the east of the loch. The dark clouds had smothered the tops of the distant mountains, choking the day of some of its light. By the time they passed the loch, a fine mist had begun to gather above the water, shrouding the reflective surface as though it were protecting a secret hidden there. The air became cooler and damper the farther they walked, and Mike pulled the collar of his jacket tighter around his throat. He wished he was wearing waterproofs like the old-timers. Once or twice he caught them giving him and Alex a backward glance, after which they chuckled together quietly. No doubt these experienced hunters thought it was hilarious dragging two city boys out on a drab day like this, to get them cold, wet and muddy and to return to the cottage with nothing but head colds to speak of the experience.

Mike rubbed his hands together, trying to bring them back to life. They were becoming numb from the cold. What he wouldn't do for a nice hot toddy made from the whisky he had bought at the shop, followed by a nice, long smoke and then a doze by the fire. He wondered what the girls were up to back at the cottage. Probably warming themselves by the hearth, reading and chatting and eating together, he thought longingly.

As he trudged on along the path, becoming irritated by his own repetitive footfalls, Mike began to wonder if all holidays ultimately ended like this, with the happy campers splitting into groups before each individual then withdrew into himself or herself. He remembered a family holiday that had gone particularly pear-shaped when he was in his early teens. His mother had booked a ten-day package deal on a Greek island as a surprise for Mike's dad. His dad was certainly surprised – he had never been on holiday for longer than a week. Mike recalled how quiet his dad had been during the flight and then the boat trip to the island. His father had only started speaking to his family during the drive to their rented villa, and even then he had seemed subdued. Mike remembered his mother's face, reflected in the rearview mirror of the hire car. She had looked terrified. Mike still wondered if his dad had driven too close to the sheer edges of the winding road on purpose to teach them all a lesson. His father had spent the next ten days sleeping by the pool or answering work calls. On one occasion he even slipped into the little town nearby to receive a fax, since their internet connection was down. His mum had tried to organize them into a schedule of family activities, including boat trips and beach picnics, but after a few days even she gave up the pretense and allowed everyone to follow their own agenda. Mike's dad took to sleeping late, then eating his meals separately, often at a taverna a short walk away. The family settled into a pattern of occupying separate spaces within the holiday villa – one in the pool, another indoors, while Mike was off exploring the coastline. Mike's mother had driven them back to the harbor when the holiday was over. She scraped the paintwork of the hire car by driving too far from the edges of the vertiginous roads. They had never taken a holiday together after that. Mike guessed they had all learned their lesson.

"I hear them," Jamie announced in an urgent whisper, bringing Mike back to the present.

Mike stopped walking, glad to take a breather. The two old men surveyed the line of trees from beneath their flat caps. Edward rummaged in the pockets of his voluminous waxed jacket and moments later produced and unfolded a compact pair of binoculars.

"It's the grouse, all right," Edward whispered, licking his spittle-flecked lips.

"All right, laddies, we'll walk close to the loch, but under the cover of those trees." Jamie pointed in the direction of the same woodland path he and Alex had followed to rejoin the girls after they had buried the dog.

"Keep as quiet as you can. Don't spook the birds."

Alex went on ahead, and Mike took a few breaths before setting off again. He was so intent on watching where the two old men were leading him that he wandered slightly from the path without even realizing it. His foot snapped a thick twig as he trod on it. With a flurry of noise and feathers, an enormous flock of birds flapped from the bushes beside Mike. They were so close that he felt the air from their wings against his face. The noise they made was frightening. He stumbled back and cried out in alarm, his shotgun tilting up as he regained his footing.

But his finger was on the trigger.

With a sharp bang, the shotgun let loose a shot. It made a sound like a purse full of pennies exploding. The thunderous recoil slammed into Mike's arm, knocking the wind out of him. He stumbled back with such force that he fell fully over and dropped the shotgun. Alex reached out and tried to grab his arm, to break his fall. Mike clawed wildly at the air, his fingertips finding the sleeve of Alex's jacket. Mike dug his fingers into the fabric, trying to remain upright, but all he succeeded in doing was to pull Alex down with him, face-first into the bushes. A whirlwind of panicked birds circled above him, loose feathers falling like autumn leaves.

"What the fucking hell are you doing?" Alex coughed through a mouthful of foliage.

As the frightened birds escaped into the branches above their heads, Mike saw at once that they were not grouse but wood pigeons. He had managed to startle them from their hiding place in the bushes when his foot had snapped the twig, but his accidental gunshot had sent them into a frenzy.

He felt like such an idiot.

Mike's eyes widened as he looked up at yet more birds now flapping terrified above the trees. His impulsive shot at the pigeons had scared the grouse – their actual prey – from their branches. Mike saw the exasperated look on Jamie's face before the old man lurched into action, cocking and aiming his shotgun into the sky. Edward followed suit, cursing under his breath as he did so. Jamie's shotgun boomed, followed by Edward's.

Mike watched the grouse disappear over the treetops. When the two old men lowered their weapons, all their good humor had disappeared too.

"You bloody fool," Edward growled.

"I'm – I'm sorry," Mike said. "The birds startled me and...."

Jamie just shook his head slowly, emptying the spent cartridges from his weapon onto the ground. He and Edward whispered something to each other. Edward then took a hip flask from his jacket pocket, and the two old friends took a drink.

"I guess that's the shoot bloody well over for today then," Alex said. He got to his feet, leaving Mike flat on his back in the bush.

"Hey, I said I was sorry," Mike protested.

Jamie wiped his wet lips with the back of his hand and gave the hip flask back to Edward. "Dry your eyes, laddie," he said. "There'll be more wee birdies to shoot at today. Perhaps leave the actual shooting to us grown-ups this time."

Mike wriggled out from the tangle of bushy branches. He dusted himself down and picked up his shotgun. Alex snatched it from him and shouldered it with his own.

"Where are we going?" Mike asked.

"We follow the birds," Edward muttered.

"Really? How far?"

"All day if we have to," came the reply.

Mike glanced back at the mist curling over the loch. It had thickened into a bank of fog that was rolling their way. He pulled a dry twig from his tousled hair and walked on, eager to catch up to the others.

★　★　★

By the time they broke the tree line, a heavy bank of fog had enveloped them. Mike's feet made distant and muffled footfalls. Alex's voice urging him to keep up was muted. It was as though all the sound had been sucked out of the world by the fog. It was blanket-thick now, and Mike could scarcely see a few feet in front of him. He called out to Alex, careless of spooking the birds again, but no reply came. The sweat at the nape of his neck felt cold as it trickled down between his shoulder blades. He turned his head this way and that, disoriented by the white wall of vapor that had anonymized the landscape, and looked for any kind of a landmark that he could get a fix on.

After a few frantic minutes, he saw a couple of dark shapes in the fog. They couldn't be more than twenty feet away – or could they? He thought perhaps the fog was lifting, giving him a reassuring glimpse of Alex and the others, but then thicker fog rolled in and obscured the shapes from his view. He prayed that the breeze, or whatever had momentarily cleared his vision, would come back again, and soon. Feeling utterly lost, he stopped walking. Looking down, he could not even see past his knees. The ground felt wet beneath the soles of his walking shoes. He pushed down with his weight and felt the uneven terrain give way slightly beneath his feet. Starting at a faint sucking noise, Mike began to wonder if he would be swallowed up by the boggy soil, lost to the fog forever. He felt panic seizing at his throat, his hungover head dizzy from the effort of trying to orientate his position in the gray void.

Mike heard something. An animal or a human voice, he could not tell. He searched the thick blanket with his watering eyes. There. He saw the shapes again, indistinct in the fuzzy distance. He wiped his eyes with the cuff of his jacket, as though in doing so he might wipe away the fog too. Eager to move from the soggy, sucking bog, he stumbled across the increasingly uneven surface in an approximation of the direction in which he had seen the figures.

"Alex? You there?" he whispered, wondering if he was doing so merely to reassure himself with the sound of his own voice. Adrift in the fog, that sound was all he had to cling on to. Even his breathing had become muted to thin rasps, swallowed by the dense shroud of mist.

On he walked, his hands outstretched partly in search of his fellows, and partly to break his fall if he should stumble over an outcrop of rock or a sudden dip in the land. Mike had begun to miss the reassuring weight of the shotgun, but Alex still had hold of it after his disastrous accidental shot.

Mike must have walked for a quarter, or even half, a mile through the thick fog without encountering a soul. He slowed his pace again and wondered if he should go back the way he had come. But which way was that? He could be walking around in circles for all he knew.

He heard the sound again.

It was low and booming, like a cough that had been slowed down and stretched out across time. The sound had come from behind him, he was almost certain of it. Perhaps he had walked past the half-glimpsed figures in the fog and they were trying to alert him to it. Perhaps he should just stand still for a while and let them catch him up. That was it, he could see them now. They were moving, and to his relief they were moving toward him. But his relief was short-lived. The figures appeared altogether too thin, somehow, the closer they traveled to him. They were taller too than he remembered Alex or either of the old men.

"Who – who's there?" The words escaped from his lips like an apology before being devoured by the fog.

Another sound, this one like chattering teeth, came as the long, dark shapes closed in. Mike narrowed his eyes, trying to focus. He felt the vibrations of footsteps through the earth as they drew near. They seemed heavier than human footsteps and more like hooves pounding the ground. The fog swirled clear for a moment, and Mike glimpsed antlers atop the tall, dark figures. He thought they might be stags, but then he saw they were walking upright on two legs. Their antlers were huge and dark, almost black.

Mike took a few fearful steps back. Then he saw another shape piercing through the fog. A shotgun barrel. A flash ripped through the fog somewhere to the left of him, and, what felt like seconds later, he heard a gunshot. In the mercurial fog, it sounded like a depth charge. Another flash tore into his vision from his right flank this time, followed by another delayed boom of gunfire.

He turned on his heel and ran into nothingness, almost falling as the ground gave way to unseen crags and hollows. Chancing a quick glance over his shoulder he saw the dark figures looming, and the black lightning shapes of their antlers snaking through the fog. Mike gasped for air as he pushed himself on. Hearing another barrage of shots, he clamped his hands over his ears. The sound was deafening as shot after shot was discharged into the fog, seemingly all around him now.

He ducked to one side, almost twisting his ankle, to avoid more black shapes up ahead. His heart was pounding at a furious rate. His legs felt shaky beneath him as adrenaline coursed through his body. Sweat and tears clouded his already impaired vision. And then he crashed into something hard and tumbled over it. The impact bloodied his lips, and he coughed at the sudden and unpleasant metallic taste coating his tongue.

He looked up at the object he had blundered into and saw it was a raised slab of stone, supported by two smaller blocks. Then the smell hit him. A stench of ripe decay. Atop the makeshift altar lay a writhing mess of dark fur and bloodied flesh. A dark tail hung limp over the edge of the flat stone. Mike had only to glance at it to know he was looking at what used to be Oscar. But it couldn't be. They had buried the dog so carefully. A hideous lapping noise came from the center of the writhing mass of spoiled flesh within Oscar's ribcage. Mike tried not to look but saw all too clearly what was there before he could avert his gaze.

Not only maggots were feasting on the dog's corrupted flesh.

A trio of newly born puppies, their eyes not yet fully opened, were eating Oscar from the inside out, like baby spiders devouring their birth mother. Their black fur was slick with Oscar's blood. One of them made little snuffling noises as it tried to loosen a piece of gristle from the hole where Oscar's beating heart had once been. Mike gagged and lurched away from the horrific scene to empty his stomach on the rough grass. He reached out his trembling hand to steady himself and felt the rough-hewn surface of a large upright stone beneath his palm.

Mike whirled around and saw the shadowy shapes of the stone circle looming through the fog. The stones seemed impossibly high, so vertiginous that he felt as though he were shrinking in their formidable presence. The altar, the intact stones, all of it was so different to when he and Alex had found and concealed Oscar. Mike blinked, vainly willing away his confusion at finding the area so changed. The fog swirled between the dark pillars of the circle, and he was reminded of dust motes he had once seen dancing in the aisle of a church—

He had been a pageboy at his uncle's wedding. Only eight years old. His parents had scolded him after the service for tapping a loose floor tile with his sandaled foot all the way through the vows. His uncle was dead now, burned to ash at a crematorium. His wife had long since left for a new life in New Zealand with her personal trainer.

—and then Mike's ears started to ring, the tinnitus rising to a fever pitch as he thought about making a break for the edge of the stone circle. But hearing a wet crunching sound followed by a whimper that froze the blood in his veins, Mike stood rooted to the spot.

How he had not noticed her before, Mike could not be sure. Had she been there all along, hidden in the foggy shadows between the standing stones, watching him?

She was dressed in a heavy woolen shawl that covered her body from throat to ground. Her bare arms were long and thin, and protruded from the shawl. In her wrinkly hands she held what looked like a knife. As she raised it over the altar where Oscar's body lay, Mike saw that it was a shard of thick, black glass. The black glass curved slightly to a sheer tip. It looked lethally sharp. She grinned at Mike, revealing stained and crooked teeth. Her look seemed to twist his guts deep inside of him. It was a look of pure delight. But in the context of what she was so delighted about doing, it turned Mike cold with fear and disgust. She had killed the first of the puppies. Its limp little body lay inside Oscar's. The woman brought the shard of black glass down and into the second puppy's body, twisting it and working it down the dog's sternum in the manner of a fishwife gutting a prize trout. She licked her cracked lips and performed the movement again, the black glass making a wet crunch as she slammed it into the third defenseless canine. The blade made an unbearable scraping noise as its tip scratched against the stone beneath.

"It is never enough," she said, her voice at once melancholy and ecstatic.

She lifted the blade again, and Mike watched the dark blood pooling at its tip.

"Never enough to restore the balance."

Her dry lips parted in a hideous approximation of a smile once again, and Mike looked on, unable to stop himself, as a droplet of dog's blood dangled and then fell from the tip of the black shard and into her mouth. She closed her eyes and swallowed. Her face flickered with pleasure, then darkened once more.

"More are needed."

Her eyes met his, and Mike felt more fear than he could bear. She began to laugh. She raised the black shard and pointed it straight at him. She turned it over in her hand, and for an instant, he felt as though it were twisting into his heart.

"Much more. More blood. More ruin. More sacrifice."

He gasped. Recoiling from the woman's gaze, he almost ran straight into the stone nearest to him. Ducking out of its way, he dove into the fog, which billowed around him, betraying his presence.

"More souls," she shrilled.

Then he heard the woman's distant laughter. To Mike, it sounded like the end of the world.

His panic drove him on and out the other side of the stone circle. After careering over a steep bank, he followed the dip of the land onto a mist-cloaked plain beyond. Clumps of sod almost tripped him a couple of times, but he managed to right himself without falling. Only when his lungs were fit to burst, and his throat burning from panicked exertion, did he risk pausing for breath.

Bent double, Mike gripped his knees with his hands and coughed. His airways had turned cold from so much damp, foggy air. A layer of clammy sweat coated every pore on his body. Panting, he made a conscious effort to slow his breathing and to calm the hell down. Whoever she was in the stone circle, the mad, murderous woman, she was gone now. Although when he blinked he could not help but see her gaunt face and accusing eyes. Nor could he rid himself of the horrific sound of her black blade, slicing into the warm, defenseless bodies of the puppies as they feasted on Oscar's flesh.

He had endured more than he could of such nightmares. As soon as he got his breath back, he told himself, he would navigate his way back to lower ground and the path that led to the cottage. Once there, he would have a stiff drink from the bottle he'd picked up at the village shop. Maybe he'd follow it with a fat spliff – and to hell with whatever Helen might have to say about it.

He was just beginning to feel better, buoyed by his intended return to form at the cottage, when he saw a shape looming within the fog. It was dark, and tall, and for a moment he fancied he saw antlers again. But as the fog swirled and reassembled into new cloudlike variations, he saw that it was a man. Mike saw the dark barrel of a shotgun protruding through the mist.

"Hey, over here!" Mike called.

The figure faded from view for a few seconds, then disappeared completely. Hadn't he heard him? And how had he passed Mike by without even seeing his shadow in the fog? Then, Mike felt something hard and painful at his back. It felt like the tip of a shotgun barrel. Mike's heart pounded, and he tried to raise his arms in surrender, but fear had frozen him.

"Don't move," a commanding voice said.

"Hey, it's me…. It's Mike…Alex?"

It sure had sounded like Alex to him. Mike felt sure his friend would realize his mistake, any second now, and drop the gun. Perhaps the two old codgers were in on the game. They were just playing a trick, that was all. A pretty mean trick, but a trick all the same. Mike began to turn around. But then he felt the shotgun push harder into his back, and now he was really scared. He remained still, his heart thumping.

"Wait, wait! Alex? It's me!"

"I know who you are, you fucking cunt," the voice whispered with a harshness to match its words. It really did sound like Alex, and yet, at the same time, it sounded like no one he had heard before.

"What are you doing, man?" Mike almost sobbed as he spoke.

He didn't care if the two old men might jump out from the fog, laughing at his expense. Humiliation would be a welcome respite from the terror he was feeling right now with a shotgun aimed at his spine.

"I know what you did, Mike," the ragged voice whispered, so close to his ear now that Mike could feel hot breath on his skin.

Mike could no longer speak. He couldn't breathe. All he could feel was the barrel of the shotgun digging in between his vertebrae. He tried not to think of the noise it would make when Alex—

It really does sound like Alex, doesn't it? Oh my god, Alex what are you.

—pulled the trigger, tried not to think of the mess and pain a shot fired at point-blank range would do to his spine. Definitely tried not to think of the confused explosion of flesh and blood it would make as it hurtled through his body and created an exit wound through his chest. Mike tried not to move, to lurch forward, although he desperately wanted to kneel in the wet grass and vomit.

"I know what you did," the voice repeated.

Mike closed his eyes against the cold wetness of his tears and swallowed. He gritted his teeth and waited for the noise and the pain – and the blackout.

Then the pressure at his back was released.

The shotgun had gone.

He stood, barely daring to breathe, unsure of what to do next. Feeling the empty air behind him with one tentative hand, Mike willed himself to turn.

He was alone in the fog.

He looked down to see if his assailant had left any footprints, for any sign in the soil and the grass that he had been there at all. Mike could see none, not even when he fell to his knees and began sobbing into a wet tangle of grass.

He had felt sure that the man with the gun had been Alex.

And he had felt sure that his friend was going to shoot him.

PART THREE

Under dark, dark skies
There are dark, dark mountains
And beneath the dark, dark mountains
Is a dark, dark road.

On the dark, dark road
There is a dark, dark turn
And beyond the dark, dark turn
Is a dark, dark cottage.

In the dark, dark cottage
Is a dark, dark window
And through the dark, dark window
Is a dark, dark room.

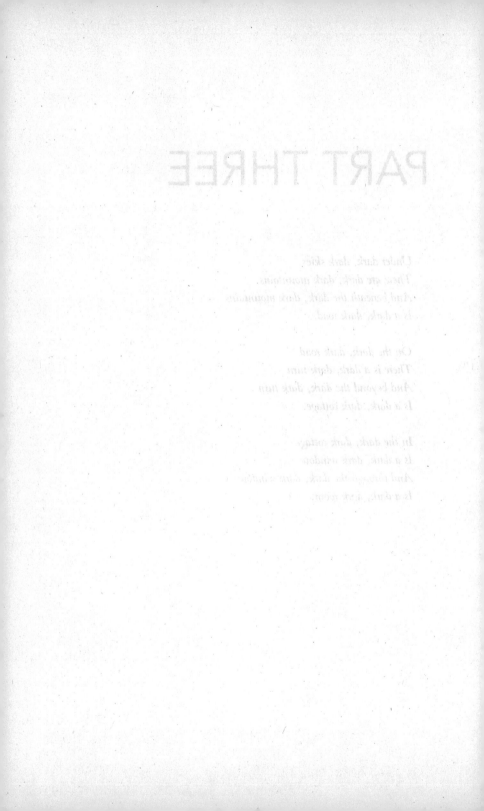

PART THREE

CHAPTER TWELVE

Mike trudged wearily back toward Hearthstone Cottage, feeling numb from the day's many traumas. He had found the path that led to lower ground only when the fog lifted. He had been wandering, lost, for over an hour since being separated from Alex and the others. His friend's words hung over him, heavy as a rain cloud, and he wanted – or, rather badly, needed – a drink. The constant, pervasive mist had worked its way into his bones, making his limbs feel leaden. He felt something close to elation when he spied the old codgers' Land Rover. It was still parked up where they had begun their ill-advised adventure a few hours earlier.

"Here he is, the city boy straggler."

Mike heard Edward's muffled voice before seeing his ruddy face reflected in the wing mirror of the passenger door. Mike circled the vehicle and found both Jamie and Edward were sitting up front, sharing a pack of thick-cut sandwiches that lay open between them atop the handbrake column. He licked his lips involuntarily at the sight of the food and heard his stomach gurgle in pained hunger. He then watched in dismay as Jamie claimed the last of the sandwiches, the thick, rustic bread filled with what looked like corned beef. His stomach made a pathetic whining sound as he watched Jamie chew, then swallow and wipe a streak of mustard from the corner of his mouth.

"Have you seen Alex?" Mike asked.

Jamie chuckled though his sandwich, and Mike saw him elbow Edward, giving him cause to chuckle too.

"Aye, about an hour ago!" Edward chortled.

Mike wondered how long it had been, exactly, since his terrifying encounter in the fog, first with the dog-murdering hag and then with the business end of his friend's shotgun jabbed into his spine.

It must have been Alex.

Mike could almost hear the bastard's voice ringing in his ears, even now.

"Where'd he go?" Mike asked dumbly, peering around the side of the Land Rover. He almost expected Alex to leap out from behind it as a finale to his performance up on the high ground.

"Back to that old cottage of his," Edward said, wiping his greasy hands on the lapels of his already rather grimy hunting jacket.

Mike stood back as Edward opened the passenger door and, with a slight groan when his knees audibly clicked, climbed down to stand before Mike.

"Better catch up with him, laddie," Jamie advised sagely. "He bagged a lovely grouse for your table tonight. Said he might let you taste some, if you help him pluck it first."

Jamie's eyes twinkled in Edward's direction, and his friend picked up the thread Jamie had started.

"You look like a plucker and no mistake," Edward chortled.

"Aye, a right little plucker," Jamie added for good measure.

Mike tried to ignore their jibes. "He shot one, you say? A bird?"

Jamie chuckled, the sound raspy and dry inside the Land Rover's cab.

"He did, sure enough," Edward muttered, "and he did'nae fall over from the recoil neither." The old man's lips curled into a sly smile, and Mike felt sick to see a fragment of corned beef jelly dangling from his bottom lip.

"Better luck next time, laddie," Jamie said before starting the engine.

Chuckling, Edward climbed back into the vehicle and slammed the passenger door. Soon, Mike was enveloped in a poisonous fog of diesel fumes. Jamie sounded the horn as they drove away, kicking up mud and stones as they went. Mike felt lighter now that they had gone. He supposed he should feel indignation that they hadn't even offered him a lift back to the cottage, but in truth he was glad to see the back of them. As he pulled his jacket tightly closed around him, he began to imagine the old men sneaking back to their Land Rover to retrieve antlers to wear in the fog to scare him. Or maybe they had already concealed them at strategic points on the path to the stone circle. He felt sure Alex was in on the joke, something that his outrageous behavior with the gun would seem to support. Mike hadn't even wanted in on the shoot in the first bloody place. He recalled how eager Alex had seemed about the venture when the two old weasels had proposed it back at the pub. A massive joke at Mike's expense, that was all it had been. And now he thought of it, Mike wondered what else Alex had been masterminding since they'd arrived at the cottage. He almost had a heart attack when they were out fishing on their first full day. Had his friend somehow engineered that little shock for him too? He wouldn't put it past him. Mike's anger now propelled him toward Hearthstone Cottage.

★   ★   ★

The fog that had lifted on Mike's descent to the path became first drizzle, then heavy rain for the final leg of his return journey to the cottage. Following the path around the loch, he felt relieved to see a curl of smoke rising from the cottage's main chimney stack. The rain was mercifully easing off, too. He pressed on, eager to warm his bones by the hearth.

He pushed the gate open, a slick coating of rain cold against the skin of his hand, and trudged up the path to the front door. It was open, and he kicked off his boots in the lean-to before peeling off his sodden jacket. He carried it with him into the cottage, where the air was pleasantly warm.

"You look soggy; what took you so long?" Helen said.

Not much of a greeting after all he had been through. But then again, she couldn't know, could she?

"Lost my way in the bloody fog," Mike answered, hanging his damp jacket on the back of the chair nearest the fireplace. He crossed to the hearth and warmed his hands, which looked pink from the rain and the chill that had accompanied it.

Helen joined him by the fire. "Didn't shoot anything?"

No, but I almost got shot myself, Mike thought grimly.

Seeing Helen's impassive expression, he just shrugged and shook his head.

"Where's Alex?"

"He's outside with Kay. Surprised you didn't see them on your way in. They're picking some herbs to have with the grouse." Helen shot Mike a teasing smile. "He was a bit luckier than you with the hunting, it seems."

"Don't rub it in. I'm bloody knackered."

"Aww, has your fragile masculinity been crushed by the failure to hunt and gather?" Helen made babying noises and ruffled his wet hair. He felt like a truant being scolded by his school ma'am. He absentmindedly looked at Helen's stomach, no doubt warm and cozy beneath her sweater. New life was gestating inside. Mike blinked away unwelcome memories of the trio of puppies gnawing away at Oscar's stomach cavity. He could almost hear them chewing. Where moments ago he had felt comforted by the warmth of the fire, he was now growing sick from it. His mouth was dry, and he felt suddenly very dizzy. It had been hours since he'd had anything to eat or drink.

"You all right?" Helen asked. "You look pale."

"Just a bit dehydrated, I think."

"I'll get you some water. Unless you want a tea? With sugar? I'll get that."

Mike almost told her that he wanted something stronger, but she would only disapprove. Instead, he sat down beside the fire and cradled his throbbing head in his hands, succumbing to Helen's mothering of him. She always could make condescension appear to be an act of kindness.

Mike shrank back into his seat, watching the flames throw vivid little orange sparks up into the chimney. The fire was drawing well, but the wind was picking up outside with the rain and Mike felt a backdraft down the chimney as it jostled with the flames – water, air, and fire battling for supremacy. He glanced up at the mantelpiece and saw the black scrying mirror sitting there in pride of place. It was a black, lidless eye, silently observing the room and everything in it. He shuddered, recalling his nightmare and the unsettling reflections he had seen – or dreamt he had seen – in the obsidian glass. Then Mike's heart skipped a beat when he heard a whining sound.

It sounded disquietingly familiar, like the last dying, pleading breath of a wounded animal. He glanced around, looking for the source, expecting to see Oscar on the rug next to him, or worse yet the stag they had left at the roadside after their accident.

Sudden pressure on his shoulder made him jolt in surprise.

"Careful! You'll make me spill it."

It was Helen with his tea. Mike heard the whining sound becoming a hiss and realized it was just one of the logs sizzling on the fire. He took the steaming mug from Helen gratefully and blew on the surface of the liquid to cool it a little before taking a sip. It was hot and sweet, and thirst quenching – though in truth it could do with a nip of the village hooch in it. Perhaps he'd sneak a slosh or two of MacGregor's Death Juice in there when Helen was occupied elsewhere.

"You're welcome," she said, towering over him.

"Oh, s-sorry, I mean, thanks," Mike stuttered.

"You sure you're okay? You don't seem with it. What I mean is, you seem less with it than usual."

"Cheers," Mike said before taking another sip of tea. It burned his lips slightly, but he didn't care. It was bringing him back to life. Antioxidants, milk, and plenty of sugar – not bad medicine, after all. "Did Alex say anything? About the shoot?"

"Only that you were trigger-happy and scared away all the birds. Honestly, Mike, you are a klutz sometimes."

Mike swallowed, and the burning sensation moved to the back of his throat. "No, I mean, did he say anything about how we got separated?"

"The fog was awful, he said. Those old blokes from the village were looking for you for ages, apparently."

"A right couple of old bastards, them," Mike said and nodded.

Mike heard Alex's and Kay's voices as they entered the kitchen. They must have come in through the conservatory door. He cringed, hearing them kissing wetly. Kay's whispers and giggles made it clear to Mike what had taken them so long. He looked up at Helen and saw she was blushing slightly. She stood over him, her stomach level with his eyeline. The distance between them felt suddenly vast, and awkward.

Helen cleared her throat and automatically smoothed down her sweater. "No need to send out a search party, after all," she exclaimed into the kitchen. "The wanderer has returned."

Mike heard more whispering and further giggling from Kay.

"Ah, the Famous Grouse-Less," Alex teased as he strode into the living room. "What happened to you, man? We were looking for you for bloody ages."

"Well, you didn't try very hard," Mike muttered.

"Try telling that to Jamie and Eddie," Alex retorted. "They were cursing your name, taking up so much of their precious shooting time."

Eddie? Mike flinched. It seemed Alex had well and truly bonded with his co-conspirators.

"Come off it, mate, they were having just as much fun as you were, trying to put the wind up me in the fog."

"What's that, old son?"

"Don't 'old son' me. You know full well what I'm talking about. Would have thought you of all people would know how dangerous it is to point a gun at someone in the fog, even if you were only having me on."

"Now wait a minute," Alex began.

Kay wandered in from the conservatory. "The bird is well and truly in the oven," she announced. Then, as though sensing the animosity in the room, she asked, "What's happening?"

Mike saw Alex open his mouth to speak but got in there before him. "Oh, I'm just asking your boyfriend here why he thought it was funny to turn a grouse shoot into a game of hunt-the-Mike."

Alex turned to face Kay. "He's having one of his paranoid stoner delusional episodes," he said. "Just ignore him."

Helen looked confused and slightly embarrassed. "What happened up there?" she asked.

Mike's mind raced. He wanted to say more, to tell her about the dead dog and the terrifying woman killing the triplets. Her knife thrusting in and out, making more holes for maggots. More souls, she had said. The memory of her voice made his head squirm. He wanted to explain how the stone circle had appeared restored and real somehow. Most of all, he needed to unpack his fear at having a shotgun – an actual bloody shotgun, and a loaded one for all he knew – pointed right at him. But the more he tried to find the words to express it all, the quicker they eluded him.

"Were you...smoking while you were out?" Helen asked, not even bothering to disguise the disapproving tone of her voice.

"No. No, I wasn't," Mike said.

His blood was boiling. That was all it was about with Helen. That was all it was *ever* about with her. Control. She had come on holiday, fully aware she might be pregnant, and had waited until they were all cozied up in the cottage before dropping the bloody incendiary bomb on him. On his life. She didn't want him to have any fun. If she could have him folding nappies before they even headed home, she would, and Mike was convinced of that.

He looked into the eyes of each of his friends, and for an instant, he didn't recognize any of them. Mike saw a trio of people with whom he had nothing in common anymore. Students who just wanted to play at mortgages and baby-boomer, flat-pack cots now that they had graduated. He felt that somehow each of them had mislaid their sense of fun on the motorway hard shoulder on their way to the cottage.

Or perhaps they had changed long before then, and he hadn't realized until now.

Their faces were just pictures in a yearbook, staring at him and judging him. Always bloody well judging him. They had done it all last term, and they were doing it now. The living room felt smaller under their collective gaze. Well, Mike was damned if he was going to be feeling smaller too. In a rush of anger he threw his tea into the fire, mug and all, and stormed out of the room. He stomped upstairs and dug into his bag until he found his stash tin. He checked that his papers and lighter were still tucked inside, then headed back downstairs. Pushing past Alex and Kay, he found the conservatory door was still ajar. As he pushed it open, he heard the crossness in Helen's voice, tinged with something bordering on concern.

"Where are you going?" she called after him.

"For a motherfucking smoke," Mike replied triumphantly.

CHAPTER THIRTEEN

Mike allowed his anger to lead him around to the rear of the cottage. He paced back and forth through the puddles that had formed near Meggie's parked car. His brain was burning with fury. Seeing the shelter of the woodpile, he walked over to it and leaned against the pile of logs there, fuming. He folded his arms around himself, as though containing his anger. Truth was, he already felt a bit embarrassed about his outburst. He knew he would have to eat a sizeable portion of humble pie in order to make good with Helen, and then some. She was unforgiving of him at the best of times, and, due in no small measure to the crappy day he had endured, she had just seen him at his probable worst.

And now, to make matters worse, in her eyes at least, he was smoking.

Deep down, he knew the real reason why he was feeling so on edge. It was a textbook case of weed withdrawal. What Helen didn't understand was that he needed oblivion sometimes in the exact same way she needed control. Perhaps that was what had made them a couple in the first place. Opposites attract, and all that. Mike sighed, wondering how their postgrad downtime could turn into such hard work. He pried the lid of his stash tin open and luxuriated in the enticing vapor of its contents. He had just begun rolling a fat blunt when he felt a few droplets of rain on his forehead and hands.

Damn it.

It was starting to rain again.

Mike glanced over to the outbuilding where Meggie kept her studio. The light was on, so she must be inside, working. He didn't really feel like company – not at all, in point of fact – but he wondered if she might join him for a smoke. It would beat standing out in the rain, trying to keep a soggy spliff alight. Worth a try. He placed his half-built jay back inside the tin and closed the lid. As he sauntered up to the window of the studio, he took a peek inside. Empty. Maybe Meggie was taking a break, or perhaps she had left the light on without thinking about it.

Not very environmentally friendly of you, Meggie, thought Mike with a smirk.

He ducked inside, glad to be out of the rain, which began to fall heavier against the window as soon as he was inside.

He could now smoke, and think, in peace. Placing his stash tin on the desk, Mike glanced idly at the unfinished sketches and watercolors littering the workspace. He sat down in Meggie's chair and continued rolling his spliff. The chair creaked slightly as he made himself comfortable, as if alerting the studio to his presence as an interloper. Joint built, he twisted the tip and tapped it lightly against the side of the desk in his own, time-honored, ritual. Mike swept away the tobacco remnants from the desk with the flat of his hand, then sparked up.

The first hit was always the best, he found, and he could feel the tightness in his shoulders dissipating slightly as he exhaled a beautiful plume of gray smoke. It smelled glorious, even better than the scent of a hot meal after a cold day out of doors. Mike chuckled to himself. He knew that in a way, this joint was like comfort food to him. But he also knew it would be swiftly followed by an attack of the munchies. That would be awkward because it would mean going back into the cottage. But at least then he would have his soft shield of smoker's fug around him. Especially if he smoked another straight after this one.

He was lost in the relaxing rhythm of these gently unfolding thoughts when he heard a shuffling sound from inside the room. It had come from over by the shelves. In his burgeoning haze, he wondered if it might be a mouse or a rat. He glanced at the floor around him and saw only discarded sheets of paper and pencil shavings lying there. He settled back into his seat and took another deep drag from the blunt.

The sound came again. The same shuffling but this time accompanied by a strange rattling noise. He stood up on instinct, the joint still held between his forefinger and thumb, and walked over to the shelves from where the sound had come. The shuffling continued sporadically, and it didn't take long for him to figure out that its source was the small cardboard box that Meggie had placed on the shelf – the one containing the injured bird.

Seeing the lid of the box move upward suddenly, Mike took a step back. He glanced over his shoulder to see – or, rather, hoping to see – Meggie returning to her studio. But he was on his own. The rattling came again. The bird was stirring; there was no mistaking that. He couldn't just leave it. What if it had gotten tangled up in there somehow? He held the joint between his lips and took the base of the box in one hand and the lid in the other. Slowly lifting it open so as not to startle the bird, Mike saw its black feathers moving. Once the lid was off, he could see the black orb of the bird's eye regarding him twitchily.

"It's okay, little buddy," Mike said, exhaling smoke.

The smoke billowed around the bird, panicking it. Mike placed his hand over the box to try to keep the bird from falling out, but that only seemed to make it more afraid. He felt the scrape of a claw against the palm of his already wounded hand. Worried that it might use its beak on him next, Mike decided there was only one thing for it.

He reached into the box and clamped his hand around the agitated bird, firmly yet gently as he wanted to avoid applying too much pressure to the bird's healing wing. He could feel the warmth of the creature against his skin. It was impossibly light and its feathers so delicately soft that he wondered how such a thing could live in the Scottish wilds at all. The bird's eye regarded him silently, reminding Mike of the dark, polished surface of the scrying mirror above the hearth inside the cottage. He wondered what that little black eye had seen in the bird's short life so far. Other than Meggie, perhaps he was the only human the bird had seen this close. It was a curious thought, and it made Mike feel more like an alien creature than even the bird was to him. He felt the bird moving against his grip, straining to free itself. It was trying to fly – that was it. Maybe it was healed and just wanted to fly free. He decided to move back to the desk. If he let it go and it fell, at least it would be on the desk and would not fall to the floor.

After brushing aside some scraps of sketching paper, Mike sat down. The chair creaked in alarm again. His eyes were stinging a little now from the smoke, and he was eager to let go of the feathered bundle so he could remove the joint from his mouth. He rolled the delicate cargo over so the back of his hand was against the desk, then slowly and deliberately loosened his grip until the bird was lying on its back in his palm. He plucked the joint from his lips with his free hand and placed it carefully on the edge of the desk so it wouldn't go out.

The bird shuddered and kicked out with its claws before partially unfurling its wings.

"Go on, it's all right," Mike encouraged. "See if you can stand before you fly again."

The bird moved its head from side to side, looking comically like it was attempting to do some sit-ups in the palm of Mike's hand. Then that shuffling noise came again. Mike was confused. The bird was out of its box now, so how was that sound continuing?

He realized too late that it was coming from inside the bird's body.

It opened its wings, and its little black eyes pulsed with panic. The bird's stomach opened, leaking blood as a violent, black swarm of flies burst from out of it. Their hideous buzzing wings brushed against Mike's face as they flew into his eyes and hair. He flailed at them with his hands, almost knocking himself backward off the chair. Turning with the swarm, he saw the flies jostling against each other as they flew toward the open door.

In a moment, they were gone.

But in their place he saw another shadow. This time it looked like someone walking past the window. He heard footsteps. Someone was coming.

He looked down at the bird, which twitched its last and then lay still. He scooped it up, not knowing what else to do other than to get it back inside its box. The bird was a hollow weight now, a vessel of bloodied black feathers. It felt lighter in death than it had in life, and the sensation made Mike feel a little nauseous. He stuffed it back inside the box, blood staining the shredded paper deep red. With trembling fingers, he wrestled the lid back into place. He got up from the desk and crossed to the shelves where he replaced the box.

Mike turned and saw the joint, balanced at the edge of the desk and still smoldering. Lurching over to the desk to retrieve it, he saw a shadow fall across the stone floor in the mouth of the doorway. A moment later, Meggie strolled into the studio. She looked surprised to see him. Then, seeing the haze of smoke around her desk, she wrinkled her nose.

"What the hell? You smoking in here?"

Mike looked from Meggie to the joint between his fingers. "Hoped you wouldn't mind," he said. "I was smoking outside; then it started raining."

"I don't like people smoking in here," she said.

"'Course," Mike mumbled. "I'll stub it out outside." He started for the doorway, but Meggie intercepted him.

"I'll take a drag first," she said, her eyes twinkling in the electric light.

Mike felt her fingertips brush against his as she slipped the joint from between them. She put it to her lips and took a deep drag, the smoke leaking from her mouth to her nostrils. Her eyelids flickered against the smoke, and she passed it back to him, her pale face now slightly flushed.

"I heard raised voices earlier," Meggie said quietly. "Everything all right?"

"I had to get out of there. Your brother winds me up sometimes."

Meggie nodded. "Me too."

"He probably thinks I'm being too fucking English about it." Alex always gave Mike a hard time about having been born in an English hospital instead of a Scottish one. Another facet of his superiority complex over him. "But if I'm going to have to go back in there, I have to do it at least partially stoned."

Meggie chuckled. It was a lovely sound. "Fair enough. Don't you think you are, though?"

"What?"

"Being awfully fucking English about it?"

Mike smiled, then laughed. "Yeah, yeah, I suppose I am."

She shrugged and smiled back at him.

"It's good to see you again," he said, "after all this time."

"You too."

He put the joint to his lips again to fill the silence between them. A raindrop fell from the curl of hair crowning her forehead and splashed onto her nose. She giggled, then stopped still as Mike reached out and brushed it away with his thumb.

"Sorry, I...." he began.

Seemingly on instinct, Meggie grabbed his hand as if to swat it away, but then she held on to it and stared at him. Mike felt a rush of repressed memory at her touch. He looked into her eyes and wondered if the same memory was awakening behind them.

"We shouldn't open old wounds," Meggie said.

Wounds? Mike only had happy memories of the last time he had seen Meggie. He was about to articulate a question when she turned his hand over in hers and looked closer at his skin.

"What's this?" she asked. "Oh my goodness. Are you bleeding? Is it your thumb again? It could be infected...."

Mike felt guilty in an instant. Before he could stop himself, he glanced from Meggie to the shelves. She looked back at his hand, and Mike knew then that she had realized he wasn't bleeding at all. The blood had come from elsewhere. Her eyes widened, and she let go of his hand. Mike felt bereft at the severed connection. After the heat of his earlier anger, her touch had been a soothing warmth. She rushed to the shelf and plucked the box from it. Mike knew she must have seen the blood on the lid, and as she opened it, he expected her to scream any instant. Instead, she walked right up to him and thrust the open box under his nose.

"Why? What, Mike? How could anyone do this to a poor wee defenseless bird?"

"I-I didn't...."

Mike's voice faltered as Meggie thrust the little cardboard box closer to his face. The black bird inside had been crushed. Blood and feathers were an indistinguishable, dark, wet tangle. Mike couldn't understand it. He hadn't harmed the bird—

It was the flies.

—the poor thing must have been infected, riddled with maggots inside—

Like Oscar, don't tell her about Oscar.

—which turned to flies and—

Mike felt sure he was going to throw up. The heat of the moment that had passed between them had turned cold. As freezing bloody cold as the grave.

"What the fuck did you do? Explain it to me please because I am having a really hard time understanding what the hell it is you thought you were doing in here."

The hurt and accusation in her voice was too much for him to bear.

"Look I tried to help it. I saw it struggling to move and then—"

That was enough for Meggie. Her eyes wet with tears, she grabbed Mike's shirt and pulled him away from the desk. Turning him toward the door, she shoved him, hard.

"You have the poor wee beastie's blood on your hands. You ruin everything," she said. "You destroy everything you touch." She spoke in quiet fury now, her trembling voice heavy with sobs.

Mike stumbled, dumbfounded, toward the doorway and toward a looming shadow. Helen was standing there, her unblinking eyes seemingly unable to take in what she was witnessing. How long had she been standing there? How much had she seen – and heard? Mike felt a cold coil tightening in his stomach.

"Helen," he said dumbly.

She was gone before he could say any more.

He turned back to Meggie, but she had her back to him. She was still holding the little cardboard box in her hands, her shoulders rising and falling with her sobs.

Mike wandered outside. The dark shape of the cottage loomed across the backyard, its windows impenetrable. He glanced back at the studio and glimpsed Meggie shutting the door. He stood in the cold, empty space between the two buildings and wished that it was still raining.

★   ★   ★

The cold forced Mike back inside. He ambled into the dining area through the conservatory door and found Alex and Kay halfway through their meal. The roasted grouse smelled delicious.

"Where's Helen?" he asked.

Alex and Kay exchanged furtive glances. Alex finished his mouthful and wiped his greasy lips on a gingham tea towel that had been left on the table next to the roasting dish.

"Upstairs," he said. "Said she was too tired to eat."

"I'm sorry. About before," Mike said.

"Big of you," Alex said, teasing.

Mike declined to answer. Hunger necessitated that he take as much mickey-taking as Alex could throw his way. If he was going to have to eat humble pie, he felt pretty sure he was acquiring a taste for it.

"We saved you some of the roasted grouse," Kay said, no doubt noticing he was licking his lips.

"But we're drinking your whisky in return," Alex said. "Cheers!"

he added with a wide grin, refilling his glass with a generous slosh of MacGregor's Death Juice.

"You're welcome to it, of course," Mike replied, though he didn't mean it.

"Come and sit with us," Kay said, gesturing at one of the vacant chairs. "Let's all be friends again."

"Aye, let's," Alex said.

He sounded pretty drunk already. Good. Kay giggled tipsily as Alex poured another measure into her glass. Mike found a clean plate and began loading it up with food. He sat in the seat farthest from Alex and Kay, reluctant to get too close to their bubble.

"Did you see Meg out there?"

Mike coughed, his food going down the wrong way. Kay rose from the table and drew a glass of water from the tap.

"Here," she said, handing it to him, and she slapped him on the back for good measure.

"Thanks." He gulped down water gratefully until his coughing had subsided. "She was in her studio."

"I'll ask her if she wants to join us," Kay said. "She might want some of the side vegetables for supper?"

"I think she wants to be on her own right now," Mike said.

Kay shot Alex a look of concern. Alex shot Mike an accusing look.

"The injured bird. It died," Mike said, hoping against hope that they wouldn't ask any more questions of him. He didn't feel like he could go into the details of what he had seen, and the weirdness of the misunderstanding between him and Meggie.

"Oh, no," Kay said. "Poor little thing."

Mike didn't know if she meant the bird or Meggie. For some reason unknown to him, Kay's rising concern was making him feel uncomfortable.

"She'll be bloody upset," Alex sighed. "First Oscar, and now the bird."

Kay looked confusedly at Alex, then Mike, who shoveled another forkful of food into his mouth as a defensive move.

"Oscar's not dead, though, just missing," Kay said. Her inflection made it sound more like a question than a statement of fact.

Alex glanced over at Mike, darkly. Mike just lowered his eyes to his plate. The game looked less appetizing when accompanied by the grim memory of what they had found up at the stone circle.

Kay seemed not to notice their silent exchange. "I'll take her a drink. She could probably use one." She shrugged.

Mike wondered if Kay was enjoying playing the part of 'concerned would-be sister-in-law'. It struck him that she always seemed to come to life when others spoke of illness, or death. One evening after a night out at the students' union, he had heard Helen complaining to a friend of hers that Kay was a bit of a – how had she phrased it? – an ambulance chaser, that was it.

Well, he thought, *the patient awaits you in her studio, clutching the remnants of a dead bird she thinks that I killed. Knock yourself out, ambulance chaser.*

"Just don't bring her in here while the grouse is still on the table," Alex said gruffly. "We'd never hear the bloody last of it."

Kay looked at the roasting dish and the delicious remnants of the game bathed in its own juices. "Oh," she said, sounding crestfallen. "You guys pop it back in the oven or something, will you?" With that, she was gone, clutching two tumblers and a bottle of supermarket own-brand vodka.

"And then there were two," Alex said, proffering the bottle of MacGregor's Death Juice. "Want some of this before it's all gone?"

Mike nodded.

"I know you're just stressed about Helen – and the baby," Alex said.

Mike flinched hearing him put it like that, in such a matter-of-fact way.

"I'd shite myself if it was me," Alex continued. He shifted in his seat. "Fuck's sake, Mike, what are you going to do? You two had your whole lives ahead of you to get pregnant. Kay says Helen's throwing her career away. She doesn't seem to hold much hope that Helen will have any chance at job progression if she turns up at interviews with a baby bump."

"And what do you think?" Mike asked after taking a welcome sip of whisky. For all their differences, Mike still valued Alex's counsel above all others.

"I have to agree with her. You have to admit, any employer's going to take issue with a new recruit planning her maternity leave before she's even passed the probationary period." Seeing Mike's expression, he added, "Sorry."

"No need to be," Mike said. "You're just being honest. It's kind of what I need right now. Nobody stopped to think I might not want to even be a dad yet. And as you said, we had our whole lives to start a family."

Alex poured more whisky, which Mike gladly accepted.

"Tell you what, I'll open the single malt," Alex said, looking disapprovingly at the empty bottle. "The vintage stuff. Proper gear. Let's get rat-arsed."

CHAPTER FOURTEEN

Mike awoke to a sudden noise. It had sounded like a child's laughter. He opened his eyes to find the room still shrouded in darkness. Turning over, he saw Helen's sleeping form next to him. The faintest glow of moonlight bled between a gap in the curtains.

It was the middle of the night.

He listened to the nighttime and heard nothing except for the faint creak of the timbers in the eaves against the wind outside. His forehead was beaded with sweat from all the alcohol he and Alex had put away in the kitchen. They had taken their last drink at two in the morning before calling it a night or, rather, a day. Wondering what time it was now, Mike rolled over to find his phone. In the Highlands, he'd found that cellular devices were only any good for telling the time. He felt around on the bedside table, then the floor, and located his mobile nestled next to the leg of the bed. Leaning over the side of the bed, he thumbed the sleep button and winced at the sudden brightness of the screen as it came to life in his hand.

Four in the morning. *Jesus.*

His head swam and he realized he was still very drunk. He began to slide from the sheets, losing his purchase on the bed. Allowing the phone to fall back onto the floor, he used the flat of his hand to steady himself against the floorboards. He had narrowly avoided falling out of bed and, he hoped, also avoided waking Helen in the process. He listened intently for her breathing. She was still sound asleep. Good, now he wouldn't have to add waking her at four in the morning to his list of many crimes and misdemeanors.

Mike pushed himself back up onto the bed and lay back against the sheets. He felt sweat trickling from his head onto the pillow. The after-burn of whisky lapped at his throat, and he wished he'd had the presence of mind to bring a glass of water up to the bedroom with him. His nausea overwhelmed his compulsion to fight it and head downstairs for a drink from the kitchen tap. He breathed slow and steady, as though willing the acid gathering at his throat to subside, then closed his eyes and drifted off to sleep once more.

The giggle came softly at first, as though in a dream. But then it built, until Mike felt sure there was a small child in the room with him.

He snapped his eyes open and sat up. His vision tilted as blood rushed to his head. Why on earth had he succumbed to that nightcap? It was what had tipped him over the edge, he was sure of it. He raised his hand to his head, brushing back his hair and feeling the sickly, cold touch of perspiration there. Hearing the little laugh once more, he turned to Helen to see if she was still asleep.

She wasn't in bed.

Was it later than he thought? Maybe she had gotten up for breakfast already. Confused, he slid his legs over the side of the bed until he was in an upright position. Now he had a clear view of the door and, in particular, the gap between it and the floorboards. Mike saw flickering light there and then two dark shadows, which moved so fast that they startled him. He swallowed in consternation, a feeling that was quickly becoming stark fear. Tension was gripping his throat, and he absentmindedly clawed at the neck of his t-shirt. But it was not his clothing that was making his throat feel tight and his chest heavy with the labor of his heart beating ten to the dozen – rather it was what he now saw, and smelled, so clearly in the room. The flickering light from beneath the door and the little shaft of moonlight from the window revealed what his senses were screaming at him to be true.

The room was filling with smoke.

Mike grabbed his hoodie from the chair next to the chest of drawers, tugged it on, and then crossed to the door. Yanking it open, he stumbled into the hallway. The rush of heat and smoke almost brought him to his knees. He pressed the cuff of his hoodie over his mouth and nose in a futile attempt to keep the fumes at bay. He coughed and wiped tears from his eyes with his free hand, leaving them burning against the acrid smoke. He ducked down the hallway with his arm still clamped over his mouth and nose and headed for Alex and Kay's room. Mike wanted to cry out, to raise the alarm, but he dared not pull away his arm for fear of being overcome by the fumes. When he reached the bedroom door, he grasped for the handle. It disturbed him that it was so very hot to the touch. He turned the handle quickly and shoved the door open.

The heat hit him full force as he realized, too late, that the bedroom was ablaze. Flames were devouring the drapes, reflected back by the window glass. The fire had spread to the divan, and Mike saw that the corner of the mattress nearest to him had caught fire. Blinking at the searing heat, he grasped for the door so that he could pull it shut and keep the fire contained inside the room. As he wrestled with the door, he had no choice but to remove his arm from over his mouth and nose. A rush of foul smoke invaded his airways. Coughing against the onslaught of smoke, he pulled the door shut. For a moment, it struck him that Alex and Kay's bed looked like it hadn't been slept in. Perhaps they'd already risen and Kay had made the bed. What he knew of Kay made that seem unlikely. Maybe it was later than he'd thought.

Typical. If that lot had gone out to leave him alone in a burning bloody cottage—

A sudden crash put any such thoughts to the back of his mind.

It sounded like windows breaking in Alex and Kay's room. The heat must have been too intense for the old, weathered glass. Even in his half-awake state, Mike knew the danger. The fire would now be fed by the oxygen outside, helping it spread. He had to get out. And he had to get out right now. He opened the door.

Fighting against the heat that he could feel pulsating through the walls, Mike placed his arm over his face again and made his way down the narrow hallway to the stairs. He could barely see them amid thick smoke. His stomach flipped at the memory of the fog on the Highlands, and the dark shapes that had hunted him there.

He steeled himself and began his descent. He could not see where the last step ended and where the next began. The last few steps were the worst, and he had to reach out his foot gingerly, searching with the tips of his toes through the smoke for solid ground.

Mike coughed his way through the smoke and heat into the living room and past the furniture. He could see the dim light of day through the conservatory windows, which seemed impossibly far away, a trick of the smoke. As he dodged the looming shape of an armchair, he realized too late that his trajectory had brought him closer to the fireplace.

He felt the heat first, then heard the rush of air coming down the flue. The entire fireplace erupted into a sudden ball of flame. He recoiled from the sharp singeing of his eyebrows and smelled the putrid stench of burning hair. Mike dropped to the floor and crawled on all fours as fast as his hands and knees would carry him. He felt the rug give way to the exposed flagstones of the kitchen floor. Even those stones, usually so cold even beneath the thickest socks, were now hot to the touch. He felt another rush of heat at his back, and heard the crashing of glass and groaning of breaking timbers. The fire was devouring the house at a frightening rate. He dared not even glance over his shoulder – to delay another second might trap him inside the house to burn along with it.

The heat was unbearable, and the oxygen thin. He gritted his teeth and let out a primal growl of desperation as he clawed his way across the hot, unyielding stone floor. Another few feet and he would be at the door. He could see its vague shape through the smoke, almost shimmering in the heat like a beacon. Mike cursed under what little breath he still possessed as he scraped his arm against one of the kitchen chairs. It too was on fire, and he could already feel the skin at his elbow bubbling and blistering from the flames. The pain willed him on, somehow, until with one final push of energy he reached up for the handle of the conservatory door. He twisted it hard, pushed against the door with all his might, and tumbled outside into the open air.

Mike swallowed oxygen down like a draught, but then he began coughing up – and throwing up – all the foul, noxious fumes he had inhaled. Grim spools of claggy black phlegm hit the blades of grass where he crouched, prostrate above the ground as though he was worshipping it. The cool sensation of the soil and grass against his fingers was a welcome relief from the oppressive heat of the cottage fire. He was just about to collapse to the ground in thanks that he had made it out when he heard a scream.

He bolted to his feet and saw flames licking at the window. Movement revealed the horrific truth – someone was trapped inside the conservatory. What he had taken to be flames licking against the glass was actually a lock of bright red hair. Meggie was trapped inside, beating her fists against the glass.

"The door, Meggie! The door!" he yelled, then realized that her route had been cut off by the burning table and chairs in the kitchen. The furniture had become an indoor bonfire, blocking her escape. He heard another crash, followed by her desperate scream. He saw the palm of her hand, so pale against the inside of the glass. She was going to die in there, a butterfly trapped in a glasshouse.

He had to do something to help her.

He licked at his dry lips and glanced around for something that he could use to aid her escape. He thought of it then, the woodpile next to the art studio, and the garden tools leaning up against it. Forgetting the black smoke that still held his lungs in a crushing grip, Mike sprinted around to the rear of the cottage. He grabbed the heavier of the two shovels he found leaning against the woodpile and, with barely a second to draw breath, dashed back to the conservatory windows. He stepped right up to the one where he had seen Meggie's hand and lifted the shovel.

"Mind the glass!" he shouted, but he could not tell if Meggie had even heard him.

He gritted his teeth and hit the glass as hard as he could. The shovel's metal scoop rebounded from the glass, and it felt as though he had tried to break open pack ice with it. A fierce shock wave penetrated the bones of his forearms, and he staggered back in bemused shock and pain before dropping the shovel. He saw Meggie's hand flailing in the smoke that had now almost completely engulfed her. He heard a faint whimper, and for one idiotic moment he could not be sure if it had come from her lips or his. The furious flames had spread from the furniture and into the kitchen proper, licking angrily at the kitchen cupboards. Even the refrigerator was on fire. Meggie was losing her struggle against the inferno. With his heart in his mouth, Mike saw her claw at the window, then fall back into the smoke and flames. Mike let out a cry of frustration, picked up the shovel once again, and charged at the glass with it.

The conservatory exploded outward before he could strike. The ball of flame had all the fury and intensity of an incendiary device, knocking him from his feet. He hit the dirt, dumbly realizing that his t-shirt had caught on fire. He sat there on the grass, patting down the flames that were licking at his stomach. Meggie had disappeared from view, but he knew she was still in there. Where once they had all sat and feasted together, now the flames were feasting on her flesh. He couldn't bear it. If only he had been quicker. What if he had tried kicking the glass instead of retrieving the shovel? Maybe she would be alive now. He clambered to his feet and made for the window next to the blazing, ragged hole of metal and glass where the conservatory door had stood just moments ago.

"Meggie!"

He knew she was gone, but he shouted her name over and over all the same. He had reached the window now, and perversely found it and the pane next to it still intact. He beat his fists against the glass, careless of the heat. He called Meggie's name over and over into the mocking flames that had consumed her. He could see his own muddy reflection in the blackened glass, a dark approximation of the scrying mirror that had once stood above the fireplace. Beyond his reflection a black shape moved, somewhere deep within the inferno.

"Meggie!" he shouted, his lungs almost bursting from the smoke and the grief.

"What the fucking hell do you think you're doing?"

It was Helen. Thank goodness. She was alive. She must have seen the fire and come back to find him out here, screaming Meggie's name into the burning building.

He turned to see Helen. She was dressed in her nightclothes, her hair tousled and her eyes wide with disbelief. Mike saw that it was night, and the garden had the stillness of those hours left stranded between midnight and morning. A gossamer layer of ground mist swirled all the way down to the loch.

Perplexed, Mike turned back to the cottage and found it intact. There was no fire. No devastation at all. He felt suddenly cold and looked down to see that he was standing alone on the grass in his boxer shorts.

"What the…?"

"Jesus Christ, Mike," Helen hissed.

Mike turned to face her once more and struggled to find the words. How had he come to be in the garden? Was he sleepwalking now – was that a thing? And, oh bloody hell, had he been shouting in his sleep too? If so, it would explain why Helen was looking at him with her eyes brimming with what looked distinctly like murderous thoughts.

"Helen, I don't know how I…I mean, I…."

A window opened then, and Mike heard Alex and Kay's laughter coming from their bedroom. Mike turned and looked up at their bedroom window. A flicker of movement caught his eye and he noticed

Meggie's curtain twitch. He lowered his gaze to the conservatory window to where he had seen – or, rather, dreamed – Meggie falling back into the flames. It had felt so real. But all he could see was a shadow across the flagstones, cast by the kitchen table.

He looked back at Helen again, dumbfounded.

She shook her head and then stomped silently past him, inside the cottage.

Mike walked across the lawn, away from the conservatory, and tilted his head back to the stars. He let out an agonized breath, which dissipated like smoke on the wind from the imagined fire of his all-too-vivid nightmares. He guessed he would be spending the remainder of the night, if not the entire rest of the holiday, on the sofa.

CHAPTER FIFTEEN

Mike walked into the darkened kitchen. The only smoke he could smell now was coming from the still-glowing embers of the fire in the next room.

He followed their glow, the fire no longer a threat to him, and stood before the hearth, warming his bones. The black glass of the scrying mirror offered a vague reflection of his face, echoing his nightmare of the conservatory glass. He blinked away an unwelcome image of Meggie being consumed by the flames. On instinct, he reached for an object on the arm of the chair nearest the fireplace. He lifted the whisky glass to his nose and inhaled deeply. The drink was near finished, with only a centimeter or so of liquid in the bottom of the glass, but it was enough to remind him of its inebriating effects. He crossed to the coffee table, where the whisky bottle stood, uncorked it and refilled his glass all the way to the brim. Turning his attention back to the ruddy-orange coals in the fireplace, he took sip after sip of whisky until the glass was almost empty. Then he filled it to the brim once more and sat down in the chair beside the hearth. Gulping back his drink, he felt oblivion approaching fast.

But oblivion, it seemed, would not come to him this time. He had almost finished the remainder of the whisky bottle – in the vague hope that it would put him down without the fear that he might walk, and talk, in his sleep again – when he had the gnawing realization that the drink was having the opposite effect and was in fact making him more wakeful. He glared at the coals in the hearth, crackling at him mockingly, like the chattering teeth of some village gossip. He recalled how bloody amused Alex and Kay had looked to see him standing in the garden, in his smalls, yelling into the night. And the thunderous look on Helen's face.

It struck him that he was most embarrassed of all to have seen Meggie's curtain twitching. He hoped against hope that she hadn't heard him shouting her name. It would be just too embarrassing to contemplate if she had.

The crackling from the fireplace subsided for a second, and he felt a throbbing at his temples. Too much whisky, or not enough, he couldn't be sure now. Then a spitting sound came from the burning hot coals, as loud as a gunshot. Mike felt furious at the noise, which had made him jump, and threw his whisky glass into the fire. The glass shattered, and the remains of his drink spat and sizzled against the embers. It sounded like a protest somehow, like the very cottage itself were hissing at him and taunting him. How could he have dreamed that it was burning down? The four walls around him had been built to last, but the smoke and the flames had seemed so real to him. And Mike couldn't fight the sneaking suspicion that the cottage itself was the problem. He'd been feeling out of kilter ever since they'd arrived. There was something wrong with the place. It didn't feel welcoming anymore, not at all. Not like the last time he had visited. The vibe at Hearthstone Cottage had changed, perhaps irreparably.

Sighing, Mike reached for his glass dumbly, then realized he had tossed it onto the fire. Picking up the bottle, he swigged from that instead. He stood, his legs buckling slightly from the alcohol coursing through his veins, leveled with the scrying mirror and stared at his reflection. He could see the room behind him stretching out in every direction — a trick of the curved surface of the glass. Wait a minute, had the mood at the cottage changed, or had he himself changed since being there?

Give yourself a break, buddy, he thought drunkenly. *Your girlfriend just told you she's pregnant and planning on playing happy families. You spent the last of your student loan on some Scottish hooch, no way you can support a family. Have to settle for the first dead-end job that offers you a new-starter date, and a new-starter rate to match, no doubt. Add that to the fact that you've been hallucinating your brain off ever since you got here. Now that's going to harsh anyone's mellow, isn't it?*

He smiled grimly at this thought, and the general ridiculousness of his situation. All he had wanted to do was chill out, party. He'd prefer to deal with the big stuff like employment, and becoming a baby daddy, much, much later. If at all. What was it his dad always said?

Make sure you can feed yourself, son, before you commit to feeding anyone else.

That was it. That, and—

I didn't, Mikey. And just look at me now. Your dear old dad's a wage slave, son. Just like the rest of them. Don't become a slave to their grind, my boy. Once they know you need the work more than they need you, you may as well kiss any chance of a promotion, and a decent pay rise, goodbye. Mark my fucking words.

His father's entire worldview was built upon how much of his hard-earned money he had to spend supporting his family. No wonder he was becoming such a bitter man in his old age. Mike was suddenly struck by something. He pictured himself, sitting in the family living room, cup of tea cradled in his lap. Then he imagined the looks on his mum's and dad's faces (but especially his dad's) when he'd say, after a lengthy sip of tea and a heartfelt sigh, that he had something important to tell them.

That girl from uni, you remember the one, Helen? That's her, yeah. You only met her twice, and only really acknowledged her once. Well, her anyway. She's pregnant! Yes, we're going to have a baby. And you're going to be grandparents! How awesome is that? We know we can count on you, Grandad, to help with the deposit for a mortgage? Fifty thou, that ought to do it. Think of all the weekends you can enjoy looking after Mikey Junior while his dad goes raving in Ibiza. Help him, Mum! Grandad's fainted from pure joy!

Mike felt his lips stretch into a grin, a distant, numb sensation that had become anaesthetized by the effects of drinking over half a bottle of single malt whisky. He looked at his face, reflected in the concave surface of the black mirror. His grin looked wider than it really was due to the curvature of the glass. He moved his head from side to side and laughed at the comical distortion of his features as though he was a punter in a fairground hall of mirrors.

But the laughter died in his throat when he saw what the mirror had to show him next.

His mouth had narrowed to a slit, which looked disturbingly like a knife wound, and which had stretched across the full width of the mirror. His eyes had taken on a dead, glassy quality, a disturbing mirror of his hallucination on the loch when he and Alex had gone fishing. But there was something else. Instinct told him not to look, but he could not take his eyes off his dark reflection. Or rather, *reflections*, because he realized his eyes were overlapping with the black, malevolent pools of another, then another, pair of eyes that seemed to be peering out at him from inside the depths of the mirror. The flesh of his face looked puffy and gray, the rims of his eyes – and all those dark and horrible others – becoming loose red sockets that oozed clear fluid. He was reminded of the gutted fish that had released its belly full of maggots—

Or had it?

Mike felt the fevered grip of madness clawing at the inside of his skull. He no longer knew what was real and what wasn't. His face was laughing back at him, and in his heart he felt only fear.

He tried to back away now, frightened of the hold the mirror had over him, but he was rooted to the spot. He willed his feet to move. Even if he could just shuffle back a few inches, it would be a start.

Then the sound of a hoof scraping against stone stopped him from attempting to move at all. He saw its red eyes in the mirror, watching him from where the sofa should be but, impossibly, wasn't any longer. The stag's antlers arced out and above its proud head, forming forks of black lightning. Mike felt a piercing pain in his heart when his eyes—

Not just mine, though, all those others.

—met the stag's.

You killed me, those red eyes sang in a pained eulogy that made Mike's ears feel like they were bleeding. *You and your friends. How will you repay? More souls are needed. So many more.*

The voice was the old woman's now, as terrifying as the moment he had met her at the stone circle. He could almost smell the blood, almost hear the sharp metal of her blade scraping against little canine bones. A sensation not unlike squirming maggots shifted inside his belly. He made a sound, like Oscar whining.

Mike braced himself against the mantelpiece. He tried to cling to what was real, and to put this phantom creature out of his thoughts and back to wherever he had conjured it from. It was born of something deep inside him. He could feel that now. Somehow, the stag was his own complex fears made manifest. Mike locked his teeth together in a snarl. He willed the creature away, just as he willed the voice of the hag from the stone circle to leave him alone too. He heard a little laugh, foul and untrue, and then the red eyes were gone. He could see only his reflection in the black mirror.

Mike let out a sigh of relief. Relaxing his shoulders and removing his hands from the mantelpiece, he straightened up and saw the mirror for all that it was. A piece of glass. He would throw it into the fire too and be rid of it. If Helen got pissy with him about it, he'd deny any knowledge.

I was fast asleep, he would say.

A haunting image of Meggie, flailing in flames, her pale body consumed by them. He visualized her clothes being burned away, exposing her skin to the heat. He closed his eyes and imagined seeing her exposed breasts blistering in the incendiary heat. His cock stiffened even as revulsion lapped at his throat. He felt aroused and repulsed in equal measure. Mike opened his eyes. Grabbing the mirror, he leaned over the glowing embers of the fire and tried to throw it into the hearth.

But the mirror was gone. His hands were empty. Perplexed, he looked around the edges of hearthstone for any sign of the damned thing. It wasn't there; it had just disappeared. Then, looking to the mantelpiece once more, he found the mirror sitting there in its usual place.

You've got to be bloody kidding me, he thought.

After reaching out for the mirror, and making sure he had a firm grip on it this time, he removed it from its roost and swung it into the fire. But exactly the same thing happened. No sooner had he let it go than he realized it was back on the mantelpiece once again, as though he had never touched it.

Okay, okay, you win.

He was clearly much drunker than he had given himself credit for. Backing away from the mirror, which mocked him blankly from its high place above the hearth, he stumbled toward the little sofa. It would be uncomfortable, but it would have to do for a bed for the remainder of the night. Or the morning. Whichever it was, he didn't really care. He just needed to close his eyes and forget about the insane things he had witnessed tonight. Mike allowed his body to fall back onto the sofa—

And kept falling.

—into a dark place, the darkest of all, black and empty as a void. He felt weightless and powerless to stop his ceaseless descent into the nothingness. He clawed at the air, or rather the lack of it, and felt something hideously slimy brush past his fingertips. Turning his head, he glimpsed the edge of the open cavity in Oscar's body, teeming with maggots. Mike tried to scream, but his teeth were locked together in a deathlike grimace. He was falling into the pit of Oscar's stomach, and through it into something – or somewhere – else. His body pitched over until he was in freefall, facedown now. He saw the dark eye of the dying stag, an impossibly huge version of the black scrying mirror, rushing up toward him. Mike braced himself for impact as he plummeted into the eye. He felt it yield, opening up to him in the way that a flower might welcome a honeybee. The viscous jelly of the stag's eye warped around him, coating him, and he rolled into it with his hands making spasmodic paddling movements through the noxious waters of the great eye. Then Mike became aware that he was swimming. The watery eye had given way to the dark depths of the loch beside the cottage. He could see two little lights blazing on the bed of the loch, far beneath him. He swam deeper, searching them out. Silt from the bottom of the loch erupted around him as he coursed his body into the deep. Clouds of the stuff fogged his vision for a few moments. Looking around fearfully, he saw a dark shape through the detritus floating all around him. It was wide and looked like a ridge of some kind, as though the mountains had slid beneath the water to encircle him. As the silt cleared, he saw the source of the two little lights.

They were the white orbs of Meggie's dead eyes looking up at him from the bottom of the loch. The skin of her face was pallid and pockmarked from the hungry kisses of the fish that had been feasting on her cold flesh. Her dead body undulated slightly beneath the wet, floating shroud of her clothing, which revealed her shape. No arousal came at the sight of her body this time; the only sensation awakening within him was a powerful and unfathomable dread.

His own body had turned to ice, and he wanted nothing more than to swim for the surface of the water, to clamber out and crawl back to the fire beside which he hoped he had fallen asleep to dream this most unwelcome of dreams. But something in his heart told him this particular nightmare was not over yet. Those two dead eyes still had a hold over him, and he knew even before it happened that Meggie's right hand would spring to life, grabbing on to his wrist and pulling him down to the bottom of the loch. He thrashed against her grip, trying to twist himself free of it, but his efforts were for nothing. His screams and protestations only forced more water down into his lungs. He was drowning, and even though he tried to fight it, he knew he had lost the battle. He felt Meggie's cold and slimy body cleave to his in the depths as he gave himself over to the blackness of death. As oblivion took him, he heard a faint sound from high above the water.

It was a child's laughter.

Mike opened his eyes and rolled over onto his side on the sofa. He threw up onto the living room floor, his vomit as cold and silty as the waters of the loch. Icy sweat coated every inch of his body. When his vomiting subsided, he wiped a dribble of fluid from the corner of his mouth with the back of his hand and groaned.

Just then, he heard the little laugh again, followed by the footfalls of tiny, bare feet.

He wheeled around into a half-seated position, holding on to his stomach, and glimpsed the shadow of a small child as it ran through the open doorway toward the stairs. Goose bumps gathered at a cold spot below the nape of Mike's neck. He wiped away the sweat, then realized his hand was still coated with the gross contents of his stomach. He willed himself to stand up and walk the few meters it would take to reach the kitchen sink. He desperately wanted to wash his mouth, face and hands, and to draw a cool drink of water from the tap. But his limbs clearly didn't share his desperation. Unable to find the energy to stand, he slumped back onto the sofa, praying he would regain the equilibrium necessary for him to clean up before anyone else awoke.

★   ★   ★

Mike didn't manage to wake up before anyone else, of course.

And whoever was up and about before him clearly had something of an appetite. The smell of frying bacon dragged him deliciously from his sleep. His belly churned, the acid aftereffects of his overindulgence still lingering there, eating away at his stomach lining. His mouth was as dry as wood rot, and his head pounded as soon as he tried to sit up.

As fragments of the night before came back to him, Mike suddenly remembered his accident. Bracing himself, he peered over the side of the sofa with one eye open against the daylight streaming into the room from the conservatory. An old newspaper, the kind that only sells advertising, lay open and facedown over the spot where he had vomited. He could see the shameful stain seeping through the front-page headline, which screamed in block capitals about 'HUNDREDS

OF LOCAL JOBS' at a new hydroelectric plant. Mike fell back onto the sofa and groaned. He had hoped to dispose of the evidence before anyone woke up. Through the haze of his hangover, he tried to listen so he could hear who was in the kitchen. After a short while, he heard Alex's voice.

"If you're still alive in there, mate, be warned. There's only a few rashers of bacon left."

Mike crawled off the sofa, avoiding the vomit-stained newspaper. He had to lean on the furniture in order to walk the short distance into the kitchen. Swaying a little, he peered through half-closed eyes to see Alex busily preparing breakfast.

"There's only three eggs, too. I'm having two, just so you know."

"I'm not sure I can eat anything."

"Not surprised. Did you really finish off the whole bottle? Mad bastard. That's a bottle of single malt you owe me."

"Please, don't even mention booze," Mike groaned.

"Not feeling so sharp myself," Alex said with a chuckle, "but it needed done, didn't it?"

"I suppose. I can't really remember...." Mike swallowed at a dry taste at the back of his throat. It tasted like soil. And salt water. The image of a looming black shape troubled him, somewhere deep in the fathoms of his memories. He blinked the image away. "Sorry about the floor. I'll clean it up."

"Aye, you bloody well will."

"Are the girls up yet?"

"What you really mean is, did your pregnant girlfriend come down here and find you comatose on the sofa with an empty bottle of whisky next to you, only to discover that it's *you* who has the morning sickness?"

All Mike could do to reply was nod, and even that nearly finished him.

"'Fraid so, Mikey, my lad," Alex said.

"Oh, fuck no."

"Oh, fuck yes." Alex chuckled again, then flipped over the bacon in the pan, making the cooking oil sizzle all the more. "You eating or what, soft lad? I'm going to smash all of this if you don't."

"I'll try a little bit."

"Good man," Alex said, cracking the third egg before dropping it into the frying pan where it began to turn white with a triumphant sizzle.

Mike frowned at the steam rising from the frying pan. He was experiencing a vague, yet uncomfortable memory of trying to shatter the conservatory window using a garden shovel. He glanced at the glass windowpane. It was intact, apart from a small, spidery shadow at the top left-hand side. Clutching the backs of the dining table chairs as he went, he shambled over to take a closer look. The pane was chipped, looking like a car windscreen might after being hit by a chunk of gravel. Could he have broken it during his sleepwalking incident? Then he remembered the injured bird. It must have cracked the glass with its beak when it collided with the window. Mike felt a pang of something like regret as he remembered how distraught Meggie had been to find that the creature was dead.

"You ruin everything you touch," she had said.

Mike's head throbbed harder, making his knees buckle. He placed both hands on the back of the chair nearest to him. Icy little beads of cold sweat gathered at his brow.

"On second thought, I'll skip breakfast. I'll only want to throw up again if I eat. Got any rubber gloves? I'll sort out the mess in the living room."

"Suit yourself, but there's 'nae any more to be had." Alex turned his attention from cooking breakfast to look Mike in the eye. The expression on his friend's face told Mike how awful he must look – and Alex himself appeared pretty rough around the edges from their late-night session.

"You look like death warmed up. Here." Alex passed him a pair of rubber gloves, along with a roll of kitchen towel and some cleaning solution. "Well, not even warmed up, just...served as is."

Mike set the cleaning items down and then tugged the yellow gloves onto his cold, sweaty hands. It was tough going, and they smelled strongly of bleach, which did nothing to quell the churning going on in the pit of his stomach. He watched Alex loading up a plate with fried rashers and slices of hot, buttered toast. It did look good, though.

"If we've run out, maybe we can head into the village and stock up?" Mike said.

Alex sat down at the far end of the table, keeping his plate of hot food away from Mike's cleaning gear.

"About that, mate," Alex said through a mouthful of fried egg.

Mike couldn't read the expression on Alex's face, but he knew something was up.

"Helen took Meggie's car, headed into Drinton this morning."

"Oh, so she's getting us some more food? Great," Mike replied.

"Don't know about that; she just headed out and took the car."

"Your sister went with her, though?"

"No." Alex sighed and put down his knife and fork.

"Kay?"

"She went out alone."

"Is she even insured? On the car, I mean?"

"I don't think she had car insurance on her mind, Mikey," Alex said impatiently. "She was in a bloody fierce mood."

Mike's stomach groaned with that sinking feeling. He watched Alex pick up the salt cellar and sprinkle more onto his already salty-looking meal.

"Helen tried to wake you this morning. Said she shook you about a bit but you were – now, how did she put it? – fucking unresponsive, that was it."

"Oh, shit," Mike said.

"Quite," Alex replied. "Then she realized she was standing in a puddle of your vomit, and that was it. She was the one who put the newspaper over your technicolor yawn. Soon after, she asked Meggie if she could borrow the car."

"Why did Meggie let her go? On her own, I mean."

"This is Helen we're talking about," Alex reminded him, picking up his fork and spearing a piece of bacon. "Would you get in her way?"

Alex did have a point. Mike was crestfallen. "Did she at least say when she was coming back?"

Alex shook his head, and washed down his mouthful with a gulp of tea. He belched, then wiped his lips with the back of his hand. "Better clean up before she does come back, though. You look like shite, man. And you stink like it too. Now fuck off, you're putting me off my breakfast."

"Thanks a lot," Mike said. "Don't look so hot yourself."

"At least I had the sense to call it a night at some point, rather than drinking myself into a stupor. You need to slow down, man. You always take it too far. You don't know when to stop."

"I just needed to cut loose, that's all," Mike said.

"Yeah, yeah," Alex muttered, sounding like he'd heard this before. Which he had, Mike had to admit. "Just bloody well cut loose with some of that disinfectant, will you?"

Mike grimaced and picked up the cleaning kit before trudging back into the living room. He sighed and dropped to his knees to begin clearing up the mess he had made. As he did so, he caught a glimmer of broken glass in the soot-black dark of the fireplace. He couldn't fathom why, but it made him feel cold to his bones.

CHAPTER SIXTEEN

It was almost lunchtime, and Helen had not returned. Mike was beginning to worry, cursing himself for overdoing it with the drink and for oversleeping. No one in the cottage had mobile reception, and the lack of a landline left Mike without any alternatives to try to contact Helen via the village stores, or the pub – not that he thought she would go there anyway—

In her condition.

—on her own in a million years. Mike rolled himself a cigarette, hating how his hands trembled so. He had the shakes, and a gnawing hunger had taken hold of him. He was beginning to regret skipping breakfast, but still, he was pretty sure he wouldn't have been fit to keep it down anyhow.

After a fitful smoke outside the conservatory, Mike ambled back into the kitchen in search of something bland to eat. Something he could keep down. Alex, good to his word, had polished off the last of the bacon and eggs earlier that morning along with the remainder of the bread. Mike stood in front of the open fridge, as though some food might appear if he willed it to do so. Only a pathetic lump of butter poked from out of its foiled wrapper, and some vegetables lurked in the salad drawer, looking forlorn.

He sighed, longing for carbohydrates, and turned his attention to the cupboards. Rifling through them, he found some out-of-date spaghetti and other dried goods, including risotto rice and a suspect-looking pack of dried porcini mushrooms. A risotto wouldn't be a bad meal, he supposed, but he didn't feel he had the energy or the wherewithal to cook it. Alex and Kay were out walking and he had no idea when they would return. Maybe they would be hungry when they got back, so he might be able to muscle in on their meal plans later. He hadn't seen Meggie since she'd gone out to work in her studio, and he was okay with that. At least it would save him the embarrassment of facing her after he'd been shouting her name into the dark the night before. Or, for that matter, facing any further accusations about the dead bird.

Putting such thoughts away, he opened the last of the cupboards and resigned himself to a lackluster meal of the dry water crackers he found inside. There wasn't even any cheese to be had with them. He boiled the kettle and brewed himself a cup of tea. At least tea and coffee supplies were still ample. But the milk was on the turn and threatening to take his stomach with it, so he drank the tea black.

Some holiday, he thought, sloshing down a mouthful of bone-dry cracker with a gulp of searing hot tea. He wished he could hear the engine of Meggie's car heralding Helen's triumphant return, laden with goodies from the village stores. But no sound came, and he retreated to the empty living room to sit down and drink the rest of his brew.

Kay had left her book of local folklore open on the coffee table. He picked it up and cast his eyes over the open pages. Evidently she had been reading up on the legend of the witch again. A sketch of the stone circle accompanied the lurid tale of how the witch had sacrificed local children there. The artist had been allowed some poetic license, depicting the stones as impossibly tall. Surely they would have rivaled Stonehenge if they had really been that big. The artist's rendition had them casting their long, black shadows over an imagined scene depicting the cowled witch standing over her tiny, sacrificial victim. The defenseless bundle was clearly an infant, and the witch's eyes glaring from beneath her cowl showed her murderous intent. The tip of a sharply curved dagger seemed almost to glint on the page, making Mike blink. He winced at the unpleasant memory of the whimpering puppies he had seen in Oscar's open belly up at the site of the Spindle Stones. Mike closed the book and dropped it back onto the coffee table, facedown this time, as if to further deny what he had seen there – and what it reminded him of.

He didn't feel like finishing his mug of tea, and left it on the coffee table next to the book. He rose from the sofa and ambled out of the living room, avoiding the black gaze of the scrying mirror looming from atop the mantelpiece as he went. The cottage felt bigger, and colder, in the daytime somehow. Climbing the stairs, he heard a couple of them creak. The high-pitched sound could be mistaken for the shrill laughter of a child, he supposed. Perhaps that was all he had heard before he had come downstairs the last couple of times his nightmares had gotten the better of him. Floorboards settling as the heat from the fire diminished would be sure to make a bit of a racket. Mike wondered if he really believed that. Maybe he was just trying to comfort himself with something explainable, something tangible.

He walked the narrow passage to his and Helen's room, opened the door and stepped inside. The air in the room was stale. It smelled of sleep and felt foggy, like the haze of unfinished dreams. Mike saw that the bed was unmade, his pillow clinging to the side of the mattress as if for fear of toppling to the floor. The crumpled mattress was bunched up at the foot of the bed, forming the peaks and furrows of an alien landscape.

He leaned his back against the door until it clicked shut. He noticed that Helen's sweater was still where she had left it, on the back of the chair that sat beside the chest of drawers. As he circled the end of the bed, Mike could see her suitcase poking out from beneath the divan. At least Helen hadn't packed her things and taken them with her. He strolled over to the window and took pause to look out over the loch and at the majestic mountains beyond.

The stillness outside began to bother him, though. He was still listening for a car engine to break the imposing silence. But none came, and he sat down on the edge of the bed, defeated. His hangover was making the sides of his head pulse in time with his beating heart. The growl of his stomach reminded him that the meager meal of dry crackers had done nothing to assuage his hunger. He pushed his body up and off the bed once more and stood at the window. It was a clear day, if a little murky over the mountains. Looking at the empty lane leading away into the distance, he realized he was done waiting for the sound of Meggie's car on his lonesome in this stifling cottage.

Seeing Helen's sweater hanging over the back of the chair made him think of his own, and he rummaged through his bag to find it. He pulled it over his head, made fists and pushed them through the sleeves. The warmth of the garment was comforting, and it felt a little like armor, somehow. Mike left the door open on his way out, to clear the stale air. It struck him that in a way he was allowing the bedroom to breathe.

After loping down the stairs, he located his raincoat on a hook above the Wellington boot rack. He shook the tangled, gossamer threads of cobweb from his hood, pulled the coat on over his sweater and set about finding his walking boots. His thick walking socks were still tucked inside the boots and were, thankfully, dry. His boots were still caked with mud from the shooting jaunt across the heathland. Instead of trailing mud through the living room, he carried them through the cottage to the conservatory door. He banged the heels of his boots together over the threshold and managed to get rid of the biggest clumps of dried mud. At least this way, he wouldn't have to worry about being told to clean up the living room floor all over again.

Mike grabbed the Ordnance Survey map from the coffee table. It might prove useful. But as he pulled it from beneath Kay's pile of books, he knocked the mug over, spilling the last of his tea over the folklore book.

Strange, he could have sworn he had closed the book, but it was open again on the page, showing the illustration of the Spindle Stones and the cowled woman. He cursed under his breath when he saw a dark stain from the spilled tea spreading across the paper. It had partially obscured the image of the little bundle that lay vulnerable to the witch's incantations on the altar stone. Mike wiped the tea stain with the flat of his hand, making it worse. It looked like a bloodstain. Eager to be away from the image, not to mention the close atmosphere of the cottage, Mike scooped up the map and trudged through the kitchen, toward the back door.

He glimpsed something dark out of the corner of his eye.

Blinking, he wondered for a moment if it was just the afterimage of the tea stain that had troubled him so much without him understanding why. A tiny screech alerted him to the fact that the dark shape had not been an afterimage but something altogether real. And the something was moving along the skirting board of the kitchen. He stood still and peered at the place where the wall disappeared behind the fridge. The dark shape reappeared, sniffing the air as he watched it from his vantage point near the dining table.

It was a rat, and a big one at that. Mike could see the red in its eyes as it sniffed the air, then looked straight at him. Great, they had rodents to contend with now. He supposed they must be common pests out here in the wilderness, but the creature's mere presence in the kitchen offended him. His stomach frothed with revulsion at the sight of the rat's slick, black fur and the pale, umbilical-like tail that uncoiled behind its fat body.

"Fuck off, vile thing!"

Mike stamped his foot, trying to scare the rat away. The interloper stood its ground, those ruddy, lifeless eyes regarding him with something akin to contempt. That was it for Mike. He dashed across the kitchen floor and swung his boots through the air like a weapon. The rat fled, darting behind the fridge. No way he could get to it now. Just to be sure, Mike sidled up to the other side of the fridge, hearing the faint hum of the cabinet against his ear.

The rat had disappeared. It was probably hiding underneath the fridge, waiting for him to leave. He shuddered at the thought of it in the kitchen, where they had been eating each day. And with the memory of food came a smell. It was sweet at first, rather like ripening fruit in a bowl. But Mike detected something else beneath the sweetness of the odor, the bitter tang of something rotten. He supposed it was coming from the rat itself, but then it struck him that what he could smell was coming from the fridge. How that could be, he did not know, since the fridge had been all but empty when he'd opened it in search of food earlier.

He pulled open the fridge door to investigate.

The smell became more pervasive and intense. The same pathetic vegetables lay inside the salad drawer, but they were not the source of the smell. Mike gagged and stumbled back from the fridge. The ruptured body of the dead bird lay on the glass shelf inside, its body a tumescent, fleshy chaos of maggots. The light inside the fridge flickered, casting a flashbulb glow over the disgusting scene. Maggots began to wriggle and roll at the edge of the glass shelf, as if they sensed freedom. Mike looked on in disgust as a few of the pale things fell onto the stone floor before squirming toward the shadows beneath the fridge. Within seconds, the rat's wet nose appeared from beneath the fridge door, sniffing. Mike watched as the slimy-furred rodent snapped its jaws, gobbling up a few of the maggots.

He had seen enough.

He slammed the fridge door against the horrid sight, and the even more awful smell, and beat a quick retreat to the conservatory door.

With his thick socks and boots now firmly on his feet, Mike stomped around to the rear of the cottage. Only one person could have put the disgusting dead bird inside the fridge for him to find. He saw Meggie through the window of her little studio. She had her back to him, and was painting at her easel. He was halfway across the courtyard leading to the outbuilding when he faltered. He heard laughter and decided to follow the sound, which was so full of childish mirth that it already infuriated him. Maybe Meggie wasn't the only one with a funny bone today.

As he made his way across the grass toward the path that led along the lochside, he saw Alex and Kay sitting on the jetty overlooking the water. Mike felt a pang of something like déjà vu and realized that his friends had reminded him of Helen. He had been sitting in almost exactly the same spot with her when she had told him she was pregnant. It felt like weeks ago, despite only being a couple of days ago. Hearing Alex's deep laugh, he wondered if they were in on the fridge joke, the two of them. He recalled how they had openly laughed at him from out of their bedroom window the night before, when he had walked in his sleep.

Mike was considering giving Alex and Kay a piece of his mind when he heard yet more laughter and saw Kay leaning into Alex's shoulder. They were kissing. He resented their closeness almost as much as he did their laughter at his expense. Deciding to leave them be, he cut a wider path around the side of the cottage. The tree cover there would conceal him until he was out of their line of sight.

★　　★　　★

It took a little over an hour before Mike cut through the trees and joined the single-track road that led to the village. The map had proven useful, showing him the quickest way across the hills. Without it, he felt sure he would have become lost. Or, even worse, that he might have ended up back at the Spindle Stones again.

He trudged down the sloping lane, grateful to see the first of the gray stone houses at the outskirts of the village. Patting his jacket to reassure himself that his wallet was still there, he couldn't help but think of a welcome pint at the pub.

First things first, he thought, *before thirst*, and pressed on toward the general store.

As he rounded the corner, he felt sure he would see Meggie's car parked up there, but the street was devoid of any traffic, parked or otherwise. And as he crossed the road and neared the shop itself, he saw that it was deserted. The glass door at the front was hanging open. The window – usually housing its lackluster display of tinned goods, lotto posters and a couple of decades-old classified ads – was completely bare and the glass was smeared with dust and grime. It looked to Mike like no one had set foot inside the shop for years, and yet he had only shopped there two days ago. He walked up to the door gingerly, calling out an uncertain hello into the dusty darkness.

There was no response.

Pushing the door open wider so he could step through, he almost cried out at the sudden, piercing sound of the shop bell clanging above his head. He regained his composure and stepped into the shop.

"Hello?" he said, a little louder and more confidently this time. "Anyone home?"

His voice echoed off the empty shelves. They were covered in a layer of dust a few millimeters thick. Dumbfounded, he strolled to the back of the shop, to the shelves where he had perused the bottles of booze. They too were empty, and decorated with dust and cobwebs. A spindly spider, its body almost translucent white, scuttled out across its web – no doubt attracted by Mike's breath against the strands – before retreating back into the shadows. Mike felt uneasy standing there in the empty shop, and turned to leave.

As he made this way back to the door, he glimpsed movement in the street outside. Was it Helen? Perhaps she had driven to the village after all. He badly needed her to see the shop with him, to tell him she saw that it was empty and derelict too. Then he would know that he wasn't losing his mind. He dashed out onto the pavement in search of her. The movement – a person or an animal, he couldn't be sure which – repeated at the very corner of the street, and was gone. He followed it, his pace quickening to a jog.

"Hey! Helen? That you?" he cried out.

Turning the corner of the street, he saw a sheet of bedraggled paper fluttering on the wind. What he had thought to be a person was just another of Meggie's bloody posters. He slowed his pace until he was walking again and stooped to pick up the poster as it fell with a drop in the wind.

'MISSING', it read. Then Mike recoiled as he saw a horrific depiction of Oscar's dead body on the poster. The dog's furry stomach lay ripped open with a trio of puppy heads hanging out, their pink tongues slick with blood. Behind them, a shadow loomed. It looked like a woman wearing a cowl and with her arms outstretched. Mike tore the poster in half, and then in half again, scattering the pieces to the wind. As they fluttered away, Mike heard whispers. They sounded like a warning. And, although he had rid himself of the shadowy thing on the poster, a much darker one now loomed over him.

Mike looked up and over his shoulder.

The source of the shadow revealed itself to be a line of thick, dark clouds gathering and rolling above the rooftops. Mike could smell and almost taste the coming storm. He turned on his heel and beat a retreat from the clouds, focusing on the clearer skies above the road that led back out of the deserted village.

He followed the road and heard a rusty, metallic squeak. He winced, reminded of the rat that he had disturbed in the kitchen back at the cottage. The wind blew and the sound came again. It was the metal pub sign, swinging in the breeze – or, rather, just the frame. The sign itself had gone, and only the metal housing remained, tarnished and bent as though it had been battered by decades of storms like the one that was now broiling in the sky over the village.

Mike made a quick detour and found the pub was in the same sorry state as the general store. What little furniture remained in the bar was overturned or broken, making the pub look like it had played host to a brawl. But how could that be? He and Alex had only recently played pool there, and drank with Jamie and Edward.

He pressed his face closer to the window and saw spots of mildew on the lining of the curtains. The green spots reminded Mike of cancerous cells, magnified. It was as though the interior of the pub was being eaten from within by decay.

A broken cue lay against the base of the pool table, and Mike strained to get a better look at it. He saw that the green baize had been torn, and the balls scattered on the floor to gather dust. Among them, sharp fragments of broken glass gleamed. Several bottles and pint glasses had been smashed against the floorboards. The debris lay in a drift against the foot of the bar, as though an invisible wave had washed it up there. It was too much to take in, and Mike backed away from the pub window, not wanting to see more.

The sky rumbled over his head, and he walked, like an automaton now, down the road that led away from the village. Within moments, heavy, freezing cold droplets started to fall from the sky. It wasn't rain, but sleet, and Mike pulled his collar tighter around him as it splashed against the back of his neck, numbing his skin on impact.

He had only passed a few of the houses when he saw the first twitch of a curtain. Perhaps the village wasn't as deserted as he'd been led to believe by the abandoned shop and the derelict pub. He slowed his progress to take a backward glance at the window where he'd seen the curtain move, only to catch it falling back into place and obscuring whoever had been peeking out from behind it.

Mike started walking again and saw another movement, this time a dark shape behind the frosted glass of a front door. The opalescent glass distorted the shape of whoever was standing there, watching him, making antler shapes at the person's head. Mike whistled between his teeth, remembering his pursuers during the shoot and the fear he had experienced as they bore down on him in the fog.

Turning the corner of the road, where the pub stood empty, and onto the main street out of the village, Mike heard the first door slam. He ignored it, but then he heard another, and another. He took a breath, choking his growing nervousness down with it, turned around and said, "Hello?"

The word died in his mouth.

Standing in the street, no more than a hundred feet away from him, was a line of people. The lashing sleet made it difficult to see their features, but Mike took them to be villagers. Something about the way they stood there, regarding him quietly through the tumultuous sleet made his flesh creep with cold terror. Mike watched as more figures emerged from the houses, and the gaps between the houses, to join the throng. With the new arrivals, the crowd stood at least three deep from pavement to pavement across the road. What did they want? Mike felt an encroaching sense of guilt, though he didn't know why. All he had done was look around the village. And yet, the dark shapes that had gathered were surely glowering at him as though he was guilty of the most terrible trespass.

"I get the message, I'm leaving," he muttered and then in quiet desperation added, "I was only looking for my girlfriend."

Mike regretted speaking the words as soon as they spilled from his mouth. The sound of his voice, muffled by the lashing sleet, seemed to act as a trigger to the dark throng gathered in the street before him. First one, then two, then all of them started walking toward him. There was something altogether unnatural about their ambling gait. Something strangely inhuman. They each walked as though wounded, but with a gracefulness that also made them seem weightless and ghostlike.

Fear shot through his veins, and Mike almost tripped over his own boots as he made an abrupt about-turn and set off at a run away from the advancing line of dark figures. He heard disquieting whispers from their ranks and told himself that it was only the wind and the sleet in his ears. Then he heard heavier footfalls and knew without even looking—

Don't look, just keep running.

—that they were running after him. A strange and disturbing sound came with them. It was rhythmic and soft, like a bolt of cloth being unraveled and then dropped onto the wet street. The beating drum of doom descending on him as, even now, he struggled to get away.

Mike risked a glance over his shoulder and saw gray skin and wet, black hair. He smelled the rot and ruin of decaying fish, its permeating odor heavy as the depths of a bottomless lake. He heard the chafing of dead skin against rough cloth and the microscopic sounds of it rubbing away to reveal soggy bone beneath. All the sounds, and all the smells, combined into a hideous concert that sought to take control of Mike's senses. If he didn't get away, he felt he would drown in them. A bleakly terrifying vision of the darkly padding figures closing in around him as he lay on the wet ground propelled him on.

He ran past the little sign welcoming visitors to the village and up onto the slope that led into the trees. He might be able to lose them in the tree cover, or at least slow them down.

If only he knew what they wanted. If only he could reason with them.

Mike darted up the slope, fighting for more air to help him do the job. When he reached the top and the ground began to level out, he weaved his way between the trees. Crashing through the undergrowth, he chanced another look over his shoulder. His eyes wide with panic, all he could see was the lashing sleet and dark columns of tree trunks stretching into the distance. He stopped and gasped for air. Just moments ago, there had been dozens of villagers pursuing him. Now he was standing alone in the forest. Mike knew he should feel relieved, but in his heart he felt only the deep disturbance that had almost taken hold of his senses. Putting the hideous sound of the wet footfalls far behind him, Mike started walking again. He focused on the reality of his own footsteps as twigs snapped and soil squelched beneath his feet. If the silent people from Drinton had wanted to frighten him, they had bloody well and truly succeeded. Dark thoughts began brewing in his fevered brain. What if Helen had been at the village all along? Had he allowed himself to be frightened away, leaving her hidden there somewhere, a captive? But once again, the old woman's whispered words came back to him—

More are needed.

—spurring him on, away from the village. Mike needed the strength of numbers. He needed to get back to Alex and Kay and Meggie. They would help him find Helen. Maybe she was already back at the cottage, waiting for him with some food and a warming fire.

Maybe.

He had walked for over a mile when he realized that he had neglected to retrace his path across the heathland, and had instead emerged from the trees and onto the same winding track road they had used to drive to the cottage on their arrival. He was cursing his mistake and considering if it would be worth turning around and taking the heathland route when he saw a white glimmer from the deep curve of the valley ahead.

Hearthstone Cottage. At last.

Judging his walking distance to be about the same if he opted for either route, Mike decided to stay on the road. If any of the freaky villagers were out for his blood, they would have caught up to him by now. Not only that, but the ground had quickly become a quagmire under the heavy and constant sleet. At least the road made it easier for Mike underfoot, even if he was deprived of the tree cover. Freezing cold and wet through, for his jacket had sprung several leaks beneath the constant barrage of heavy weather, Mike mustered up what little energy he had left. He pushed on toward the tiny beacon of the distant white cottage, holding it in his mind like a totem.

★   ★   ★

The sleet had become rain and was finally easing off when Mike approached the outskirts of the valley floor where they had met their accident with the stag.

As he drew closer to the place where the dark, still waters of the loch began, Mike saw Meggie's car at the roadside in the distance. It was overturned, resting on one crumpled side.

As he ran to the crashed car, he wanted to call out Helen's name, but the ringing in his ears was all too deafening. Reaching the car, he saw that the driver's door was wide open, a deep dent giving it the misshapen appearance of a broken jaw. A spider's web pattern of broken glass was all that remained of the windscreen.

He looked inside the car, his heart beating frantically. Broken glass littered the passenger's and driver's seats. One windscreen wiper pirouetted spasmodically into thin air, and Mike momentarily mistook the whine of its little electric motor for that of a wounded animal. He reached through the driver's side window, which had also shattered, and turned the ignition key to kill the electrics in the car.

The mechanical whine gave way to the breath of the wind, which crept across the surface of the loch, bringing a damp chill to Mike's skin. He stepped back from the car a little and blew on his hands, massaging some warmth into them. Just then, he saw a bloodstain on the lip of the car door, next to the handle. He walked around the vehicle and into the scrubland beside it.

Helen was nowhere to be seen.

PART FOUR

Under dark, dark skies
There are dark, dark mountains
And beneath the dark, dark mountains
Is a dark, dark road.

On the dark, dark road
There is a dark, dark turn
And beyond the dark, dark turn
Is a dark, dark cottage.

In the dark, dark cottage
Is a dark, dark window
And through the dark, dark window
Is a dark, dark room.

And in the dark, dark room
There is a dark, dark hearth
Upon the dark, dark hearth
Is a dark, dark mirror
And in the dark, dark mirror
There is a dark, dark truth.

PART FOUR

CHAPTER SEVENTEEN

"Hey! Stop!"

Mike waved his arms frantically, trying to attract the driver's attention.

Edward and Jamie's Land Rover had sped past him, kicking up wet dirt as it went. They must have seen him. He was, after all, the only living, breathing thing in the landscape. He punched the air and saw the vehicle slow down, its red brake lights glowing hot in the middle distance. He jogged after the Land Rover, cursing his sore feet and aching limbs for preventing him from moving faster.

"Where ye going, laddie?"

It was Edward, his ruddy face peering out at Mike from the gloomy driver's cabin. Jamie sat beside him, regarding Mike with a pitying expression.

"Back to the cottage. There's been an accident.... My girlfriend, I have to make sure.... Did you see the wrecked car?"

The old men's expressions remained the same. Mike wondered what it would take to rile these two.

"Aye, we saw that," Edward mused. "Didn't look like anybody was about. It's a write-off, that car. Like the one you wee youngsters hired, eh?"

"I don't care about the bloody car," Mike said, more gruffly than he'd intended. "I just need to make sure she got back okay."

"Hop in, laddie," Jamie said with his usual tone of authority.

"There was a bloodstain, on the car door." Mike faltered at the memory of the red smear and all it might entail. "And my girlfriend.... Well, she's pregnant, see."

Edward raised his eyebrows and glanced at Jamie, whose face broke into a wide smile.

"Didn't think ye had it in ye," Jamie muttered.

"Aye, but she did, didn't she?" Edward showed his teeth when he grinned.

Mike pretended not to hear that one. "Can we just get back to the cottage? Please?" he said, clambering onto the passenger seat beside Jamie.

"Just trying to calm you down," Edward said, his voice clipped. "You've had a bit of a shock."

Mike remained silent. His concern for Helen had drained him of all patience with the two elderly jokers. He thought it perhaps best for all of them if he stayed quiet for the journey to the cottage, and so he did. The atmosphere in the driver's cab felt tense. Mike noticed that Jamie had shuffled along the seat as far as he could, the distance between them as icy as the weather outside. All the while, Mike scanned the edges of the loch, trying his best to detect any movement. At one point, a dark shape shifted and Mike almost called out to Edward to stop. But the movement quickly revealed itself to be a host of black crows swaying on the lower branch of one of the many pine trees clinging to the edge of the loch. Mike had never seen so many, clinging on to a branch together like that.

After what felt to Mike like an age, but was in fact only a matter of minutes, the Land Rover reached the track leading to the cottage. He had already released his safety belt before Edward had pulled over, and with a quick word of thanks, Mike opened the passenger door and scrambled out of the vehicle. He shoved open the gate and raced up the path to the front door. It was shut, and locked. He banged on the door but was too impatient to await an answer, and so he skirted around the back of the cottage to the conservatory door. That too was locked. He made a quick about-turn and ran across to Meggie's studio. Her painting stood on its easel, with her brushes and paints lying abandoned on the desk nearby.

Mike ran back around to the front of the house. Maybe someone had heard him knock, and he had hardly given anyone time to answer. He rounded the corner of the cottage to find Edward and Jamie standing on the doorstep.

"Anyone answer?" Mike asked, breathless.

"No, laddie," Edward said, removing his hat and scratching at his thinning gray hair.

"Can't imagine where they've gone to," Mike said and then had a thought. "Wait a minute, what if Helen made it back here, and then they took her to the hospital?"

He couldn't shake the image of the bloodstain on the car door. She was injured in the crash. She would need medical care. But then he realized something else.

"Bloody hell. Meggie's is the only car we have. So they couldn't have driven her anywhere, after all. Unless they managed to call an air ambulance or something."

"We did'nae see any *helicopters* when we were out driving, did we, Edward?" Jamie's eyes twinkled.

Mike didn't like that look, which had an accusatory air about it, like Mike was overreacting, or inventing his story about the bloodstain.

Edward shook his head. "No, I can't say that we did," he said dryly.

Mike bristled at the old man's tone. It felt like he was being humored.

"Why don't you use the spare key?" Edward said, as if it was the most obvious choice of all. "Check she's not at home and asleep, with a concussion or the like?"

"Spare key?" Mike replied, pointing at the combination lockbox, which hung open and empty beside the front door. "There isn't one."

Edward shrugged, then bent down – quicker than his age ought to allow – and began lifting the plant pots beside the porch door. After a few moments, he held up a shiny object between his thumb and forefinger.

"The *spare*, spare front door key," Edward said with a grin.

Its gleam almost outshone the triumphant smile he was wearing. He handed it over to Mike, who took it gratefully and slid it into the lock.

"How did you know where to find it?"

"Why, laddie, I knew because I was the one who put it there."

Mike was taken aback. "You? What business have you got having keys to the cottage?"

Edward's cheeks flushed with indignation, or was it embarrassment?

"Now, now, laddie, there's no need to take that tone with young Edward here." Jamie moved closer to Mike, puffing his chest out like some prize cockerel.

"It's all right, Jamie," Edward said gratefully. "The boy is just worried about his girlfriend, that's all." Before Mike could reply, he continued, "Your friend Alex, his father sometimes employs folk from the village to clean and maintain the property. I delivered a trailer of logs for him not so long ago. You'll have seen those around back?"

"The woodpile," Mike cut in. "Yeah, I saw that. But that still doesn't answer why you would need the front door key."

Edward smiled, all teeth again. "Alex's pa expressly asked that we put the kindling wood indoors. To keep it dry, you ken?"

Mike felt suddenly very stupid. He turned his back to hide his frustration and set about unlocking the door.

"Now you know our secret," Edward said. "All the houses in the village keep a wee spare key lying around somewhere. But don't tell your city friends, will you?"

Mike pushed his way inside the cottage. It felt lovely and warm inside, and he could smell a wood fire burning.

"Aye," Jamie called out from behind him, "don't be telling the likes of them."

Mike wrestled off his damp jacket and hung it on one of the hooks above the Wellington boots. He quickly scanned the rows of clothing and footwear, eager to see any sign of Helen's return to the cottage, but found none.

Not bothering to kick off his boots, he opened the interior door into the living area and heard what sounded like applause. He was already two steps over the threshold when he realized his mistake. The clapping sound was flesh upon flesh, but not in the way he had expected.

A blazing fire roared in the hearth, backlighting the living room in a hot orange glow that danced like fireworks on the walls of the room. Standing over the hearth, her naked skin glistening with perspiration, was Kay. Behind her, Alex stood with his trousers around his ankles, thrusting into her. They were both deep in the throes of their combined passion, Alex grunting and Kay crying out with each ecstatic thrust. Mike stood, frozen to the spot, not knowing how to react. Between Kay's grabbing hands on the mantelpiece, the scrying mirror reflected the flickering firelight like the pupil of some monstrous, voyeuristic eye.

"Bloody hell, it's a long while since I've set eyes on anything like that!"

Edward's voice cut through the heat of the room like ice.

Alex struggled to detach himself from his lover, pulling his trousers up on instinct and then attempting to protect Kay's honor by standing in front of her.

Mike turned to see that the two old men were gawping at Kay, who turned around and screamed the moment she realized they were standing there.

"Jesus hell and b-bloody Christ, Mike," Alex stammered, "why the hell didn't you knock?"

"I did.... I mean, we did. But there was no answer. And the door was locked."

"How on fucking earth did you get in then?" Alex was absolutely fuming, his face almost blood-red from this humiliating *coitus interruptus*. "Would you gawping bastards actually mind?" Alex shot an angry look at Mike, then at the two old-timers, before gathering up Kay's clothes. They had been cast off over the back of the sofa.

Mike saw an open bottle of wine on the coffee table, along with two glasses. Clearly, one thing had led to another.

"Well?" Alex thundered. "Give us a bloody minute, yes?"

Edward and Jamie retreated to the doorstep.

"Bloody hell, you guys, I'm so sorry," Mike said, averting his eyes as Kay held her clothes against her body, before she made her way over to the foot of the stairs.

"I...I found Meggie's car," Mike blurted. "It's a wreck. There was blood on the door handle, glass everywhere. No sign of Helen."

Kay stopped for a moment. The seriousness of what Mike had just said registered in her eyes. "I'm just going to get dressed," she said. It sounded like she didn't know what else to say.

"Fuck's sake, Mike," Alex said. He tugged on his t-shirt, and only then did his expression change. Mike's revelation had, for the moment, diffused the awkwardness of the situation. "You checked the car properly, right?"

"I looked all around, and even under it," Mike said. "Mate, she wasn't there. I was hoping she had made her way back here, but...."

He almost lost it then, his teeth chattering and his eyes burning with the tears that wanted to come.

"Chill. Just chill. Bloody panicking won't help find her." Alex always seemed to know what to say. Even after he'd been walked in on. Mike needed his friend's strength. "She can't have gone far. Maybe somebody saw the accident, picked her up. We can phone the hospital."

"How can we? The phones never bloody work."

"They will on higher ground. Let's search the path that goes around the loch. She may have walked blindly. She would be in a state of shock if the smash was that bad, right?"

Mike nodded.

"If we find her, good. If not, the path leads us to higher ground and we can phone around – also good."

Kay emerged from the stairwell, now fully clothed. Alex filled her in on the search party plan, and she set about filling a couple of plastic bottles with water to take with them. She also retrieved a thick woolen throw from the back of the armchair and slung it over her shoulder. "If we find Helen, and we will," she reassured, "we'll need to keep her warm. She might be freezing out there, poor thing. I'll grab the first aid kit, too."

"One other thing we haven't considered," Alex said as he rooted out his own coat. "Meggie may have found Helen already."

"Oh?" said Mike and heard the hopeful tone in his voice. He would have to cling on to that for dear life, use it to tell himself that Helen may yet have survived the crash.

"Aye, she headed off out for a walk about an hour ago," Alex said.

Mike saw Alex and Kay exchange an unspoken look. For reasons he didn't want to fathom right now, he found that their silent connection was making him feel weirdly jealous. Mike grabbed his jacket from the coat rail and flinched at its cold dampness as he tugged it on over his clothes. Alex and Kay pulled on their walking boots, and then they were all set.

"Which way do we walk?" Mike asked. Then, answering his own question, he suggested, "We should walk the perimeter of the loch, see if she's there. Then go uphill."

"Oh, we won't walk," Alex said. Then, off Mike's look, he added, "We'll get those two old bastards to drive us."

★　★　★

Edward and Jamie maintained what was, for them at least, a respectful silence as they drove up the rough track that led to the lochside.

The terrain became bumpier the farther they drove, and Mike had to cling to a rail inside the back of the Land Rover to keep from falling from his bench seat. Alex and Kay sat opposite him – they had made it clear neither of them wanted to sit up front with the two lecherous old men.

Mike's thoughts kept returning to the crashed car and the alarming sight of the blood on the door. He willed the Land Rover to go faster. Edward made a bad gear change, and the gearbox protested with a mechanical groan. The vehicle lurched left, and they were onto the loch path proper. Mike peered out through a gap in the Land Rover's canvas awning, eyes alert for any sight of Helen. The rain had stopped, making visibility much better, but he realized he didn't even know what Helen had been wearing when she had gone out that morning. Mike was just about to ask Kay about this vital piece of information when he heard something that silenced him.

It was a woman, shouting.

Every hair on Mike's body seemed to stand up in response to the sound, a primal reaction to what he could only now hope was Helen.

"Hear that?" he called to Edward and Jamie in the driver's cab.

Edward nodded, and manipulating the steering wheel as though it were the wheel of some huge seafaring vessel, he altered the Land Rover's course in the direction of the sound.

Mike thrust his head through the gap in the canvas, eyes fixed on the line of trees by the loch. The light on the water shimmered, casting everything in the foreground into silhouette.

"There!" he exclaimed. "Stop the car!"

The Land Rover lurched to a halt with a squeak of its elderly brakes. Hearing the voice cry out again, Mike tussled with the metal bolt of the Land Rover's tailgate. His hands trembling, it took him a couple of attempts before it was released from its housing, and him along with it.

He jumped down onto the damp earth and stones, which felt reassuring beneath his feet. The afternoon light was almost blinding, reflected off the surface of the loch. He narrowed his eyes and saw a dark shape moving between the trees. He heard the voice again and struggled to understand what it was saying.

Hold on, baby, he thought. *I'm coming. Help is coming.*

He blundered across a thicket of grasses and weeds, heading straight for the young woman—

It's her, it must be her. Jesus god, Helen, I'm glad you're alive. I'll look after you right from now on, I promise you.

—and then all at once, she moved from out of the tree cover and into the light. She moved her head, and Mike saw the shape of her hair, then its color.

Red.

Red hair, like—

Meggie's.

It *was* Meggie.

Mike stopped still then and felt the breath leave his body deflated.

He understood what she had been calling out. It had been a name, but not his. Not a human's.

Oscar's name. It's Meggie and she was shouting for Oscar. And Oscar's bloody well dead, isn't he? And Helen's not here, and—

Mike screamed then, or at least made a strangled, croaking attempt at a scream. He had to let rip, had to let it out. This was too frustrating, not knowing, not being able to do a bloody thing about it.

As Alex and Kay caught up to him, looking shocked, he reeled around them and stomped back to the Land Rover, then straight past it. He glimpsed dried blood on the license plate, the marker from an altogether more successful hunt. To Mike, the stain was a cruel reminder of Meggie's crashed car and the only clue he had that Helen had even been driving it.

He decided to leave Alex and Kay to explain to Meggie what had happened, and walked on. His heartbeat had become a thundering tattoo, and his brow felt clammy with sweat. His fingers became numb from how tightly he was curling them into fists. Every fiber of his being now ached with a gnawing need to find Helen, and to make sure she was okay.

CHAPTER EIGHTEEN

Mike led the charge up the steep, winding path to the higher ground.

If they couldn't find Helen up there, he had argued, then maybe they would be able to see her from a higher vantage point. Edward and Jamie had offered to scour the wooded area adjacent to the bank of the loch farthest from the cottage side. Mike hadn't had a problem with that – the two old geezers were experienced hunters, and he hoped their tracking skills might now be put to efficient use in finding Helen. Though, a nagging feeling at the back of his mind made him distrustful of the old men. He couldn't help but still feel riled at the way they had gawped at Kay back at the cottage when they'd caught her in flagrante with Alex. And maybe, rather than out of the goodness of their hearts, they had only offered to search the woods to avoid having to climb the sheer path to the heathland.

Grunting from his exertions as he neared the top of the path, Mike tried to put such unhelpful thoughts away. They were elderly, and he was in his twenties, so he could hardly blame them for taking the easier path. Besides, even he was out of breath by the time he had scaled the path. Despite his eagerness to push on ahead, he felt the sharp stab of the beginnings of a painful stitch in his left side and opted to take a quick breather where he stood.

He glanced behind him and saw Alex, Kay, and Meggie following him up the path. They looked almost as knackered as he felt. Mike saw Kay reach out to join hands with Alex, the couple helping each other up the sloping path. This simple gesture made him want to find Helen all the more. Meggie trailed a little farther behind her brother and Kay, keeping a regular walking pace. The lack of urgency in her movements made Mike feel that she had perhaps tagged along out of a sense of duty, rather than a genuine desire to help him find Helen. He watched Meggie as he drew deep breaths into his lungs, wishing for a cooling drink of water. Meggie was constantly looking from side to side of the path, her keen eyes peering out across the landscape. He wondered if she was looking for Helen at all, or only for her precious dog.

If only she knew.

"No sign?" Alex's voice roused Mike from his thoughts.

Mike shook his head as he watched Alex unlink his fingers from Kay's. The move was deliberate, Mike thought, but only served to accentuate the close bond between his friends.

Meggie appeared over the brink of the hill and produced a water bottle from the folds of her raincoat. She drank thirstily, then strolled over and offered it to the others. Kay and Alex each took a sip, slaking their thirst gratefully. When the bottle was offered to Mike, he refused it. His mouth was dry as dust, but he could only think of covering more ground. Before it got dark.

That's a good one, he thought. *Things got pretty bloody dark already.*

As if in collusion with his thoughts, he heard an animalistic moan. He wondered if it had only been the wind in his ears, but then he heard it again. It was a plaintive sound, which meandered across the heathland, so slight as to be almost undetectable. But he *had* heard it, and it was something to latch on to.

Without a word, he strode off across the scrub in the direction of the strange, unearthly moan. Hearing it again, he broke into a run, taking care not to twist his ankle or trip on the uneven ground.

"Mike?" Alex called from somewhere behind him, but Mike's attention was so fixated on that tiny sound that he dared not look back for fear of not being able to hear it again.

He ran on and, hearing more cries from the others, knew then that they too were running after him. His body went into autopilot, darting this way and that to avoid snagging his feet on treacherous outcrops of thistle, sudden tangles of brambles or roots hidden within clumps of tall grasses. The high-pitched whimper became clearer as Mike ran on. He heard Meggie call out Oscar's name from somewhere in the distance between them. When she called out again, he hollered over his shoulder for Meggie to keep quiet. She fell silent as she drew closer to him. The two of them listened intently.

There.

They ran on together, and Mike knew instinctively where the sound had drawn them to before they got there.

The site of the stone circle was, from this distance and angle, a narrow, dark oval of tangled grass and outcrops of stone. Crouched on all fours at the center was Helen. She was digging madly in the dirt, her fingers and clothes caked in the stuff. Mike felt a wave of elation on seeing her alive. As he neared her, Mike saw that her hands were covered with blood, the drying, congealing red stains merging darkly with the soil at her fingertips. She must have torn her skin by digging so frantically in the rough ground. Mike turned cold as he realized exactly where she had been digging.

Hearing a sudden gasp of revulsion from Meggie, he realized that she had seen it too. Mike tried to put his hand over Meggie's eyes, to turn her away, but she fought him off and shoved him aside. Sobbing, she approached the exposed earth where Helen knelt, still scratching, still digging. Helen had unearthed Oscar's dead body. A writhing yellow halo of maggots surrounded the corpse, expanding ever outward as Helen continued to disturb the earth.

"Helen? What the...?" Mike could hear the confusion and despair in Meggie's voice, echoing his own. "Are you...? Are you all right?"

"Babe?" Mike approached Helen now, eager to get her away from the hideous scene of Oscar's burial. As he neared her, he could smell the ripe corruption of decaying dog flesh. The stench made him gag.

Swallowing, he willed his reluctant feet to move closer to Helen. The smell was unbearable. He had to look away for a moment as he saw a wriggling maggot emerging from the pale jelly of Oscar's eyeball. The dog's tongue was speckled black with thousands of tiny flies. Mike watched in revulsion as they skated across the filmy surface of saliva coating the dead pink gray of Oscar's gaping mouth.

Reaching out with a trembling hand, Mike grabbed a hold of Helen's wrist and pulled her upright, as though extracting her from a nightmare. She did not resist and, as she reached his eye level, looked back at him blankly, as if he weren't even there. Gently, but firmly, he led Helen away from the dead dog. As he did so, Meggie fell to her knees, crying over the remains of her pet. He knew from the sheer force of her sobs that she had been holding on to the hope that he might still be alive. All this time, she had allowed herself to believe that he would come back. And now she knew—

"Oh shit, you found Oscar."

The words were out from Alex's mouth before Mike could convey any kind of warning to him. Kay had caught up to them too and was looking in horror at Meggie and the dog. A cold silence permeated the Highland air.

"Oh.... You bastards," Meggie hissed.

She glared up at Mike and Alex from beside the rotting, ruptured remains of poor Oscar. Mike glanced guiltily at Alex. He found the same incriminating expression on Alex's face that must have been etched on his own.

"You buried him up here, didn't you? Let me think... Let me think all this time that he would come back. How could you do this? How could you...?"

"We didn't want you to see him," Mike said.

"Aye, we were—"

"Only trying to help?" Meggie's voice trembled with rage. "How could you even think this was the right thing to do?"

Mike saw Kay's incredulous look.

"Did you guys really...?"

Kay looked at Alex like she no longer knew him. Then her eyes met Mike's. He broke eye contact and glanced at the ground. But, however bad things were for Meggie right now, he knew he had to focus on Helen. She was staggering away from the horrible guilty secret that lay at the center of the Spindle Stones. Mike caught up to her, stopped her and rounded on her, touching her face with his fingers and finding her skin to be freezing cold. She might be suffering from exposure. He started taking off his jacket.

"Helen, I looked for you everywhere. In the village...." He lost his thread for a moment, remembering the shapes in the sleet, pursuing him, then the bloodstain on the crashed car. Mike took a breath and tried to find his resolve. It was buried somewhere deep inside him, somewhere beneath the layers of dread and revulsion. He quickly wrapped his jacket around Helen's shoulders.

"Jesus, Helen, you're bleeding." Kay's voice sounded so thin on the cold air that Mike thought he might be hearing things.

He took a step back from Helen. To his horror, he saw that Helen was in a far worse state than he had realized. His relief at finding her turned to abject horror as he saw the bloodstain on the crotch of her jeans. She was drenched in it. The blood had spread out in a dark rose petal from between her legs and across her inner thighs.

"Oh my god," Alex said.

Kay ran across to Helen, pushing Mike's jacket away from her shoulders and replacing it with the blanket she had carried with her. Mike stooped to scoop up his jacket, watching as Kay took over comforting Helen.

"Oh, Helen," Mike said, "my Helen...."

She swooned, her face as blankly white as a snowdrift, and Kay only just managed to catch her fall. Mike joined Kay, and they each supported Helen with a shoulder.

"We have to find Edward and Jamie, right now," Mike said. "We need to get her to a hospital."

CHAPTER NINETEEN

"I still think she'd be better off being cared for at a hospital. By medical professionals."

Mike knew Kay's words made perfect sense, but Helen had been adamant that she wanted to return to the cottage to sleep.

He had given in to her partly because her freezing skin made him want to get her warm as soon as possible. Alex had revived the fire in the hearth as soon as they returned. Even Meggie had helped. When she had gone outside after they got back, Mike assumed she would retreat to her studio. But she returned a few minutes later, her arms laden with firewood from the log pile outside. Alex took the firewood gratefully and tried to broach the subject of Oscar once more, but Meggie's look made it clear that he was not to go there – possibly ever again.

Mike had remained silent too, putting all his nervous energy into fussing after Helen. He was worried about how much blood she had lost and, on Kay's instruction, made a pot of tea. He wished they had fresh milk – Helen loved her tea quite weak and milky – but at least there was some local honey left with which to sweeten it for her. He knew Kay had only asked him to make tea in order to stop him from pacing up and down across the creaking floorboards. As Kay and Meggie took over nursing Helen, running a hot bath for her and making up a hot water bottle for her to sleep with, he had been forced to back off and give them some space. He had retreated only when he was satisfied that Helen had taken a few sips of tea.

"How is she?" Mike asked as soon as Kay and Meggie emerged from the stairwell and into the living room.

Meggie sighed. "Sleeping. The herbs I added to her bath seemed to calm her down a wee bit."

"Didn't know my sister was a witch doctor," Alex said.

"Why do you always do that?" Meggie asked. She sounded hurt.

"What? Chill, I was just—"

"I'm going to do some painting," Meggie said, her voice loaded with finality. A heavy silence hung in the room after she had left.

Mike cleared his throat, eager to know more. He still felt frustrated at the lack of anything he could do to help. "Did you get any sense out of her? About the crash?"

"She said...." Kay's voice trailed off a little, and her eyes darkened. "You guys, she said she saw a stag at the side of the road. She said she swerved to avoid hitting it."

"Another stag?" Mike's mind raced. "In pretty much the exact same spot where we hit one? That's impossible, don't you think?"

Alex shrugged, and then he looked thoughtful for a moment. "It's unlikely. Not impossible."

Kay looked troubled – certainly the most troubled Mike had seen her since he had walked in on her and Alex. "Events do seem to be replaying themselves, don't they?" she muttered.

"What's that?" Alex hadn't been listening to her, seemingly lost in his own thoughts.

Mike considered all he had seen since they had come to the cottage. He felt his body twitch at the muscle memory of being chased out of the village by the silent mob. He glanced at the fireplace and the black mirror that sat above it. His thumb throbbed where he had cut it. Reaching out with his right hand, he touched the back of the armchair nearest to him, feeling that he needed to make contact with something tangible.

"There's another possibility, of course," Mike heard himself say.

"Aye, what's that?" Alex asked.

"She thought she saw a stag. I mean, really thought she did. But it wasn't there."

"What, like a hallucination, you mean?" Kay asked.

"Exactly what I mean," Mike said, then decided however mad he might sound he would have to broach the difficult subject with them. Of seeing things. Of losing his bloody mind. He gripped the back of the armchair tighter, feeling the tips of his fingers turning numb and enjoying the reality of the sensation. "Can I ask...? Have either of you...? Have you seen anything strange since we've been here?"

"Strange like what?" Alex asked.

Mike could hear the indignation in his friend's voice. He knew he shouldn't have asked, but he had no choice. Perhaps if he phrased it differently.

"Or heard anything? I don't know, it's just that since we came here, I've been having these weird dreams...."

"Like when you were sleepwalking?" At least Kay sounded like she was being a bit more patient with his questions.

"Yeah, like that. Kind of, anyway. I mean, I know it was a laugh for all of you, but when I was dreaming, it really did seem like the cottage was burning to the ground. It was fucking terrifying, and really bloody *real*, you know?"

"Not really, mate," Alex said, sounding exasperated. "Listen, you were pretty bloody drunk. Best part of a bottle of whisky, and the rest of it."

Mike recoiled. "If you're going to lecture me again—"

"No, no, I'm not. I understand that Helen's news came as a bit of shock to you. Came as a shock to all of us."

"Yes, it really did," Kay added.

Alex went on. "Your smoking and your drinking probably just got the better of you, that's all. You're reading too much into all of this." Seeing Mike's wounded look, he added, "It's bloody terrible what's happened to Helen. We all just have to pull together and do what's best for her. Take care of her."

"I agree," Kay said.

Great, so now they were putting on a united front for Helen and not even listening to what he was trying to say to them. Mike wanted to talk about his waking nightmare at the loch, of the child's laughter he had heard in the night, and about the stag he had felt in the room with him when they'd all gone to bed. He desperately needed to unburden himself of the dark reflections he had seen in the scrying mirror, and the fact that it hadn't been him that had killed the injured bird in Meggie's studio. But...

But...

But, most of all, he wished he could tell them how sorry he was that Helen had crashed the car. Her miscarriage was his fault, and his alone. If he hadn't hit the bottle so hard the night before, she'd still be pregnant. She'd still be pissed off with him for something else, no doubt, but she would still be pregnant. Mike couldn't find any of the words he needed to articulate any of those thoughts, so he simply sat down in the armchair in silence.

"Din'nae blame yourself, mate," Alex said, placing a reassuring hand on Mike's shoulder. "What's done is done."

This only served to make Mike feel even worse. He chewed at his dry, chapped lower lip, not even flinching as he tore some skin away from it, tasting the salt tang of his own blood. The throbbing in his thumb had become an itch, and he tried not to scratch at it, but the urge was too great. He felt the hard, liquid lump beneath the surface of the damaged skin shift slightly as he scratched at it. A sharp stab of pain accompanied the queasy sensation that it might burst if he scratched too hard.

Seeing him flinch, Kay noticed his hand. "Jesus H. Christ, Mike, that looks infected. Have you put any antiseptic on it lately?"

Mike shook his head. Kay tutted, like she might do to a petulant child, and went into the kitchen. She returned with the first aid kit and, placing it on the coffee table, searched through its contents until she found a tube of antiseptic cream.

"Here," she said. "Put some of this on it right now before it gets any worse. Rinse it first, under the faucet."

"She means 'tap'," Alex said as he leaned across the armchair to take a better look at Mike's wound too.

"I know what I mean, thanks all the same," Kay said, "and so does he."

Alex's nose wrinkled. "Bloody hell, Mikey, I can smell it from here. That's nasty."

Mike went into the kitchen and peeled back the bandage. He saw a shock of purple around the wound site. Rinsing it under running water gave rise to fresh agonies, and he retreated to the living room. He unscrewed the cap of the tube of cream and applied some to the wound. It stung a little, and the angry buildup of fluid beneath the skin prickled like pins and needles. The cream smelled faintly of root beer, only slightly masking the offensive smell that was coming from his damaged hand. He hadn't noticed it until Alex had said something about it.

"I think we should take them both to the hospital tomorrow, don't you?" Kay suggested to Alex, as if Mike wasn't even there in the room with them.

"Aye, not a bad idea," Alex sighed. He gave Mike a pitying look before wandering off into the kitchen. "Come on, Kay, let's have a cup of tea and get some air."

Kay nodded, asking Mike, "Would you like a cup?"

Mike just shook his head and waited for them to go out. He gazed into the dead ashes in the fireplace, then glanced at his hand. The wound was turning from purple to a dark shade of gray – almost blackening – like the contents of the hearth.

★   ★   ★

Alex worked his magic on the dried goods, turning them into a passable risotto. They ate by the fire, with their bowls in their laps. Earlier, Kay had tried to encourage Helen to eat something, but she would only take a couple of mouthfuls before curling up to sleep again under the duvet.

"Is it safe for her to sleep so much?" Mike asked, wiping food from the corner of his mouth with the back of his hand. Even his wound felt a little better, no doubt due to Kay's quick thinking with the antiseptic. Seeing the question in Kay's eyes, he continued, "I'm just concerned she might have a concussion, after the crash."

"I don't think so," Kay said. "Me and Meggie checked her out pretty thoroughly. No sign of any head wound, but she's clearly exhausted from loss of blood. Thank goodness she was wearing a safety belt in the car. We'll keep a close eye on her and, as soon as the Land Rover comes in the morning, get the both of you to the hospital."

Mike polished off the last of his meal, watching the flames dance in the hearth. He still didn't like the fact that they were relying on favors from the two old men. The way they had looked at Kay, and their sly murmurs about him on the day of the hunt, they couldn't be trusted, those two. Mike felt a burning sensation at the back of his throat and coughed. He reached for the glass of water that Kay had poured for him. Gulping it down, he thought maybe he had coughed due to a grain of rice that had gone down the wrong way. But as he breathed again, he realized something else was the cause.

"Is it just me, or is it smoky in here?"

Alex glanced up from his bowl and looked to Mike and then the fire. His face fell. Mike followed the line of his gaze and saw it too. A backdraft was pushing smoke back down the chimney. It puffed out, then curled out and over the mantelpiece. Mike watched as dark gray wisps of smoke snaked over the polished surface of the black scrying mirror.

"Blimey, must be windy out there," Mike mused.

He saw Kay's eyes widen as another plume of smoke erupted from the fireplace. This one was much larger, billowing up the full height of the wall above the hearth before spreading blackly over the ceiling.

Alex and Kay put their supper bowls down onto the coffee table. They both stood and took a few steps back from the fire, which was now churning out so much smoke that it was becoming an indoor fog, filling the room. The smoke was so thick, and so acrid, that it made Mike's eyes water. The smell and taste of it reminded him of his sleepwalking nightmare—

Events seem to be replaying themselves, don't you think?

—and he dashed into the kitchen without pausing to speak another word. Seeing the risotto pan on the hob, he quickly searched out the next biggest one he could find. He crossed to the sink, filled it two-thirds full from the cold water tap and carried it back with him into the living room. The water sloshed from side to side in the pan, spilling over the edge a couple of times and wetting his feet. He slowed his pace as he neared the armchair, intent on not spilling any more of the water.

Standing over the fireplace, with the smoke searing his eyes and clogging his airways, he emptied the water onto the fire. The flames hissed and died as he doused them. The veil of smoke hung heavy in the room, but at least the fire was out. Kay opened a window to the night, and Alex picked up a throw cushion and started wafting the smoke toward the open window. Within a few minutes, the worst of it had cleared. Mike dropped to his knees and placed the flat of his good hand into the aperture of the chimney. He couldn't feel any draught there at all.

"There's no ventilation at all. Something's blocking it," he said.

"I don't see how," Alex said. "It's been fine until now."

"Put your hand there," Mike said. "You'll see. Or rather, feel."

With a puzzled look, Alex joined him next to the fireplace and tried as Mike had suggested.

"You're right," Alex said after a short while. "It's weird, though, the fire has been drawing so well up until now."

The interior of the chimney was still warm, but no longer hot now that Mike had put the fire out. He stood up and took the length of broken antler from the mantelpiece. He caught the pale maggot-like reflection of the antler in the black mirror as he did so.

He dropped to a crouching position and shuffled closer to the fireplace until he could reach up and into the chimney aperture with the antler. Using it in the way that an archaeologist might use a trowel, he began scraping away at the chimney opening, working his way around until he felt something heavy shift beneath the pointy end of his makeshift tool.

"Careful, you guys," Kay said. "I've heard about chimney fires in old places like this. Just be careful that whatever it is blocking the stack isn't alight or we'll need to get you to the hospital way before morning comes."

"Right you are," Mike said as matter-of-factly as he could.

Kay's words had increased his anxiety about what he might find blocking the chimney, but his curiosity was too great. There was something lodged up in there, all right, and he just had to work it loose if he could. He adjusted the angle of the antler bone and thrust it into the tight space between the chimney and the heavy object. Then he twisted the antler with both hands, rocking it back and forth. This brought more smoke and black soot raining down on his arm from above, but he persisted, feeling certain that he was almost there.

"Mike——" Alex began, then quickly covered his mouth and nose with his arm as, with a snapping sound, the antler and everything else above it gave way.

The thick, black soot of ages came thundering down into the fireplace, billowing up in a great cloud that choked Mike and sent Kay retreating all the way to the open window. Mike coughed and waved his hands around in front of the cloud of soot, tossing the antler aside. He saw that the end of it had snapped off, and for a few seconds he thought his efforts had been in vain. But then, as the soot settled in a dark carpet across the hearthstone and the surrounding floor, Mike saw that an object had fallen from the chimney and was now lying on the grate.

He had succeeded in unblocking the chimney, that was for sure, and he brushed aside the soot to find that the mystery object was a dirty cloth bundle. The fabric looked years old, worn through to mere strands in several places. A collection of irregularly shaped objects was contained inside the bundle, and Mike wasted no time in setting about untying and unraveling the ancient wrappings to take a look at what they were.

It was a tight tangle, and he had a hard job loosening the final part of the bundle. He pulled at both ends, then shook the bundle out over the fireplace. The objects rattled onto the blackened hearth, free at last, and Mike waved away the soot they had kicked up so he could get a better look at what they were.

"What is it?" Kay asked, and Mike sensed some fear and trepidation in her voice.

He felt those same emotions too as he reached out to pick up the object nearest to him.

It was a human skull.

He blew the soot from its hollow eye sockets and felt his jaw drop. The skull was tiny. It must have belonged to a child, no older than an infant. He held it up to the light from the table lamp and tilted it this way and that, not quite believing what he was seeing.

Alex took the skull from him, and Mike heard his friend whistle through his teeth at the dreadful sight of it. Rooting through the other contents of the bundle, Mike began to piece together what he now knew to be the rest of the child's skeleton. All the pieces were there – rib bones, femurs, a curved spinal column – a grim anatomical model of a life that had been snuffed out all too soon. A little jawbone glinted with its row of tiny teeth.

Mike had to stop looking through the bones when he found the fingers. They were so small and so delicate. He left them where they lay, starkly yellow white against the black soot on the hearth. As the last fragments of soot rained down from the unblocked chimney like black snow, Mike retreated from the hearth and rose on his trembling legs.

"Is that…? Are they a child's bones?" he heard Helen say.

He turned and saw her standing in the doorway. Kay gasped at the sight of her standing there in her nightdress. None of them had heard her coming down the stairs. They had each been too intently focused on the matter of what had been blocking the chimney to notice.

"Helen, it's maybe best if you—" Mike started his sentence but didn't finish.

Helen screamed. Her eyes were wide open to the horror of what she was seeing. And, as she screamed her throat raw, her nose started to bleed. She automatically swabbed at her nose with her hand and then, pulling her hand away, saw the blood there. The dark red trickle dripped into her mouth, making her all the more terrified. Mike saw a few droplets of blood fall onto her white nightdress, an image of her bleeding at the stone circle coming back to haunt him.

Kay sprang into action, putting her arm around Helen and turning her away from the fireplace. But it was too late. Helen had seen everything; Mike listened to Helen's frantic cries as Kay walked her back upstairs.

As Helen's anguished wails rang out from the upper floor of the cottage, Mike looked at the disjointed space between the child's skull and its jawbone. Then he couldn't help but stare into the hollows where bright little eyes once must have shone.

The skull, too, looked as though it were screaming.

CHAPTER TWENTY

Mike tossed and turned on the sofa, falling into, and lurching out of, sleep—

And in his dream, which he knew was a dream even as he dreamed it, he and Helen were on the doorstep of his parents' house. They had left Hearthstone Cottage, with its dark fireplace full of secrets, far behind them. Mike reached for Helen's hand and took it in his. Her fingers felt icy cold. He lifted her hand to his lips and kissed each digit, as though attempting to bring her fingers back to life. She looked at him blankly, and her thin lips curled into a wan smile. It will be okay, her eyes seemed to say. He pushed the doorbell, and they waited, icy hand in hand until the door opened, all by itself, like magic. Mike led Helen over the threshold, and they were all of a sudden standing in the living room next to the fireplace—

Don't remember my folks having an open fire, how strange.

—and the fire was raging. My, my, it's drawing so very well, Mike mused as he watched the angry flames licking at the dark insides of the chimney. He heard his mother's cry of delighted astonishment to find Mike and Helen in her living room. Behind her, a shadow loomed, as long and as tall as a stag's in the dying light of a midwinter sun. Mike knew it was his father. He could smell the pungent musk of his sweat. He could feel his simmering disapproval from across the room.

"What's wrong?" he heard Helen ask.

Then he realized it was his mother.

"What's wrong what's wrong what's wrong what's—"

He felt Helen's cold fingers tighten around his, crushing his hand. The old wound in his thumb seeped pus and ruin, and there was the dreadful stench of something dying. Mike stepped away from Helen as the fire raged behind her. She was bleeding again, the profusion of the blood flow rivaling the fury of the flames in the hearth. Something twitched beneath, and he saw a little cloth bundle crawling across the hearth.

"Mum, Dad – we were having a baby, but now it's dead and I don't

know what to do, there was so much blood – so much blood – so much – and I think she's in pain and—"

The dark shape of his father stretched itself in the shadows.

SO PROUD OF YOU, SON. MORE DEAD MOUTHS TO FEED.

His mother started to laugh, tears of mirth falling from black eyes. Helen's nose was bleeding too. He looked down to see the hearthstone had become a grave marker—

HERE LIES MICHAEL CARTER, SO MUCH BLOOD, MORE IS NEEDED.

—and the crawling, shuffling thing on the hearth started to wail through its cloth.

Mike felt its dead touch.

"What's wrong what's wrong what's WRONG—"

Mike shocked awake again, his hand clamped around the sofa cushion.

His wound was throbbing like crazy, the skin surrounding it livid once again. The antiseptic cream seemed to have made it feel worse rather than better, and he began to resent Kay for insisting he apply it in the first place.

As he lay there, sleep deprived, Mike wondered if he should have asked Meggie about one of her herbal remedies, like the scented bath she had prepared for Helen. Then he began to wonder if Helen was sleeping okay and if he should have gone to bed upstairs after all. Kay, still playing matron, had suggested that Helen might sleep better if he crashed out on the sofa. Well, suggesting was putting it mildly – she had pretty much ordered him to sleep downstairs. Easy enough for her to say. She was, after all, shacked up in a cozy, soft bed with Alex.

Yawning and turning over with his butt hanging uncomfortably over the side of the sofa, Mike pulled the blanket over his shoulders, but in doing so exposed his feet. Ever since he had doused the fire, the room had grown increasingly cold, and he was beginning to feel a chill in his bones. The sensation of something brushing past his feet came just a few seconds later.

Mike sat bolt upright, startled. Blinking as his eyes adjusted to the scant moonlight from the windows, he glanced around and caught the vague, inky shadow of someone – or something – moving—

Or was it shuffling?

—past the fireplace and into the stairwell.

"Helen? That you?" He knew in his rapidly beating heart that it was not Helen.

The shrill sound of a child's laughter seemed to underline the fact for him. Whatever had brushed past his feet was not human, nor was it even a living thing. Mike's eyes were drawn to the little cloth bundle where it still lay on the hearthstone.

"We need to lay you to rest if I'm bloody well going to get any," he muttered.

Another childlike laugh; then footfalls on the stairs provoked him into action. Mike tossed the crumpled blanket aside and followed the sound up the narrow stairs and onto the landing. Again, he saw the shadow flicker across the wall farthest from him. It looked like someone was standing there, in the doorway to his and Helen's room. But it wasn't small enough to be a child. It looked to be an adult, standing slightly hunched over the door handle. The door was ajar, and Mike felt an urgent pang of concern for Helen. She was sleeping alone in there. What if someone had sneaked into the cottage? His blood pumped at the thought that Helen might get another scare after all she had been through. He narrowed his eyes to try to make out who the figure was, and for one horrible moment he imagined it to be one of the old men from the village, skulking around in the dark and intent on another stolen glimpse of young flesh.

"Hey!" Mike growled. "I see you."

The figure halted and turned to face him.

She stepped into the light, and Mike realized his mistake. It was Helen, after all. And she was naked. Her hair fell across her shoulders in tousled rivulets. The cold had turned her skin to gooseflesh. Seeing him, she smiled, and Mike's heart thumped harder. She looked like she had the first time he had met her – completely gorgeous, healthy and happy to see him. Helen laughed, a high-pitched giggle that sounded like pure joy, and ducked into their room. Mike followed.

He found her lying on their bed. She held her hand out to him, beckoning for him to join her. He climbed onto the bed and crawled to her like a child. Her fingers found his shoulders, then his waist, and then began unfastening his trousers. She kissed his neck and nuzzled her nose beneath his chin. She felt warm and vital against him, and her hair smelled of earth and rain, the tantalizing after-scent of whatever it was Meggie had added to her bath. She chuckled as she took him warm in her hand, coaxing him fully out of his clothes and into a heightened state of arousal.

"We can try again," she whispered into his ear as she pulled him inside of her.

Mike gasped. It had never felt quite as tactile as this. His every nerve ending was alert to her softness and her warmth. As they began to fuck, Mike felt Helen push harder against him, grinding with her hips. She moaned, then laughed again. The sound startled him since her lips were still so close to his left ear. She felt so wet – too wet – and he tried to pull away from her slightly but couldn't. She had her legs locked around the small of his back. He felt a wave of nausea as he craned his head down as far as his chest would allow and saw scarlet between them. She was bleeding again, this time profusely, and they were both slicked in the stuff from the waist down.

"Helen, please," he protested.

She now had such a tight grip on him that he was finding it difficult to breathe. Mike tried to brace himself by shoving his hands beneath the pillows, but the pull of Helen's body was simply too great for him to overcome. His lower vertebrae made a hideous cracking sound, and he felt a hot sting of agony in the small of his back.

All the while, Helen's laughter became shriller. It sounded like the laughter of the phantom child that had awoken him. Mike bit down on his lower lip, hoping against hope that he was still asleep – and that this was just another of his horrific nightmares. But as Helen licked the blood from his lip, laughing horribly, he feared he was not going to wake up from this one.

Then the pressure eased, and Mike was able to breathe again. The rhythm of Helen's body subsided, giving way to a pleasant rocking motion.

"Fuck me," she sighed. "That's what you want to do, isn't it, Mikey? That's all you ever really want to do." But disturbingly the voice was no longer Helen's.

He saw another flash of red and recoiled, thinking there was more blood on the pillow. But then he saw locks of red hair. He was not sleeping with Helen. It was Meggie who now cleaved to him as he thrusted into her on top of the bedsheets. She looked up at him with twinkling eyes. Mimicking Helen's voice, she whispered, "We can try again, Mikey."

Mike held her wrists down on the bed and tried to pull away from her. But her legs were still clamped around his back.

"Let me go, witch," he gasped.

Meggie burst out laughing. The sound, a cruel mockery of his discomfort, made him wince. His arousal had diminished, leaving only a sense of confusion, and despair. He gritted his teeth and barked his frustration into the pillow. Then he felt Meggie begin to struggle beneath him. Her legs fell away, relieving the pressure from his spine. He pushed down on her wrists and lifted his upper body from hers.

"Where's Helen?" he shouted at her. "What have you done with her?"

The struggling form beneath him spat something that sounded like his name.

"Get off me," Meggie said, her voice sounding weird now. "Get off me!"

He let go of one of her wrists, feeling ashamed of his anger. She thrashed out with her free hand and scratched him across the face.

"What did you—" he began and then realized his mistake.

The terrified, angry face looking up at him was not Meggie's or Helen's.

It was Kay's.

"Oh my god," Mike said, jolting back from her. He scrambled back across the bed and saw now that it was Alex and Kay's bed, not his. "Oh my god, I'm sorry, so sorry."

He tumbled off the mattress and stood up. He was still partly clothed, at least. But how had he come to be in the wrong room? He held a hand up to Kay, hoping she would give him a moment to try to explain himself. But he didn't even know where to begin. Sleepwalking, that was it. He had been sleepwalking again. Kay screamed something unintelligible at him, and he began backing away from the confusion of sound and fury, still holding a placatory hand up in the air.

The bedroom door opened, and Mike backed into whoever had entered the room. For a split second, he imagined he might feel the barrel of a shotgun in the small of his back again, like he had during the hunt in the fog—

I know what you did.

He knew that it was Alex even before his friend grabbed his shoulder, spun him around and punched him square in the face. Mike's nose cracked and erupted with blood. Everything went fuzzy. The room tilted and became the hallway, and then he was spiraling head over heels down the stairs.

He came to a rest on the hard floor and heard the echo of a distant thud.

Mike blacked out.

★   ★   ★

The sound of a door slamming roused Mike from a fitfully deep sleep.

He tried to sit up but felt his head spinning and had to lie back down again. He felt the lumpy and unyielding surface of the sofa at his back. Exploring his extremities with a shaky hand, he felt another lump forming around his eye. It wasn't a dream after all. Alex really had punched him in the face.

Mike felt his lower back twinge painfully, and he reached down with his other hand to apply some pressure to it in a vain attempt to stop the agonizing throbbing. Touching the site of the pain brought with it flashes of memory. He remembered Helen's face, then Meggie's, and finally Kay's. But most of all – most upsetting of all – he remembered his friend Kay's screams. He glanced over to the foot of the stairs where he had been sent sprawling by Alex. The aftereffect of his friend's understandable rage was now spreading to every nerve ending in his face and spine. Mike coughed and felt a painful tightening beneath his ribcage on the left-hand side of his body.

Tears came to his eyes from the effort it took to sit up. From somewhere achingly far away he heard a car door slam, and then another. A muffled voice called out, unmistakably Scottish, and unmistakably Alex's. Mike leaned forward, gasping in pain as he did so. Several empty liquor bottles lay on their sides on the coffee table right next to him, though he couldn't recall drinking any the night before. The dry, wormy taste in his mouth told him otherwise, and he pushed the bottles away from him in disgust.

He stood and lurched forward too quickly, and too soon. Losing his balance, he almost toppled over the coffee table. The little cloth bundle still lay on the hearth where he'd placed it the night before. A protrusion of infant bone through the flimsy wrapping made his stomach flip.

Mike bolted for the doorway.

Feeling hemmed in by the confined space by the front door, Mike swayed a little as he searched out his boots. He heard a car engine revving up outside, and, neglecting to locate his footwear, he unlatched the front door and heaved it open. He lurched outside and daylight hit him, cold and muted by thick gray clouds that hung heavy over the landscape. He shivered, realizing he had only his t-shirt and jeans on. His socks were already wet from the damp earth beneath his feet, and he struggled to remain upright as he staggered down the path that led from the front of the house to the lane. Edward and Jamie's Land Rover was parked a little way beyond the front gate. As he skidded down the path, he saw Jamie bundle a piece of luggage into the rear of the vehicle. He heard the old man mutter something and guessed that there were passengers in the back.

"Hey! Hey, wait!" Mike gasped as he reached the gate.

"Let's go." Alex must have been sitting in the back of the Land Rover with the luggage.

Mike dashed through the gate, socks now encrusted with wet mud, and reached for the canvas flap at the rear of the Land Rover. His fingers just brushed it, knocking it aside, and he saw the occupants of the vehicle huddled together at the partition between the driver's cab and the luggage area. Kay had her arm around Helen, whose face was obscured by her hair. But Mike knew, even without seeing her face, that Helen was crying.

"Hey! Wait!" Mike protested.

He saw Helen recoil at the sound of his voice and fell silent at the way she had burrowed herself further into Kay's arms. He couldn't bear that she could ever feel threatened by him. Kay didn't look at him either, but he could see fury and disgust etched in her eyes as she glared at the floor of the Land Rover.

Sitting opposite them, Alex signaled the driver by banging the flat of his hand against the grille separating the cab from the passengers. Edward was behind the wheel, and, as Jamie clambered into the passenger seat beside him, Mike heard the gunning of the engine. The rear wheels started to spin, not quite gaining purchase on the wet ground. Mike had one hand on the tailgate of the vehicle, his other hand waving frantically to try to attract Alex's attention. Even if Helen and Kay were blanking him, perhaps his old friend would give him a moment to explain what had happened the night before.

"Just a minute, mate, please – I can explain—"

The engine roared, and Mike felt himself being pulled violently forward by the Land Rover. The spinning wheels kicked up mud and sludge. Worse still, clumps of loose turf and stones pelted against Mike's body until he felt as though he were being paint-balled. The Land Rover skidded to one side slightly, wrenching Mike's wrist at a torturous angle, and he was forced to let go.

His sudden disconnection from the vehicle, and its passengers, sent him sprawling backward into the mud. When the Land Rover roared away with a cloud of exhaust fumes swirling, mist-like all around him, Mike felt the mud spatter his t-shirt and his face.

He sat, plunging his bare hands into the sodden earth to steady himself, and watched the Land Rover speeding away down the bumpy lane. The red taillights of the Land Rover became angry pinpricks of light as it drove Helen and his friends farther away from the cottage. They had actually left without him. Without a word. The pain in Mike's throbbing thumb and twisted wrist had nothing on the hurt he was feeling inside.

That Jamie had been loading Helen's luggage into the Land Rover meant that she must have been expecting at least an overnight stay at the hospital. Rather than speak to him and settle their differences, they had chosen to run out on him. He couldn't quite believe it.

Mike dragged himself out of the mud and began to feel a nagging doubt. Had he seen more luggage in the Land Rover before it had sped away? He couldn't be completely sure if Alex's and Kay's bags had been packed in there too. He trudged back up the path and decided to take a look. It would help to know if he was on his own or if they were coming back.

He peeled off his ruined socks as he crossed the threshold, and padded inside. Leaving wet, muddy footprints on the crofter's stone floor, Mike grabbed the handrail of the stairwell for support and forced his bruised and aching body up to the first floor. He sloped along the passageway and leaned against the wall at one point for support when his legs almost gave way beneath him. He rounded the doorway into Alex and Kay's room, where he had inexplicably found himself an unwelcome visitor the night before, and saw to his dismay that his suspicions were correct.

The room had been cleared of Alex's and Kay's belongings. The wardrobe door was wide open, with nothing left hanging inside. The chest of drawers was partially opened too, revealing dark empty spaces where their clothes should have been. Their luggage had gone with them. Mike imagined how they must have waited for him to fall asleep before quickly packing up to leave. Perhaps they arranged it with Jamie and Edward even before his latest sleepwalking incident. Helen blamed him for everything; that much was clear. And his friends along with her. Their postgraduation party had ended with none of his friends willing to look him in the face, nor willing to speak to him, nor hear him out.

Fuck.

A single cold tear trickled down Mike's cheek. He felt numb and alone, standing on the threshold of one empty room, with his back to a host of other equally empty rooms. Glancing upward, he saw the Haelu runes hanging there—

Health, wealth, happiness. And what was the other one? Blessings. That's a fucking joke. Blessings.

—and allowed his feet to carry him away and down onto the first step. He sat at the top of the stairs and put his spinning head into his hands. His flesh wound throbbed as the stress he was feeling surged through him in a rush of blood.

Mike stared into his hands, his vision blurred by yet more bitter tears, and he sat like that for quite some time in quiet despair, until, prompted by the sight of the Haelu charms, he realized something.

He had not seen Meggie with the others in the Land Rover.

She must still be at the cottage.

Wiping his eyes with the back of his damaged hand, he struggled to his feet.

CHAPTER TWENTY-ONE

The cottage was unoccupied. Meggie had to be outside, somewhere.

Mike ran out through the conservatory and rushed around the side of the cottage, past the woodpile and to the outbuilding. The lights were on in the studio. Something moved in the window and Mike's heart skipped a beat. But what he had mistaken for Meggie was the shadow of a cloud formation moving across the window. He turned and looked up at the sky. The clouds were rolling over their peaks at a frightening speed. A storm was brewing over the mountains. The wind picked up from across the loch, a cold warning that lashed across his face, stinging his cheeks. He turned away from the chilly blast of the oncoming storm and headed inside the studio.

"Meggie? You in here?"

He knew she wasn't, but he had to say something. Had to hear a human sound, even if it was only his and his alone.

"Talking to myself again," he heard himself mutter. "First sign of madness, that."

He slouched over to Meggie's work desk, sat down in her chair. He picked up a tube of acrylic paint, then, seeing that it was a blood-red color, put it straight back down again. A couple of paint brushes lay abandoned on top of the desk. They had been swabbed on some old newspaper pages that lay crumpled and blotched with paint beneath them. The red-stained sheet bore the headline 'TRAGIC HIGHLAND CAR ACCIDENT', and Mike wondered if Helen had made the news.

Of course she hasn't, he told himself, *that newspaper looks months old.*

He lifted the paper and found another front page beneath it. This one was even older, the edges of the paper spotted with rusty stains. It proclaimed, 'KINTAIL DAM PROJECT CONFIRMED,

WILL CREATE 800 NEW JOBS'. His father's legacy, and Alex's. Mike's fragmented nightmare came back to him, his father standing stag-like in the shadows—

SO PROUD OF YOU, SON.

—while Helen bled out. The shuffling cloth-thing snapping its tiny bony fingers at his ankles—

Thunder rumbled overhead, so loud and so impossibly close that Mike saw the desk tremble.

He stood bolt upright, startled by the noise and the movement, and knocked Meggie's chair over behind him. He was about to right it again when he saw the painting that Meggie had been working on, standing on the easel near to the window. He supposed the light must have been good over there, ideal for a painter's colors, on a clear day. Not like today. The sky was boiling black with clouds so thick and so pregnant with rain that they looked more like smoke than vapor.

Forgetting the toppled chair, Mike walked over to the painting to get a better look. The storm clouds outside had cast a dirty shadow over Meggie's meticulously rendered scene. Mike hugged himself, feeling cold at the sight of it. She had almost completed the painting, with only a couple of patches still needing brushwork. The painting depicted the Spindle Stones, beneath a turbulent sky not so dissimilar to the one that was churning outside the windows.

Another rumble of thunder followed by an earsplitting crack sounded from above the studio roof. The electric lights flickered, making it look like the lightning in the painting was real. Mike peered closer at the painting and, more specifically, the figure standing at its center. The old crone, the exact same one he had seen – or hallucinated – at the stone circle was depicted there. She loomed over her sacrificial altar, Meggie's delicate brushwork accentuating the strange carvings in its stone surface. The woman held a sharp dagger aloft, a spike of lightning reflecting from its sharpened silver tip. Mike felt cold seeping into his bones, and the hairs on his body stood on end in response to the electricity in the air, conjured no doubt by the immense storm gathering outside.

Lying prone atop the stone altar was a little cloth-wrapped bundle.

The lights flickered again, then burned incredibly bright, and as they did so, Mike noticed a detail his eyes hadn't picked out before. The woman's hair was poking out from beneath her cowl, wherein her dark eyes glowered. The wisps of hair were sunset red, like Meggie's.

The light bulbs popped in a sizzle of heat and went out.

He heard a child's laughter.

Hard rain began to fall.

★　★　★

Mike rushed outside, afraid to be alone any longer in the darkened studio. His feet slid on the uneven surface of the courtyard, and he had to reach for the pole supporting the washing line to steady himself. Lightning flashed over the mountains, turning them into a jagged black gash on the skyline. He blinked against the sudden barrage of lightning flashes, their afterimages describing the distended grin of some immense jack-o'-lantern. He thought he was still seeing things when a slight figure moved down by the waterside. He held the flat of his hand over his eyes to shield them from another flurry of lightning flashes. The figure moved, her hair flapping in the fierce wind.

"Meggie!"

If she could hear his voice above the noise of the rising storm, she didn't show any sign. Mike left the studio door banging in the wind. Bracing himself against the lashing onslaught, he moved as fast as he could alongside the cottage to the gate. He had to grip the little wooden gate with both hands to wrench it open, such was the force of the storm. Meggie had reached the far end of the jetty, her hair a fiery halo around her head. She had her back to him. Mike pushed through the opening between the gateposts and let go of the gate. It banged in the wind behind him, beating a tattoo as he struggled across the lane and down the slope leading to the lochside.

"Meggie!"

Unbelievably, given the weather conditions, she appeared to be untying the little fishing boat from its mooring on the jetty. A blinding flash of lightning lit up the entire surface of the loch, turning its black waters to silvery white for just a moment.

"Meggie! Wait!" Mike shouted above the deafening tumult of thunder and hammering rain.

The storm had traversed the peaks of the highest mountains and was sliding down across the landscape, its deepening shadows unfurling like the tentacles of some mythical, maritime beast. Meggie either couldn't hear, or didn't care to listen to him. Mike saw her drop the unfastened rope before she climbed over the lip of the jetty and down into the waiting boat. He saw the outlines of the oars as she lifted them, then the bobbing of the boat on the water when she used the oars to push away across the loch's surface.

Mike battled the full fury of the storm, and, willing his last reserves of strength into his limbs, he ran down to the jetty. The wind dropped for a few seconds, then returned with renewed force, making waves lap madly at the end of the jetty. Cold water coated his face in icy little droplets. But he barely felt them, chilled now by what he was seeing, rather than the unforgiving kiss of nature.

Meggie had taken the boat halfway out across the loch.

She had abandoned the oars and was kneeling inside the boat, which rose and fell with the undulating surface of the water as it churned in the high winds. She was in danger of losing the oars, but Mike saw that she was intent on something else entirely.

He recognized the solid shapes of the weights from the kitchen's weighing scales as she transferred them to Alex's keep-net. She then took a length of rope and fastened it to the net's binding. Meggie let the net rest for a moment, propped up against the narrowest wooden seat of the boat. She seemed to be gazing out across the water, at the bankside nearest the road. Mike followed her line of sight and saw a familiar dark shape looming there. It was a stag, its antlers standing proud against the backdrop of tumultuous gray skies and wind-bludgeoned trees. Mike watched as the stag, which seemed to be casually observing Meggie from the lochside, lowered its head to the water to take a drink. Mike could see the pink of its tongue lapping up the dark waters that sloshed up and over the bank and across the beast's darkly shining hooves. Mike could no longer discern where the stag's black hooves ended and where the dark waters of the loch began.

Another stag, its features distorted by the movement of the water, was reflected on the breaking black mirror of the loch's surface. It was as though the two were joined, inseparable twins to one another. Its thirst slaked, the first stag lifted its head once again, and Mike felt the gaze of its unfathomable eyes pierce into his brain and twist the breath from his body.

Gasping for air, Mike stumbled back and tore his gaze from that of the animal.

He now saw that Meggie had stood up in the boat, which teetered dangerously, rocking from side to side. Mike was about to shout a warning to her when he noticed she was holding the net filled with weights over the side of the little wooden vessel.

No, he thought, *don't*.

And the futility of that thought crushed any hope left in him, heavy as the rain that was flattening the grass beside the loch, drowning it.

Meggie let the weights drop into the water. The uncoiling rope followed them, snaking eagerly beneath the surface and into the depths. She stood proud for a second, the funeral pyre of her flaming red hair lifted by the wind. Then the other end of the rope pulled taut where she had tied it around her ankles.

Her feet were pulled from under her, upending her body.

Mike heard the sickening crack of her skull as it hit the side of the boat, and then she disappeared from view beneath the black waters. A trace of bubbles was the only sign that she had been there at all. When they too became lost to the undulating water, Mike saw only the empty space in the boat where she had been standing just moments before. Thunder roared in the sky over the loch, and lightning flashed. Heavy droplets of rain pricked at the surface of the loch, carving it into gooseflesh with each tiny impact.

Mike sprinted across the last remaining rain-soaked planks of the jetty, feeling them buckle and give way slightly beneath his feet.

Roaring with the thunder, he drew all the breath that he could into his lungs.

And dived into the loch.

CHAPTER TWENTY-TWO

The pressure of the water around Mike was all too strong.

His limbs protested at the strain it demanded of them to push his body deeper into the blackness of the loch. But he couldn't give up now. He had already let Helen down, and he was determined not to fail Meggie. Bubbles spiraled around him, and it chilled him to the bone to think that each tiny bubble contained Meggie's breath. If he didn't catch up to her – and even then, he would somehow have to remove the rope from around her ankles – then the bubbles swirling past him might be her last signs of life.

It was so impenetrably dark, and so deep now, that Mike only had the bubbles to go on. He had to trust that following them down would lead him to Meggie. The urge to open his mouth and let in water was almost overwhelming, if only for the chance it would afford him to scream at the fatigue spreading through his body and the frustration of not being able to see more than a few inches ahead.

Then, a ray of hope came in the form of yellowy tendrils of light that snaked from above and down into the depths. The clouds must have broken in the sky far above the surface of the water. Mike's heart pounded when he saw what he hoped was Meggie's dark shape sinking deeper below him. He saw a starburst of silt erupt around the impact of a smaller object and realized that it must be the net, weighed down by the weights. It had hit the bottom of the loch first.

Mike focused on the now dissipating cloud of silt and pushed himself deeper. Then, just as suddenly as they had appeared, the helpful tendrils of light from above were gone.

Plunged into isolating darkness once more, Mike had to trust his trajectory and hope that it would lead him to the spot where the netted weights had fallen. A few more agonizing seconds, and Mike felt sure he would run out of air. His every instinct was telling him to resurface, to fill his lungs with air and try again. But Mike knew in his heart that his body would be too tired to attempt another dive, and even if he could, it might be too late for Meggie.

He stretched his fingertips out to their maximum reach in front of him, and then, with dazzling clarity, the tendrils of light returned, illuminating the lochbed in a preternatural glow. What he had mistaken for a crack in the clouds was the lightning that had come with the storm. It must be raging on directly over the loch, and the elemental threat of it had now become an advantage for Mike as another luminescent shaft of light revealed Meggie to him. She was lying in a fetal position on the lochbed, gently curled up in a shimmer of silt as though she was sleeping and wrapped in a blanket.

The bubbles had ceased rising, and this simple, incontrovertible fact propelled Mike on toward Meggie's prone body for all his life was worth.

Contact.

His fingers found her wrists, and he lifted her from the lochbed so that he could see her face, hoping to rouse her. Meggie's eyes were wide open, pupils dilated and fixed in a catatonic stare that froze the blood in his veins. She looked so still and so innocent somehow that it broke his heart just to look upon her. Then he remembered the rope tied to her ankles and swam along the length of her body so that he could untangle it.

Meggie had tied the knot tight, and no doubt the force of the weights had pulled it even tighter. He cursed his clumsy fingers as they slipped from the smooth surface of the rope. The silt that clouded his vision was making his task all the more difficult too. Mike redoubled his efforts. Come what may, he had to return Meggie's body to the surface. He couldn't leave her at the bottom of the loch with only shadows for company—

The shadows.

They had seemed to rise up all around him, looming darker than ever in the deep. He recalled how, in the dark visions he had glimpsed in the scrying mirror, the shapes in the loch had seemed like a row of black teeth with its bed forming the jawline. But now they seemed to be taking on sharper and more distinct outlines as they closed in around him.

Ignoring the encroaching darkness as best he could, Mike untangled the last length of rope from around Meggie's ankles. The rope snaked free, a pale tentacle undulating on the undercurrent of the loch.

Mike wasted no time, feeling his lungs bursting from the need for oxygen. Mouth-to-mouth might revive Meggie, but he wouldn't be able to try it until they were both above water. He hoisted Meggie's arm around his neck and pulled her upward. His toes were against the soft silt. He looked upward and saw sparks of lightning breaking the surface of the loch, which looked impossibly far away. Bending his knees, he pushed against the lochbed, but something held him down.

Startled, he saw Meggie staring at him, her mouth slightly open and a trail of bubbles leaking from her pale lips. He felt her arm tighten around his waist. Her free hand clutched on to the rope that was still attached to the weights. She was holding him fast. He kicked and struggled, water seeping between his teeth – briny, cold and foul.

He kicked and thrashed, hearing the sound of his own terror in his ears. She meant to drown him. Oh god, she really did. Mike screamed, a terrified, liquid scream of agony, as he curled his hands into fists and pummeled against Meggie's shoulders. She did not budge, her grip clamshell tight around his body. His vision swam, a confusion of dark water, slimy fronds and lochbed detritus, and his world seemed to topple and tilt around him.

Tumbling sideways through the water, he saw the loch inverted before his panic-stricken eyes. The bed was above his head now, an indistinct ceiling, with the fathoms of cold black water a hideously unforgiving abyss beneath his feet. Tumbling ever on, his body spiraled with Meggie's until their feet touched the bottom of the loch again.

The water fell upward like rain.

Meggie's eyes, black as coals, bore into him.

And she let him go.

Mike took one step back across the lochbed, then another. It felt more solid to him. His lungs were at breaking point and he opened his mouth to scream.

And breathed.

Air.

There was oxygen.

He coughed and heaved at the sudden, impossible and icy rush of it in his airways. His eyes swam with tears where there had, only a moment ago, been loch water for as far as they could see. He looked up, and his sense of perspective was utterly shattered. The loch waters had retreated and hung suspended above his head, forming a frothy night sky. He looked down and saw that the lochbed had become dry and firm. Furtive movement at the periphery of his vision revealed its source to be grasses and shrubs, sprouting in the shadows where only water weeds had held dominion, until now. The liquid sky above his head flashed with lightning, describing the sharp outlines of the shadows that had seemed so threatening underwater.

Mike saw now that the shadows were the roofs and walls of cottages and other buildings. There was an entire ruined village on the lochbed. Some of the structures even had intact windows, the glass reflecting the flashes of lightning so that Mike could make better geometric sense of them. He saw the remains of a shopfront, with the pockmarked steeple of a church teetering high behind it. A tall, thin structure was revealed to him by a further watery lightning flash, and Mike saw with wonderment that it was a lamppost.

A lamppost at the bottom of the loch. He could scarcely believe it.

He felt pressure at his hand, then. Looking down, dumbfounded, he saw Meggie's fingers curl around his.

"Welcome to the village," she said.

Her voice sounded muffled and drowned. Hearing it, Mike wondered if he too had drowned and gone to hell.

"The true village," she continued.

"No," Mike spluttered, "the village is up the road. We went there. We all did."

She smiled horribly. "To put up posters of my dead dog, you mean?"

Mike tried to find the words. He was standing at the bottom of a loch, in the middle of a drowned village, with the water churning above him in the sky.

He had no words.

"That village is not the true village," Meggie went on. "Your father brokered the deal that drowned this little place, to make way for the Kintail dam project. The locals agreed to rebuild, in return for money. You've seen for yourself how they've paid the price. Their community is clinging to the edge of nothingness. All the children left, leaving the old ones to die alone. Do you know how that feels, Mike? To die alone?"

Mike swallowed, tasting something hideously salty at the back of his throat.

"I don't suppose you do," she said.

Meggie's voice was having a seismic effect on his body, the oily ebb and flow of her tone making him feel seasick.

"You might, yet, though," Meggie said. "The sins of the father and all that...."

He saw them then, the shapes emerging from the ruins of the village. They each moved with a strange gait, like they were treading water. As the procession of shapes ambled toward him, Mike's sanity began to unravel. He felt terror pierce his heart to see how many they were, and how dark. The old witch from the stone circle was their vangaurd. She loomed behind Meggie, a dark sentry with her robes flowing as though she were underwater.

Mike glanced up at the loch-water sky and felt something snap in his psyche.

I guess we all are, he thought madly, *underwater*.

Then he heard the shrill chime of child's laughter, hollow ice bells breaking, and saw a small child emerge from behind the old woman's skirts. The thing – Mike thought the word 'child' would be too much of a kindness – stepped through Meggie's body as though she were a ghost. The thing's head was the last part of it to emerge from Meggie's belly, and as it did so, it left its shadow behind. Meggie's belly pulsated sickly, left pregnant with the darkness deposited there by the child-thing. As it took its place in front of Meggie, it looked straight at Mike. Its face was impenetrably dark, but he saw a flash of teeth and the reflection of something darker still in its eyes. The small creature chuckled – a mournful sound that made Mike want to weep for the world's ending.

He heard the same dreadful sound echoed in Meggie's throat, and then that of the old witch.

There they stood before him, forming a chilling triptych. Mike saw that Meggie's eyes were black too, inexorably linking the three of them together. Meggie grinned at him, all teeth, as if sharing his realization. Ever since he had arrived at Hearthstone Cottage, he had heard the child's laughter—

The Maiden, Meggie's voice said inside his head.

—and he had seen the terrifying old woman at the Spindle Stones—

The Crone. Hey, now, you're really getting it.

—and now he was seeing Meggie, pregnant with the dark inside of her—

The Mother. Oh, well done, Mikey!

Mike heard a sound like glass breaking in reverse. Like the world un-making itself.

We three as one, inseparable in sisterhood, insufferable to men and the world of men.

The black figures of the villagers – led by Meggie and the child-thing, and followed by the dark presence of the old woman – closed in around him, with no footfalls to be heard on the lochbed save for the faintest wet, dragging sound. Timbers of the ruined village's buildings creaked on the dark horizon like the hulls of ancient shipwrecks. The tenuous physical forms encircling him began to solidify, making a circle around him.

Mike struggled to breathe, feeling pressure against the chambers of his heart. The pressure spread through his veins, gathering at his temples in an agonizing throb. He threw back his head to scream and heard the sound again, of glass shattering in reverse. The sound grew to a fury in his ears. He clamped his teeth together and shut his eyes tight against the conflagration of noise and pain.

Something shredded at his hair and flesh.

It was as though he were being dragged through a tangle of thorns and out into—

Mike gasped and tried not to fall back.

He reached out for something, anything, to hold on to, and his fingers found purchase on a ledge in front of him. He opened his eyes to see the deep black vortex of the scrying mirror. The ledge he was holding on to with both hands was the mantelpiece. He was back inside the cottage and somehow outside of it at the same time.

Meggie lay at the center of the obsidian vortex, dead, or dying, he didn't know which—

Oh, I'm both, Mikey. I'm dead and dying, dream and dreaming.

—and her body was as pale as the time he had seen it—

Imagined it?

—seen it in the loch when he and Alex had taken the boat out for their fishing trip. Her eyes were lifeless orbs, reminding him of those of the fish he had gutted. He wondered if her horribly distended belly writhed with maggots, too—

Oh but it does, Mikey. Do you want to see?

He really did not. Didn't want to look and didn't want to hear her voice inside his head anymore. But even if he closed his eyes he knew he would still be able to see her there, at the center of the dark. And even if he smashed the mirror and gouged at his eardrums, he knew he would still hear her. Meggie's body moved, as if carried along by some invisible wave, her limbs rearranging themselves and settling once again.

I have been here all along, Mikey. Waiting for you to return to me. To us.

Mike gagged, overcome by nausea. Meggie's soughing voice and the spiraling black of the mirror were making him feel seasick to his core. He gripped the mantelpiece tighter, his knuckles turning white and his palms coated in a sickly film of cold sweat.

You know I'm dead, don't you?

Mike fought the urge to vomit.

Poor Mikey. I've always been here. My time at the cottage has taught me so much. The veil is so very thin at Hearthstone Cottage. It can see into your soul. See you for who you really are. And if you let it, it will show you.

Mike's vision was filled with the black vista of the mirror. He choked down bile, wishing to be released from its gaze. But it held him fast.

Hearthstone Cottage is populated by dreams for some, and nightmares for others. Tell me. How have you been sleeping, Mikey?

The teasing tone in Meggie's voice wormed into Mike's inner ear. He pushed against the mantelpiece with all his might.

She likes you, the wee child. So does the old woman. And you know I do, Mikey. But there are other spirits lingering here. Some are not so kind. You will meet them all.

Her mocking laughter tipped him over the edge. He pushed again and was able to detach himself from the mantelpiece for a split second. Long enough to thrash out with his right hand. He felt a dark warp of immense energy fold around his fingers as he swatted the scrying mirror from its perch, sending it toppling over and onto the hearthstone.

Mike heard the sound of glass breaking in reverse once again, only this time much louder. Another sound – that of the world inhaling – followed before becoming a deafening crash that threatened to split Mike's skull open.

And then, silence.

He looked down at the fragments of curved black glass. The mirror had been smashed to pieces on impact. Mike took a step back, relieved to find his mind and body free of the mirror's reflection and the dreadful grip it had held over him.

But then he felt that something was wrong before he even heard it.

And he heard that something was very, very wrong before he even saw it.

Meggie's laughter became a low whisper, singing discordantly inside his head.

Oh, imagine how many years bad luck that will be for you!

The next sound was of glass scraping against the rough stone of the hearth. It set Mike's teeth on edge to hear it, and he clamped his hands to his ears in a futile attempt to block out the sound. With dawning horror, Mike looked down to see the source of the sound was a fragment of broken black glass, moving as if by the direction of some invisible hand to join another piece nearby. The pieces locked together with a sickening snap, and they in turn joined to several others.

The mirror was remaking itself before his disbelieving eyes.

I spent so many dark, lonely hours gazing into this looking glass, Meggie's voice intoned. *Or is it more appropriate to call it a seeing glass? Maybe it is.*

Mike heard, or rather felt, her sigh.

So many hours until I had the answer. Until I knew what to do.

A thunder crack resounded in Mike's fevered brain.

Until I learned what it wanted, Meggie said. *You'll learn too.*

The broken pieces of mirror were gone, leaving behind only the bare stone surface of the hearth. Looking up at the mantelpiece in dread, he saw the mirror sitting in pride of place again, exactly where it had been before. The last few pieces were — and this seemed incredible even to Mike, after all he had witnessed — moving across the mantel to join with the mirror. It was as though some powerful magnetic field held dominion over the fragments. Mike could feel the pulse of the mirror's dark power coursing through the fabric of the cottage, and through the rough stone. And as each mirror shard began to slot into place, Mike began to see what was reflected there. Instead of his own image, he could see the sweep of the landscape outside the cottage.

He felt compelled to lean closer to the reflective surface.

In the absence of his own reflection, there was only sky and a line of tall trees. Where the loch should have been, Mike was astonished to see rows of cottages and a church steeple against the skyline. This must have been how the village looked before the dam project flooded the land and drowned it. Mike understood now how his father's pet promotion project had altered the land forever. What was it that Meggie had said to him about the sins of the father?

He put the unfinished thought aside, seeing something new enter the circular frame of the mirror. Builders, dressed in clothes from long ago, were lashing together the timbers of the cottage. As the final shard of the mirror clicked into place so, too, did the stones that formed the structural walls of the cottage. And then Mike saw a reflection of the men carrying an enormous slab of stone into the room behind him. He guessed from the shape and size of it that it was the same hearthstone that lay beneath his bare feet. The image was so vivid he felt as though he could turn around and see the men hoisting the stone over his head and into place. But something else caught his attention, rooting him to the spot.

The men, each grimacing from the effort of manipulating such a hefty stone, were turning the slab over. Mike saw the arcane inscriptions there before they began to lower the stone into place. He recognized them in an instant.

The hearthstone in the fireplace was the altar stone from the Spindle Stones.

It had been laid inscription side down, leaving the rough underside as a neutral surface for the hearth. The witch's occult pictograms had been hidden beneath the cottage floor, but had still resonated through the centuries with whatever dark power she had conjured during her rituals. Mike thought of the little cloth bundle he had seen depicted in Meggie's painting and felt sick to wonder how much blood had been spilled over that stone – the exact same stone he was now standing on.

More souls were needed, Mikey.

He felt warmth at his feet and smelled an unpleasant metallic tang. Mike looked down to see a slick of blood seeping upward through the stone, coating his bare skin. Hearing a muffled, dragging sound, he glanced across to the edge of the hearthstone and started at the sight of the little cloth bundle, twitching and shuffling toward him.

She really does like you, the wee bairn.

"What the fuck *is* this?"

Feeling the hideous touch of cloth at his right foot, Mike kicked out at the little bundle. Bones rattled horribly as it skidded across the hearth. He recoiled, leaving bloody footprints on the hearthstone.

"Jesus bloody Christ! Is this a nightmare? Or is it real?"

We have a winner! And a runner-up, actually. It's both, you poor boy. Don't you see? You've made the world from your own Id, all the lust and paranoid fantasies from your fragile male psyche. It's been a thing of beauty, Mikey, really it has, to watch your fears and desires unfold. Never knew you had the half of it in you. But the cottage did. The cottage gave you the power to project it all, to make it real. All it wanted was to show you. Show you who you really are. And now the cottage wants something in return. Word to the wise from someone who knows about these things. It's best not to refuse it.

Mike felt a cold wave of panic wash over him. He tore his gaze away from the mirror and turned to face the empty room. The walls were shifting and then reassembling around him, a constant loop of making and unmaking that made it seem as though the cottage was breathing – a living thing.

Perhaps it is, Mike thought darkly.

He turned back to the mirror and saw a woman reflected there, lying on the floor, her legs parted in readiness to give birth. Dark figures stood around her, the shadows of their cowls concealing their faces. But Mike knew that he was seeing the spectral villagers again – and echoes of what had once happened here at the heart and hearth of the cottage.

One of the figures was stooped over the pregnant woman's prone body, holding her hand tightly and whispering incantations over and over, her voice cracking from the continued effort. It was the witch. Mike thought of the cloth bundle and a thought – too hideous to contemplate – began to form in his mind.

"She lived here, didn't she? And children died here. She cursed them and stored their bones in the walls of this place."

But why would she do that, Mikey?

"For whatever her dark magic gave to her. The book that Kay was reading said she wanted revenge on the villagers...."

Meggie chuckled and then sighed. He could almost feel her breath inside his head. It made him feel queasy.

She only ever wanted to help her community. If there was a difficult birth, the villagers called upon her. If a child was sick, they called on her then, too. Women always pay the price, don't they, Mikey?

"You make her sound like a victim, or a saint even," Mike said.

Oh, you're not listening. Not properly.

Meggie's voice took on a harder edge, making him wince as she spoke.

Her name was Elsa. And for all the times she helped them, the villagers loved her. But when her magic failed, they began to blame her – not just for the death of an already stillborn child but for all sorts of things. Failed crops, tainted water. The good Christian men of the village ordered that she be put to death. A scapegoat for all their barely hidden sins. Imagine how that feels, Mikey? To make protecting your community your life's work and then to have it turn on you like that. Tell me, would that not make you vengeful?

Mike remained silent, but he heard the truth in Meggie's words.

On that fateful day, she cursed the world of men. She's interested in you, Mikey, because your father was offered her cottage as a prize from his paymasters, in return for flooding the village she once called home and displacing its people to a pathetic shadow of the community she helped to build and protect.

Mike saw the dark shapes again in the mirror and felt their confusion and despair at being so lost. He thought of the sunken village in the loch, where the bodies still lay. Because his father's company had wanted to avoid the cost of relocating them. The cemetery where he had seen the headstones bearing his name was a sham, set dressing for a soulless collection of buildings that could never replace the real village. That place had been drowned under the supervision of his father. And for what? Money and a promotion.

"But he didn't take the cottage," Mike said. "Didn't even get his promotion. Your dad took that from him, Meggie Buchanan."

Only because your father fucked up. But he set it all in motion, with his wheeling and dealing and dubious cost-cutting measures. Bodies left to swell and rot in the loch. Heart ripped from out of the community. Cold, empty streets abandoned by a cold and empty man. Left behind and forgotten by your father, Michael Carter.

Mike felt ashamed to hear his surname alongside a roster of accomplishments such as those. As this feeling took seed inside him, the images in the mirror began to distort, then grow clearer. The woman on the living room floor looked different somehow – younger, and her hair had become distinctly reddish in hue. He thought it might be the glow of the fire that was creating these impressions, but then he saw her face clearly for the first time.

It was Meggie.

You would do well to feel ashamed, Mikey.

In the mirror image, Meggie was weeping and holding on to the little, blood-smeared body of her dead child. The infant corpse was so tiny Mike knew it couldn't have nearly reached full-term.

That night when you and Alex argued, remember that?

Mike saw a flicker of it in the mirror. He and Alex had drunk a fair bit that night, the last time they had stayed at the cottage. Mike couldn't even remember what the fight had been about. That they were picking up where their respective fathers had left off – well, he knew that much at least. He saw himself at the kitchen table, hurling abuse at his best friend, accusing Alex's father of being the source of all Mike's misery. If only Alex's father hadn't shopped him to his bosses at the company for his dodgy dealings with the contracts, then Mike's father wouldn't be so unhappy. He wouldn't hate Mike so much. If—

If?

If only—

If you're honest with yourself, you wanted rid of my brother that night, didn't you?

Mike saw, in the mirror, an image of Alex storming out of the cottage, slamming the door and climbing into a cab. Just as Helen and the others had abandoned him in the Land Rover that morning.

Events do seem to be replaying themselves here, don't they?

Mike swallowed against a bitter, dry taste in the back of his throat.

You wanted Alex gone so you could be alone. With me, Meggie said. *I know because I wanted it too. The cottage helped me see that. All those pretty things you said to me—*

"I don't remember," Mike said quietly. "I'd had quite a lot to drink and—"

And so you fucked me and forgot me.

"That's not what I…. That's not how it…."

That is exactly *how it happened,* Meggie reminded him.

Mike saw a reflection of the two of them standing over the hearth, deep in the throes of their combined passion, their bodies lit by fire. Just as he had walked in on Alex and Kay with the two old-timers from the village.

You left early the next morning, didn't you? Didn't even say goodbye. I thought you might have gone to get us some food. Stupid teenage girl. I waited all day, until the sky went black, Mikey. Imagine how that feels? Can you, even?

"Meggie, I'm sorry, I-I had to clear my head. I felt so bad about Helen; I had to get back to her and—"

I was less than nothing to you. I was your revenge. You used me up and then didn't have the guts to even acknowledge me. Don't worry, I didn't pine for you for too long. It was easy to forget you, and I guess you know all about that, about forgetting, until I started throwing up in the mornings.

Mike swallowed. "Bloody hell, Meggie, why didn't you contact me?"

Oh, I tried, Mikey. Meggie sounded wounded now. *But you blocked me. Shut me out. Deleted my messages, even changed your address. I thought of confronting you, really I did. Just rocking up at your door, or one of your happy-clappy nights out with Helen. But I couldn't.*

"Why not?"

She laughed – a hollow, bitter sound that rang inside his head.

Get this. I didn't want to hurt you. I suppose that's what makes us so different. Opposites attract, so they say.

"But I didn't know. I would have tried to help...."

We'll see, Meggie said in a cryptic whisper.

Mike closed his eyes. He desperately wanted *not* to look, so afraid of what he might see. But her whisper coiled in his brain like a command, and his eyes opened. He saw her, reflected in the mirror. She was at his shoulder, still clutching her tiny, dead child—

Our tiny, dead child.

—and the sight of it made his eyes swim with tears. It looked so frail, so vulnerable and cold. He wished he could warm it by the fire. He knew that Meggie had felt that too, knew that she had swaddled the lost little form in its cloth wrappings, trying to will it back to life as she placed it on the warmth of the hearthstone.

I tried to have an abortion, Mikey. Only they called it a 'termination procedure', which didn't really make it any easier. I went to the clinic and everything. Drove myself there in my crappy old brown car and sat in the driver's seat until it got dark. Didn't even unfasten my seat belt. Then I drove back here. I had told my folks I was off traveling. I'd already dropped out of art school. I was too worried that I might start showing. What would people think? What would people say about me?

She fell away from him, then.

And, as Mike felt the cold distance between them, he wondered if that was what she had felt too, all that time she had tried to get in touch with him. He wanted to tell her he was sorry but knew any such words would be meaningless given what she had been through.

What he had put her through.

I felt so tired after the drive; I just put it down to all the stress. But as I got out of the car, I saw the blood on the seat—

In the mirror, Mike saw a bloody handprint on the door of Meggie's car.

I made it back here, crawled inside the living room. And I lost her. Really lost her. I had a miscarriage, Mikey, right here in this room. I felt the little life leave me, and it was the emptiest feeling I've ever experienced. I felt so alone. In the hours I spent trying to justify getting rid of the child, I had realized I wanted to keep her—

Mike heard something shuffle and twitch on the hearthstone. *Don't look, don't look, don't look,* he told himself, keeping his eyes fixed firmly on the mirror.

She came to me then. Elsa did. Told me she could make all the pain go away, but that there would be a price to pay. I agreed to pay it, gladly. Our daughter's soul would be hers, increasing her power, and I would remain with them—

"Oh, no, Meggie."

Mike saw in the mirror an image of Meggie staggering out of the door that led down to the lochside, her body weakened from the loss of so much blood. Her shoulders were bent forward from the strain of carrying the fishing net filled with weights. Mike's fingers brushed the mirror's surface – a futile gesture – as she walked on and into the water, the blackness of the loch closing around her until she was gone.

I've been here ever since, Mikey. Living, but not living. Waiting, but not waiting. Replaying the blissful days and dark nightmares that only Hearthstone Cottage can bring. As my body lay at the bottom of the loch, my soul has been in limbo inside this place. I am tethered to its power. Anchored by the hearthstone that is the source of all things. In a way, Mikey, I became another sacrifice to the stone circle. And just as dear Elsa offered up souls to the stone circle, now so too must I.

As Meggie's words chilled him to the marrow of his bones, a sudden spike of freezing, sharp pain shot through the core of Mike's being. The force of it made him double up and almost rocked him from his feet. The dark intrusion spread out and coursed through him like a tsunami of ice, and, unable to stand it any longer, he fell to his knees, trembling and convulsing.

"My god, Meggie, make it stop, make it st—"

What came next shook the words from his mouth.

CHAPTER TWENTY-THREE

Loch water spewed in cold torrents from Mike's mouth and onto the hearthstone, which hissed, hotly.

You are tasting the same deep water that I tasted.

Meggie's voice was ever musical above the torrent.

The same crushing fathoms that stilled my beating heart and made tributaries of my lungs.

Mike gagged as the fronds of something slimy trailed across his throat with the unceasing flow of the dark loch water. He thought of the graves and the rotting bodies, still lying there on the lochbed. Death, drenched forever beneath the waves.

Bitter, isn't it? Meggie said.

Coughing and heaving from the hideous evacuation of so much water, Mike pulled himself erect, holding on to the mantelpiece for fear that another wave might pass through him. As he fought for breath, spitting silt from his mouth, an image in the black mirror began to take shape. He could see a Highland sky over the peaks of the mountains and something else in the foreground. He thought it might be the reflected furniture in the room, but then he realized he was looking at the backs of Alex's and Kay's heads. And, noticing the headrests, he saw they were sitting in car seats.

Mike blinked and the image began to clarify.

He was seeing them from the back seat of the same 4x4 that he, Helen, Alex and Kay had written off after hitting the stag. Mike looked down expecting to see the hearthstone, but instead saw the solid floor of the car's plush interior.

He was inside the vehicle again.

And it was moving.

Mike reached out and pressed the flat of his hand against the passenger window. It felt cool and hard to the touch.

Real.

This was real.

He turned to look at Helen. She looked so alive, her skin flushed with expectant energy. His gaze fell to her stomach, and he wondered if new life grew there still.

"What?" Helen said, looking puzzled at the way he was staring at her tummy.

"Nothing, babe," he muttered. His voice sounded clearer, too. Away from the cottage. Away from the cloying dark and the endless nights.

Mike's mind reeled at the implications of this new, entirely altered, reality.

He was being given another chance.

That must be it.

He looked again out of the window. The landscape on the left-hand side of the road had opened up, giving full view of an enormous, stunning loch. The still surface of the water was like a mirror, reflecting every detail of the sky above it. Tall, ancient trees lined its banks, and, between them, the stark white of a small building stood out from their dense green foliage. Mike tilted his head with the car's movement around the loch and peered out at the building he knew so well.

"Hearthstone Cottage," he said quietly.

The windows looked so dark, and so impenetrable, as though shrouding the cottage's secrets from view.

"It looks…smaller than I'd imagined," Helen said.

Kay hissed through her teeth. "Beautiful!" she exclaimed. "It looks freaking beautiful!"

Alex cracked a smile at her enthusiasm, playfully tousling her hair.

"Thank you for bringing us here," Kay said softly and kissed Alex on the nose.

Alex's eyes were taken off the road for just three seconds.

But three seconds was all it took.

"Alex!"

Helen's horrified scream jolted Mike from the stunning view. He almost screamed too, from the sudden pain of her fingernails as they dug into the flesh of his forearm. The gasp died in his throat when he glanced through the windscreen. A massive, dark shape loomed dead ahead on the dirt road in front of them. It was a stag. Mike saw, almost in slow motion, steam rising from the creature's back in subtle wisps like the smoke from his joint.

"Christ!" Alex yelled, gripping and yanking the steering wheel to the left.

The car drifted as it went into a skid. Mike felt the entire rear end of the vehicle lift from the ground. He saw the stag's eyes, twinkling dark in the daylight. Then the car hit the dirt, righted itself on its new trajectory, avoiding the stag as it hurtled onward.

Mike heard the panicked cries of the others as the car crashed off the road. All at once, the interior of the vehicle became a tumbling metal barrel. Objects were strewn above Mike's head as the car continued rolling, over the graveled edge and into the loch. The impact of the car in the water came as a massive thud, which shook the bodywork so hard that Mike felt sure the car would split open in the water.

The bodywork buckled at the sudden impact, water pressure distorting the doorframes and trapping them inside. Water flooded into the vehicle, dragging it farther down into the loch, and Mike became aware of each of his friends clawing desperately at door handles, trying with all their might to wrench them open.

Mike looked across at Helen and saw her nose bleeding profusely. Droplets of red fell onto her lip, and she spluttered—

Seeing movement, as if in a dream, Mike glanced to the front of the car and saw the Ordnance Survey map slide and fall from the dashboard—

In the passenger seat beside Alex, Kay was struggling and wriggling. Mike leaned forward and saw the extent of her panic. Her foot had become twisted and trapped under her seat. Alex had hold of her lower leg and was trying to work it free—

Mike saw the door release next to him and thumbed the catch. The impact had mashed the surrounding doorframe into a tangle of metal. His thumb was torn open by an exposed piece of metal. He lifted his thumb and watched as blood billowed, upward, from the wound—

He was aware only then that the car had completely filled with water, and he was drowning.

So much for a second chance, he thought.

Mike felt a hand at his shoulder and knew that it was Helen's.

But he could hold on no longer. The pull of the void was too great. He gave himself over to the spiraling blackness of unconsciousness.

Opening his eyes, he found himself standing on the hearthstone once more. Or perhaps he had never left. The images played on in the black scrying mirror, and he watched, a captive audience watching four people trapped inside the sinking car.

You can go back if you want to, Meggie's voice intoned, buzzing inside his ear with the incessancy of a fly. *You can live.*

"But?" Mike asked.

He knew there would be a 'but'.

Clever Mikey. That's a good wee laddie. You do have to choose. Helen or you, I'm afraid. That's the way this works. More souls are needed. She won't take no for an answer.

Mike wondered for a moment if Meggie meant the witch or the cottage before he asked, "And the child? Mine and Helen's?"

If you choose Helen, then the life that's sparking into existence within her will live on, too. For how long, no one can know. But the wee child will live.

"I'm sorry for what happened to you, Meggie. If I could change things back, start over, I would."

Go you. I think you might even mean that, Mikey.

Mike watched as Alex, reflected in the mirror, beat his fists against the windscreen with all his might, unable to break free. In the back of the car, beside Mike's unconscious body, he saw Helen pivot around side-on in her seat. Lifting her legs up, she kicked at the passenger window, her desperation increasing with each attempt.

"Go on, Helen," Mike urged.

You made your choice then?

He nodded.

Goodbye, Mikey.

His heart raced to see hairline cracks begin to form where Helen had kicked the window. He held his breath, willing her to succeed with every atom of love he had left in him. Helen kicked again, hard, and the window gave way. Shards of glass erupted out and into the murk of the loch water.

Helen clambered out first, followed by Kay, who was helped out through the jagged escape route by Alex. Mike watched from somewhere deep inside as Alex turned to pull him out of the window. But the car began to sink farther toward the lochbed, and Mike saw the anguish in Alex's eyes. The anguish when he realized that Mike was already dead.

After struggling free, Alex linked arms with Helen and Kay, and together they kicked out in the water, rising to the surface. And, as the mirror image faded, Mike saw his own body sinking, trapped inside the twisted hulk of the wrecked car. Sinking into the murk.

The mirror's surface became an unyielding sheet of polished black glass once more, its inward curve holding all of the darkness inside of it. Hearing distant sounds, Mike took a few steps back from the hearthstone. The living room was bathed in stark, still light from the conservatory windows. Dust motes hung in the air, as if frozen in time.

Mike moved through the static space and over to the windows.

In the distance, beside the loch, he saw an ambulance, its lights flashing slowly. Helen and the others were being treated by a trio of paramedics. Metallic-silver thermal blankets had been draped around their shoulders to warm them after their ordeal in the cold waters of the loch. Edward and Jamie, with their Land Rover, were helping the startled stag away from the roadside and toward the trees, where it could once more run free.

Hearing a distant bark, Mike saw Oscar trotting down to the lochside.

Two other shapes moved there, apparently unseen by his friends. The sunset red of Meggie's hair glimmered on the breeze as she walked back into the encompassing waters of the loch. A little child walked with her, and Mike saw that they were holding hands. Trapped behind the glass of the window, he watched as they both slipped beneath the surface of the water and disappeared from his view.

Oscar barked, then ran up and onto the lane where he greeted Helen with enthusiastic tail wags. It felt good to see Helen petting Oscar and ruffling the fur around his ears.

It felt right.

But nothing else did.

Mike placed his palm against the glass, feeling the timeless throb of the cottage's dark energy all around him. He saw Helen look up for a moment – saw her look straight at him.

Could she see his hand against the window?

She looked away, following Oscar as he scampered over to Alex and Kay.

Mike slammed his fists against the window as he called out to her soundlessly.

It was as though Helen had taken all the remaining light with her. Mike felt the room darken with gathering shadows, until he too was just a shadow.

Trapped inside Hearthstone Cottage forever.

FLAME TREE PRESS
FICTION WITHOUT FRONTIERS
Award-Winning Authors & Original Voices

Flame Tree Press is the trade fiction imprint of Flame Tree Publishing, focusing on excellent writing in horror and the supernatural, crime and mystery, science fiction and fantasy. Our aim is to explore beyond the boundaries of the everyday, with tales from both award-winning authors and original voices.

·

Other horror titles available include:
Thirteen Days by Sunset Beach by Ramsey Campbell
Think Yourself Lucky by Ramsey Campbell
The Hungry Moon by Ramsey Campbell
The Influence by Ramsey Campbell
The Haunting of Henderson Close by Catherine Cavendish
The House by the Cemetery by John Everson
The Devil's Equinox by John Everson
The Toy Thief by D.W. Gillespie
One By One by D.W. Gillespie
Black Wings by Megan Hart
The Playing Card Killer by Russell James
The Siren and the Specter by Jonathan Janz
The Sorrows by Jonathan Janz
Castle of Sorrows by Jonathan Janz
The Dark Game by Jonathan Janz
House of Skin by Jonathan Janz
Dust Devils by Jonathan Janz
The Darkest Lullaby by Jonathan Janz
Will Haunt You by Brian Kirk
Those Who Came Before by J.H. Moncrieff
Stoker's Wilde by Steven Hopstaken & Melissa Prusi
Creature by Hunter Shea
Ghost Mine by Hunter Shea
Slash by Hunter Shea
The Mouth of the Dark by Tim Waggoner
They Kill by Tim Waggoner

·

Join our mailing list for free short stories, new release details, news about our authors and special promotions:

flametreepress.com